Gabriel's Journey

Gabriel's Journey

Mary Collis

The Book Guild Ltd

First published in Great Britain in 2018 by
The Book Guild Ltd
9 Priory Business Park
Wistow Road, Kibworth
Leicestershire, LE8 0RX
Freephone: 0800 999 2982
www.bookguild.co.uk
Email: info@bookguild.co.uk
Twitter: @bookguild

Typeset in Adobe Garamond Pro

Printed and bound in Great Britain by CPI Group (UK) Ltd, Croydon, CR0 4YY

ISBN 978 1912362 332

British Library Cataloguing in Publication Data.
A catalogue record for this book is available from the British Library.

For my brother
whose eventful journey through life inspired this novel.

1

A strange awakening

For a long while, Gabriel had lain motionless. He was afraid to move, fearful of opening his eyes. When eventually he summoned the courage to tentatively raise his eyelids, he could see pale green curtains drawn across a small window, sunlight gently seeping through and casting a pale green glow onto the white cover draped across the bed. The room was cold and clinical, sparsely furnished with only a bed and a small bedside cabinet. On top of the cabinet sat a small, metal safe secured with a tiny padlock. The intense whiteness of the walls and the glint of metal instruments lined with mathematical precision on a nearby trolley heightened his feelings of alarm and desperation.

Still frightened to move, he lay there feeling vulnerable and fearfully apprehensive. The silence was oppressive; the only sound being that of his beating heart. A key turning in a lock broke the silence followed by the sound of a heavy wooden door opening. A young girl with Aryan features and long blonde hair tied back in a pony tail entered and walked purposefully towards the window and opened the green curtains. Sunlight flooded into the room revealing parallel striations on the gleaming white floor tiles, reflections of the steel bars running vertically down the pane of glass. The girl moved towards the trolley and wheeled it along purposefully until it touched the bed. She reached for a syringe filled with a transparent liquid. Gabriel sat upright in the bed, not wanting to believe what he was seeing, he told himself that it was all a bad dream and that soon he would wake up. When the young girl took hold of his arm and he felt the stabbing sensation of a needle penetrating his skin he knew it was not a dream.

Gabriel opened his mouth, he wanted to ask the girl where he was and why he was there, but he couldn't speak. He could feel his heart rate slowing, as the injected medication began to take effect. He could no longer feel the thumping throb in his chest and he felt calmer but his body had stiffened as if paralysed. He felt himself slipping back into a state of almost semi-consciousness where strangely he could see and hear everything that was happening around him but his body was incapable of movement or of speech.

Gabriel was aware of comings and goings in the room, he could make out two men in suits having an intense conversation but they were too far away from him to hear what was being said. They were both tall and heavily built, he tried to estimate their ages, but it was difficult, finally he guessed that they were probably in their late forties or early fifties, one was wearing tinted glasses and had dark hair with traces of grey. The other carried a black briefcase which he proceeded to open, extracting a thick cardboard file banded with a red ribbon. As he lifted up the file Gabriel was alarmed to read the words Top Secret emboldened in black letters across it.

Gabriel's heart started pounding again, the panic within him stronger than the medication given to calm him. He knew that there were secrets from his past that were best left buried, episodes and events that he had never dared speak about to anyone but which he had cleverly managed to keep at bay. Had the naivety and indiscretions of his past finally caught up with him?

The young girl was now moving busily around the room, wheeling what looked like a small computer to the side of his bed and then attaching small white wires to his chest and his arms. When she had finished he became aware of a monotonous bleeping sound and a hazy picture of moving green lines on the screen she'd placed by his bed.

Another much older woman appeared; she was short in stature, dressed in black and walked with a distinct limp. Gabriel knew that he had seen her somewhere before and when she spoke the shrillness of her tone sounded familiar. She spoke in broken English with a distinct foreign accent, she was saying he'd run away from her and that it was not her fault because she had tried to stop him. She was becoming extremely agitated and one of the suited men moved purposefully towards her and, taking her by the arm, led her firmly out of the room.

Gabriel's mind was awash with questions; who was this woman, why was she saying he'd run away, who or what had he been running away from? The word "running" triggered a shadowy picture of a recent event, a memory recalled in a series of flashbacks. He could see himself running, running fast, he was in a desperate state of panic, he was running past shops, cafes, past people standing at bus stops, there were flashing signs from pedestrian crossings, people standing waiting because the light was red, but he kept on running across the road, cars' hooters sounding, he could see himself on the other side of the road now and still running.

Then the voices in the room grew louder and the memory faded. The woman in black had returned and she was arguing with the two men in suits. Another man wearing a white coat entered the room, Gabriel suspected he might be a doctor and thought that perhaps he'd been involved in an accident whilst running away from whatever it was that he couldn't remember. Perhaps this was a hospital, but why would there be bars on the window and a lock on the door? The white coated man moved towards him, bent

3

over and scrutinised his face intently, he was so close that Gabriel could feel the warmth of his breath. He wanted to speak, to ask him what had happened, but still the words stubbornly refused to come.

Finally the white coated man turned towards the two men in suits announcing that he recognised the man lying in the bed and identifying him as the one they had been seeking. One of the suited men was flicking through the pages of the official looking file and announced that he matched the description of the man they were looking for. He took out a piece of paper from the file and showed it to the others who looked at it with interest and nodded in agreement.

Gabriel desperately tried to make sense of the situation. He could not understand why they had been searching for him or what it was he was supposed to have done. He wanted to shout out to them, to tell them that his name was Gabriel Jones but still the words refused to come. Now another man entered the room wearing what looked like a porter's uniform. Gabriel recognised the red anorak the man was holding, it was the same one he'd been wearing in the flashback he'd experienced just moments ago. The porter handed it to the suited man with the tinted glasses who put his hand into the inside pocket and retrieved Gabriel's old brown tattered wallet. Gabriel watched with annoyance, as the man systematically examined its contents, removing his Oyster card, the various loyalty cards that he'd collected over the years but rarely used and finally his numerous bank cards. He heard him say that the signature was indecipherable. Then he read out the name G.T. Jones printed in silver capitals on the front of the card. The two men looked confused and asked if this was the only means of identification they had. The porter passed over a crumpled piece of paper, informing them that he had found it in one of the pockets, but that he didn't think it was important, it just looked like rows of random numbers, followed by strange symbols. The suited men studied the scrap of paper for what seemed a long time.

If the situation had not been so serious Gabriel might have laughed as he listened to their explanation of what the numbers could mean. They surmised that the numbers must be UK telephone numbers because each row began with either the numbers 01 or 02. Then one of them pointed out that each row consisted of only nine numbers and that UK telephone numbers including a dialling code always have more than nine numbers. The man with the glasses took a pen out of his jacket pocket and carefully copied the numbers into a note book, observing that they might be significant.

Frantically Gabriel tried to move, he wanted to give a sign that he was listening to their conversation. He wanted to tell them that his name was Gabriel Jones, that he was a lecturer at Oxford University and that there was nothing sinister about the numbers on the piece of paper. It was simply his way of recording the pin numbers for his credit and debit cards without the risk of anyone else knowing them. He simply added the four pin numbers to various five number national dialling codes and the symbols were simply to cause confusion.

Knowing that he had no control of the situation his fears grew but he tried to stay calm. He tried taking deep breaths; he knew that he must try to find the strength to move his body. "Stay calm, stay strong." These words he repeated over and over again like a well-rehearsed mantra. He eventually managed to raise first one foot, then the other, with more concentration he managed to move them little by little until they were both slightly overhanging the side of the bed, he felt angry that with all the effort that he'd made no one in the room seemed to have noticed the change in his position. The suited men and the white coated man were immersed in a discussion and the porter was now involved in a heated argument with the woman dressed in black.

Perhaps it was anger and frustration that finally propelled him with a gigantic sideways push of his body to be sitting almost upright on the edge of the bed; his feet suspended a few inches from the floor. Instinctively he wanted to raise his body from the bed and stand up straight but that required more strength than he was able to muster. He managed to slide himself forward on his bottom until his feet touched the floor, but putting his full weight on them was a step too far and he fell, landing in a crumpled heap on the floor.

In the background music was playing, it was coming from the area just outside the door where the group of men were assembled, deep in conversation. On hearing the commotion caused by the fall they reacted immediately, one shouting, "Quick, he's on the move." The white coated man approached, shouting at the young girl who had given Gabriel the injection and reprimanding her for not administering the correct dose. He told her that it was essential that the correct dose was given to this particular patient. She looked embarrassed, left the room and soon returned with more medication, the white coated man watched as she injected Gabriel who noticed this time she used a much larger syringe to dispense the medicine. Two porters arrived and carefully lifted him onto the bed and once again he found himself lying in a horizontal position completely motionless.

It wasn't very long before he started to feel sleepy; he was still aware of the sound of music playing in the background and found it comforting in a strange sort of way. He was almost thankful for the medication they had given him, he could breathe more easily, his heart rate felt normal and he was calmer. He knew the situation he was in had not changed but his panic reaction to it had eased, at least for the moment. The music stopped and a voice announced that the programme was being interrupted in order to broadcast an important news bulletin. It was then that Gabriel realised that the music had emanated from a radio in a nearby room. As Gabriel slowly ebbed into oblivion he was aware of a distinctive BBC voice announcing the government's decision to withdraw British troops from Afghanistan.

2

Revisiting the magic that was Afghanistan

Gabriel had travelled to Afghanistan in the summer of 1973, a time when Afghanistan was a symbol of something other than war. Having grown up in South Wales during the post war years of austerity and from a poor background he was a symbol of the social mobility accessible to his generation. When he graduated with a university degree and was recruited into the London Civil Service, his dad congratulated him, saying proudly, "Well done son, now you have a job for life." His dad's comment, expressed with so much pride, had the unexpected effect of unsettling Gabriel, the words "a job for life" led him to envisage a steady, safe but ordinary life that was already mapped out for him. This was not something that Gabriel wanted; he wanted to see and experience as much of the world as he could before settling down.

And so in the early summer of 1973 he set out to hitch-hike across Europe travelling through Yugoslavia and Bulgaria, to Turkey. It was in Turkey where the trail to the East began. Gabriel had been told to find the Pudding Shop, the nickname of the Lale Restaurant, a cafe near the Blue Mosque in Istanbul, the only place in the city where tourist information about transportation to Asia was readily available. It was in the Pudding Shop that he met Alf and Helen an ageing crazy, long, haired pair of hippies, colourfully dressed in 1970s obligatory hippie attire, bandanas round their foreheads and strings of multicoloured beads around their necks.

They were happy to have his company along the long journey east in their old blue VW camper van decorated with pink and yellow flowers. It was a long trek through the Iranian desert. Every morning they started out very early to avoid the worst of the heat, and by mid-morning would find themselves stopped in the wilderness. The van frequently broke down. Luckily, Alf had trained as a motor mechanic in his previous life and somehow his sweaty tinkering with the aid of a box of old tools and Gabriel's strenuous efforts at a push-start got them back on the road.

Along the way Alf and Helen enthralled him with fascinating stories of their travels, one of which was how they had managed to develop a lucrative import-export business in lapis lazuli beads and bangles, bags made from karakul skins and handmade Afghani fur coats, all were fashionable in the UK and Europe in the late '60s. They told stories of how some people, obviously not them, as they were keen to emphasise, were attracted by the plentiful availability of drugs like hashish and opium. One way of smuggling hash back through Iran and Turkey before heading home, so they had heard, was to go to an infamous souvenir shop in the capital which would seal it inside a spice jar or weave it lace-like into the inside of a small multicoloured Afghan carpet.

Between the borders of Iran and Afghanistan there was a wide stretch of no-mans-land before they reached Herat, the first major town where the customs officers searched the van rather haphazardly before introducing the trio to the patron of a nearby small hotel. It was clear that the customs man and hotel owner had a vested interest in detaining the travellers long enough at the border to tempt them into booking a room at an inflated price. When Alf insisted that they could not pay the asking price, the customs officer hurriedly signalled to them to go on their way. That night they slept on the thin mattress in the flower power van for the last time.

Finally they reached Kabul and Gabriel was captivated by the beauty of the city. The Afghan capital sits high in the Hindu Kush, overlooked by the snow-capped peaks with the Kabul River flowing through a narrow pass between them meandering placidly through its heart. Kabul was amazing, some modern buildings rising above bustling bazaars where you could purchase yarn or lentils or the garlands of paper flowers that were used to decorate cars during weddings. The narrow streets were filled with people wearing colourful flowing turbans and gaily striped chapans (cloaks). Afghan trucks were a riot of colour, the cabs heavily decorated and the body panels painted with colourful scenes. Gabriel's plan was to stay in Kabul for a while and then cross the country into India, finally ending in the mountains of Nepal and Kathmandu.

Alf and Helen drove him to the Peace Hotel which they informed him was a good place to stay and instructed him to haggle over the price of the room. The hotel was next to the more famous, more expensive Sigi's Hotel and close to the infamous Chicken Street, the city's enclave of hotels and restaurants, a ghetto of global hippies and hedonists, where you could get high in any one of a number of coffee shops, carpet shops, fur shops or spice stalls.

After successfully negotiating a reasonable price, Gabriel was escorted up a small flight of stairs to a very basic, small room with a single bed and a small cupboard with some lonely metal hangers precariously suspended on a rung, shared toilet facilities were at the end of an unlit corridor. From the small hotel window he looked down on the street below, the sidewalk tables set under gay umbrellas beckoned, he left the hotel to explore.

Gabriel chose a cafe occupied by travellers of various nationalities congregated around the small tables in groups.

Tentatively he moved towards a group speaking in English, explaining that he had arrived in Kabul that day and asked if he could join them. As he came to realise, their immediate warmth and acceptance of him into their midst was typical of the traditional hospitality of the country and the welcoming atmosphere of Kabul in those days. He sat listening to them trading stories of the roads they had travelled and the roads that lay ahead, whilst drinking tea and smoking. There were four of them altogether, two American trainee lawyers from Boston, Ivan an athletic looking Russian who spoke perfect English with only a trace of a foreign accent and Max, a medical student from England. Gabriel became close friends with Max and the friendship continued for many years after the Afghan adventure. Max was ambitious and became a senior consultant at a London teaching hospital. A group of young Afghan women were walking along the sidewalk close by, Max, called out to them, they turned and waved, they were obviously already well acquainted, he stood up and beckoned them to come and join them.

Afghanistan was unquestionably poor and backward, but it seemed to be making remarkable progress in its efforts to embrace modern life. The young girls wore attractive western style miniskirts, they were all carrying small piles of books, Gabriel was reliably informed that they were students at Kabul University. His eyes were drawn to one particular girl; she had long sleek jet black hair, a swarthy complexion and the most beautiful bright green eyes. She must have been aware of his obvious attraction to her as he watched her purposefully remove a chair from the table opposite and carry it effortlessly across, placing it next to his. For once he was lost for words and grateful that she, sensing his awkwardness, started the conversation. She introduced herself as Azita, explaining that her mum being of Persian origin had named her after a story about an ancient Persian princess. She went on to tell him that she was a student of engineering and that she hoped to graduate that year, that she had lived in Kabul all her life and that she had three brothers. She paused, and Gabriel started nervously to talk about himself and his life, wishing he could make it sound more exciting and interesting than he knew it really was. To his surprise Azita appeared to be interested, she was listening intently, he grew bolder, and decided to elaborate on the only real exciting thing he could ever remember happening to him. It had happened a few years earlier when he was still an undergraduate, it was the last week of the summer term and he'd successfully completed his second year of an International Politics and Modern Languages degree. He dreamed of becoming a photographer achieving fame for capturing significant world events and images on camera. One afternoon he walked into a London second hand shop and felt lucky to find an Ilford Advocate camera. The shop owner explained that it was English made and interesting in a number of respects, being finished in ivory enamel on a cast aluminium body with a wide angle 35mm focal length lens. When Gabriel bought the camera that day he was unaware of how important it was to become in capturing images of people and places during his future travels.

Later that day whilst enjoying a quiet drink in a student bar, Gabriel had been joined by his university tutor and another older man whom he did not recognise. The older man spoke English with a heavy foreign accent and introduced himself as Vicktor, they chatted with Gabriel buying him a few drinks. Vicktor explained that he worked at the Russian Embassy and asked what Gabriel intended to do during the long summer break before his final year at university. Gabriel told him that he intended to look for some manual work to earn enough perhaps to take a short holiday somewhere in Europe before returning to university in the autumn. Vicktor offered to find him some work for the summer which he said, involved translating some boring government papers from English into Russian. Gabriel had jumped at the opportunity; a desk job was preferable to his previous summer job on a rain soaked building site. Gabriel's interest in communism and the Soviet Union had been triggered in his late teens when he and a young friend had attended covert meetings held in a small smoke filled back room of the Swansea Labour Club. One particular evening after a few beers they'd naively signed a piece of paper and joined the Communist Party.

Gabriel spent two months of that summer working on translations at the embassy and at the beginning of September, a month before the start of his final year at university he was asked if he would like to travel to Leningrad to make what they called a drop. He didn't understand what that meant at the time but didn't want to miss what he knew was the opportunity of a lifetime, the chance to travel to Russia. It was later that he realised they wanted him to deliver the papers that he had systematically spent the summer translating.

This was the mid 1960s and Gabriel was aware of the cold war and that students were a fruitful target for spy recruitment, but in spite of the offer of a trip to Soviet Russia at a time when obtaining a visa to travel there was virtually impossible for ordinary people, he never felt like a real spook. Nevertheless he tried to give Azita the impression that he might have been. It worked and she was visibly impressed that Gabriel had visited Leningrad. She gave him a broad smile and he sensed a definite twinkle in her eyes. Azita explained that Afghan students were keen to further their studies abroad and that she had a choice of going to the US on Fulbright scholarships or to the USSR to study for a technical profession. Gabriel's story seemed to have stimulated her interest in him. She took his hand in hers and offered to show him around Kabul the next day.

When Azita and her friends waved goodbye, Gabriel took leave of his new friends and headed back to his hotel, through a narrow alley, past the sweet aroma of hashish, and the huddled forms of men warming themselves around a wood fire glowing in a barrel. Kabul had never seemed more magical.

Gabriel had intended to spend only a few days in Kabul

then find his way across Afghanistan through the Khyber Pass to Peshawar, crossing at the Lahore-Amritsar border into India. One morning he went to the main Kabul bus station where he joined a long queue of international travellers making enquiries about the long-distance Afghan bus to Pakistan. A fellow traveller at the bus station told him he had made the trip several times and warned Gabriel to be prepared for a very bumpy and harrowing journey. At certain points along the road there were steep sheer drops on one side with a mountain straight up on the other and the drivers played a game of chicken frequently overtaking each other in the most dangerous places. The traveller suggested that if Gabriel was seriously considering making the journey it was worth paying a few pul to one of the local tribesmen who gathered around the bus station to go and sprinkle incense around the bus and chant a blessing to ward off any evil. There was a brief moment of indecision before Gabriel left the line and made his way back to the cafe where he knew he would find Max and the others. His mind was made up; He would spend the rest of the summer with his new found friends and with Azita. The desire for further travel and adventure had soon faded.

Long summer mornings were spent in the congenial effortless company of Max and his acquaintances. They were young, naive, and living in a dream whiling away the hours sitting in their cafe bathed in the Afghan sunshine, smoking and reflecting on the meaning of life through the haze of hashish filled water pipes. In the afternoon Gabriel would meet Azita who kept her promise to show him the "real" Kabul. She led him on foot along the Kabul River to the Monday Market a lively bazaar in the centre of the Afghan capital. They wandered through a maze of alleyways lined with brightly coloured canvas-covered wooden stalls where bearded Pashtun merchants displayed their wares: nuts, spices, dried fruits, tea, slabs of raw meat, live turkeys, blankets, beads of lapis lazuli. They passed knife sharpeners, sparks flying at them from their spinning wheels and turned down one of the alleyways into a bird market, where bright green parakeets and budgies flitted by the hundreds inside bamboo cages.

It was at this market that Gabriel met Darius, Azita's elder brother, a handsome man, smartly dressed in a western style suit in his late twenties. He was seated with other similarly smartly dressed Afghan men of a similar age, they were deep in conversation but he looked up and smiled as Azita called out to him, he stood up and looked suspiciously at Gabriel. Azita quickly introduced him as her friend from England and Darius politely shook my hand before returning to his friends.

Later Azita explained to Gabriel that Darius was over protective of her, in a brotherly way and that he'd recently returned from Moscow having taken advantage of the Soviet aid which offered scholarships to students interested in studying film. He was working at the Arena Cinema where Azita and Gabriel passed many enjoyable evenings watching dubbed foreign pictures courtesy of the free passes given to them by Darius. Afterwards they would dine lavishly at the Khyber Restaurant next door to the cinema. It was a popular meeting place in Kabul located on the first floor of the Finance Ministry in Pushtunistan Square.

One evening Gabriel accompanied Azita to what she called, "The House of the People" located in a modern concrete soviet looking building a few streets away from the cinema. They climbed the stairs to the second floor, removed their shoes and entered a smoked filled, fluorescent-lit room. At one side of the room a throng of Pashtun men of all ages sat cross legged on a green-carpeted floor. Standing amongst them Gabriel recognised Darius, dressed in traditional tribal clothes addressing the small crowd in his native language Dari. Azita told Gabriel that when Darius returned from Moscow he'd told her that the experience had opened his eyes to different ways of living and being.

Gabriel already suspected that Azita and her brother were involved in one of the many underground political factions operating in Kabul at that time. Azita explained that the Soviets and the Americans competed with aid programmes, and things had improved in Kabul, but outside of Kabul life was very different. There were huge areas where the people had very little and the government could do little because they were largely uneducated and influenced by tribal leaders. The government regime was constantly changing and even that day on Radio Kabul they had been told of an allegedly Pakistan-backed plot to overthrow the latest regime.

Azita went on talk proudly about her brother Darius saying that he passionately believed that things could change for the better in Afghanistan if the right people were in power. When Gabriel asked her who were the right people, Azita was evasive, saying only that the situation in her country was complicated. She placed her fingers on Gabriel's lips, a gesture which invited no more questions and took his hand saying they should stop being so serious.

She led him to a small side kitchen from which wafted aromas of spices, they stood in line to be served with strips of beef sizzled in huge pans of sesame oil and served with unleavened bread. Musicians in the centre of the room played local instruments and several men around the outside had hand drums. There was a communal singalong that reminded Gabriel of the camaraderie of Welsh pubs on a Saturday night. When they'd finished eating a young Pashtun boy appeared, poured Gabriel a cup of Afghan green tea, followed by a water pipe of hashish which he sipped contentedly allowing the music to waft over him.

Later Azita and Gabriel returned to the Peace Hotel where the caretaker was asleep with his head on the desk. Carefully they removed a large metal key marked No. 22 from the wooden block on the wall behind him and crept quietly up the stairs, suppressing their desire to giggle. The electricity had failed and the room was cold and dark, undeterred they pleasantly passed the hours by candlelight, wrapped in thick furry Afghan blankets. In case they fell asleep Gabriel set his small travel clock with its luminous hands to midnight. Azita's parents, whom she described as being very open minded, had nevertheless imposed a night curfew on her. When the alarm sounded they crept down the stairs, Azita barefoot, shoes in her hands. Once out in the street they walked hand in hand until reaching the corner of the hillside where Azita's small family home nestled amongst other flat roofed mud constructed houses.

As the weather started to turn colder and the cafe umbrellas fluttered in the wind Gabriel knew that the time had come to go home, after all, this idyllic life could not last forever. Max had already gone. It was with a heavy heart that he said farewell to Azita, they promised to write to each other and to meet again one day but they both knew it would be a brief memorable chapter in their lives but it was now over.

On the first of October Gabriel packed his rucksack, looked around the small room that had been home for a short while and headed down stairs, handed the key in at the desk and made his way to the airport on the east of the city. He had budgeted for extensive travel, but the decision to spend all his time in Kabul meant that he had more than enough money left to pay for a flight home. He found that he could travel to Frankfurt on Ariana Airlines and from Frankfurt take a connecting flight on BA to Heathrow. As the plane slowly ascended into the red glow of the Afghanistan sunset and the city that he had found to be so magical receded into the distance Gabriel was on his way home to a grey bland rainy London.

3

Déjà vu

In those half moments between sleeping and waking Gabriel was drowsily aware of the uncomfortable, paper thin, hard mattress beneath him, it reminded him of his bed in the Kabul hotel and he reached out for Azita expecting her to be lying next to him. Quickly realising that he was still in the hospital, tentatively he tried to move and to his surprise his body responded, he stretched his arms and legs with sheer joy at the simplicity of the task. His elation was soon disrupted by the shrill sound of a woman's voice saying, "It OK, it over now, you go home soon." Seated in a chair close to his bed was the woman he'd seen earlier shouting hysterically, the one that said she'd seen him running away. Gabriel sat up and looked closely at her; she had a foreign appearance, perhaps Indonesian he thought. He knew her from somewhere but was struggling to think who she was or where he might have met her before.

Gabriel asked her who she was but, ignoring the question she repeated, "It OK, I take you soon." At that moment a man in a white coat entered the room, the stethoscope around his neck confirming Gabriel's thought that he was a doctor. "Good

17

morning Mr. Jones, you have been a good boy, you've made an excellent recovery, you have really done very well." Gabriel didn't like his condescending tone and he certainly didn't trust him. The woman got up from her chair, took the doctor's arm and walked over to the corner of the room, where they engaged in a hurried conversation. She was getting angry, her voice was raised but they were too far away for Gabriel to hear what was being said. Finally the doctor waved his arms in the air dismissively and marched out of the room.

The woman pulled a suitcase from under the bed and proceeded to lay clothes, shirt, pants, trousers and socks neatly on the bed. "Come, you get dressed, we go now." Feeling that it would be futile to ask questions Gabriel did as she asked, slowly he discarded the thin pale green gown he was wearing and replaced it with the everyday clothes she had laid on the bed. "Quickly, hurry, we must hurry," she cried. "We must leave now."

Once he'd dressed, she took his arm and holding on tightly, led him along a corridor until they came to a flight of stairs; rather unsteadily he managed to descend them, at the bottom of the stairs a door opened out into the street. Once outside she tried to wave down cars passing by, Gabriel first thought she was hailing a taxi but soon realised her movements were not random as he had first assumed but she was deliberately signalling to black saloon cars with darkened windows. After a few minutes one of them stopped and pulled up alongside. She pushed him into the car shouted something through the open window to the driver and then got in beside him. Gabriel's head felt heavy, it was as if he'd been on a night out and drunk far more than he should have. He was becoming more and more convinced that he'd been given drugs, maybe they were prescription drugs or something more sinister, he'd no way of knowing. He felt like an onlooker watching a drama play out, it was like watching a serialised drama but he could not make sense of what was now happening because he'd missed an episode.

As the car moved off he was determined to fight the fog he felt himself slipping into and try to get some awareness of his bearings, he was looking for a landmark, something that he could recognise, something that would tell him where he was, he assumed that he was in England but had no idea where. A sign on the corner of the road said Dunston Road, this meant nothing to him, as they turned out of the road he could see in the distance a bridge and a wide murky river. There was a lot of traffic, when they pulled up at traffic lights he recognised the red circle transected by a blue band indicating a London tube station. "I'm in London," he shouted. The driver laughed and the woman answered impatiently, "Yes, you in London."

They moved away from the narrow streets onto a wide thoroughfare, lots of traffic including red London buses, with London Transport written on the side clearly identifying them. Gabriel felt more secure knowing that he was in London and not in some distant city that he would not be able to negotiate if he managed to escape. No sooner had he thought this, than they moved onto a dual carriageway with fast moving traffic and a sign M4 Heathrow Airport appeared. Again a feeling of despair, of not knowing where he might be heading, but his fears were allayed as they turned off the dual carriageway and he was able to make out another road sign with an arrow pointing north to Wembley.

They continued the journey in silence passing through rows and rows of suburban houses, finally turning into a green leafy suburb arriving at a gated block of flats. The woman got out, opened her handbag took out a bunch of keys and opened the gate, it swung slowly open and the car pulled into a designated parking space. Gabriel was slow getting out of the car feeling still very hazy, although strangely aware of what was going on but not really being there. The woman again told him to hurry and forced him to walk more quickly than he felt able towards a door, where she pressed a button and spoke briefly into an intercom. When the door opened, facing him were more stairs and a lot of them. The woman told him to hold on to the banister, then took his arm and led him up the three flights of stairs and opened the door to a small flat.

As soon as he entered he experienced an overwhelming sensation of "déjà vu", but although some things seemed very familiar other things were completely strange. He knew the layout of the place, there were a number of rooms and all the doors were closed but he headed straight to the bathroom because he desperately needed to go in there. The little room was very feminine with pink fluffy towels and a collection of multi-coloured perfume bottles. Washing his hands, he looked into the small mirror placed on the wall above the sink, for a moment he could not believe the reflection that looked back at him, his face was thinner and older than he remembered, there were bags under his eyes, his hair was turning grey and his beard was draped raggedly around his chin. He wetted his hair and brushed it lightly with his right hand, thinking, *I'm still a good looking bloke*, he'd always known that.

When he'd finished in the bathroom he found the woman in the small kitchen busily taking packets out of a small fridge and assembling them in an orderly fashion on the work surface near to the cooker. He opened one of the cupboards hoping he might recognise something that was his, something he might have chosen to buy and bring to this place, some indication that he might have been here before. The contents of the cupboard revealed haphazardly arranged, multicoloured, garishly designed plates and cups, certainly nothing that corresponded to his particularly aesthetic taste. The phone rang, the woman answered in a foreign language, it didn't take him long to recognise that she was speaking in Japanese. Of course, why hadn't he realised she was Japanese, he'd lived in Japan and although he couldn't speak the language he could understand some words. She was telling someone that he was here with her, that he was safe, that she would watch him, that she would make sure he contacted no one and that she would not let him out of the flat. It was only a brief conversation, she replaced the handset, turned to him and said "that my friend." He thought it best not to tell her that he understood Japanese and that he knew what she'd said.

She returned to examine the contents of the fridge, "This food not good, I must go shop, buy something for us to eat, I go buy steak, you like steak, I cook you nice meal." She had a disconcerting habit of closing her eyes whilst talking and always starting with the phrase, "How you say," a rhetorical question she used to precede whatever approximate English translation she could think of to convey her meaning. It was a phrase that would come to irritate him. Then she quickly put on a short coat, picked up a walking stick and a small backpack, turned to him and said, "I back soon, I lock door, keep you safe."

"No, no, don't lock the door," he protested.

"Yes, I must, they told me I must, you must be kept in safe," she said, as she turned the key in the door behind her. When she had gone Gabriel sat down on a small and rather uncomfortable settee, he was frightened, so many questions raced through his mind, who had told her she must lock the door? Who were they protecting him from? Who was looking for him? So many questions for which Gabriel had no answers. The only thing he was sure of was that he was in London. He'd lived in London for many years and knew that if only he could escape he'd know where to go, he had good friends in London, and if he could get to them he was convinced that they'd help him.

The time passed slowly, he wandered around the small flat, there were two small bedrooms, one looked almost like a student bedsit with a whole wall devoted to books and A4 folders. It was barely furnished, just a single bed very low to the floor, a small bedside table with two drawers. Inquisitively he opened the top drawer; it contained a few items of old fashioned women's underwear. Closing it quickly, not wishing to investigate these

21

items any further, he opened the drawer beneath, it also contained a woman's clothing, black trousers and black polo neck jumpers, exactly the same as the woman who had brought him here was wearing that day. He decided that not knowing her name he'd call her the "woman in black". This he felt was an apt description of someone he'd come to think of as remote, mysterious and ambiguous.

He opened the door of a narrow small cupboard built into the wall, it was filled with neatly stacked identical yellow boxes bearing the Kodak logo. Again he had that distinct sense of familiarity. He took one of the boxes in his hands and held it almost tenderly trying to recapture the memories that he felt the objects within held for him. Gently he opened the box to find photographic slides of the type commonly used in the old days with a projector. Holding a few of them to the light he managed to discern they were photos of rather magnificent historical buildings and splendid fountains. Examining the contents of the box more closely he saw that each of the slides was numbered, the number corresponding to a neatly compiled indexing system which revealed this box contained images of Rome. All assembled methodically in alphabetical order starting with the Arch of Constantine and ending with the Vatican. He carefully replaced everything back in the box and held it close to him for a long while before reluctantly returning it to the cupboard along with the intangible memories he felt it held for him.

He moved to the book shelves that lined the wall. There was a row of hardback books about the history of railways, history of architecture and many books on the subject of photography. On the narrower shelf below was a row of about twenty paperback novels written in Japanese and all by the same author Haruki Murakami. He reached to the top shelf where he could see a single black folder, as he pulled it from the shelf the contents emptied onto the floor, he panicked, he was fearful that she would return and discover that he'd been looking through her belongings. He hurriedly picked up the sheets of paper from the floor and stuffed them randomly back into the folder replacing it on the shelf. He went to walk away but stopped noticing a black and white photograph lying face up on the floor. He picked it up meaning to replace it in the folder, but looking more closely saw that it was a photograph of himself but only half an original photograph. He was standing outside a typical Japanese house and looked relaxed and happy. It was obvious that someone else had been standing next to him in the picture, a neat line had been drawn and a pair of scissors used to carefully remove the other person. Who was the other person and why had someone found it necessary to physically separate him from whoever it was? He put the photo in his pocket and returned to sit on the settee and wait for the woman to return.

He didn't have to wait long, she soon appeared laden with carrier bags as well as a full backpack which she removed from her shoulders, placed on the floor in front of him and said, "Look what I've got you." The contents revealed an M&S black bag, he opened it to find pants, tee shirts and pyjama trousers, the colours and style were not those he personally would have chosen, nevertheless he felt it was expected that he say, "thank you".

As promised, she cooked a meal, steak surprisingly cooked rare, just as he liked it, accompanied by a bowl of green salad and a bowl of boiled potatoes. They sat in silence at opposite ends of a small table near a large window overlooking a garden enclosed by tall trees. While they ate, he tried to scrutinise the "woman in black"as he'd mentally named her; she was small in stature and was overweight for her height, she had short cropped black hair maybe she looked older than she actually was, but he thought she must be at least sixty.

When they'd finished the meal she asked if he'd like to watch the television and said they only had pre-recorded programmes, explaining that there was no reception in the flat because of the surrounding trees. She pointed to a stack of DVD's piled high next to the television, "Choose whatever you want, I no mind," she said. Looking through them he saw they were organised alphabetically, starting with various Agatha Christie dramas followed by various recorded football matches, rugby matches, Top Gear and so on, there was quite a collection to choose from.

He felt very tired and surprisingly relaxed after the meal. He still could make no sense of the situation he found himself in, he was in a place where he suspected he'd been before and a place which he felt held happy memories, and with a woman he thought he'd met before, but who was a complete stranger to him now. He decided to watch a Wales v England rugby match, one of the Six Nations matches from 2012, and he remembered Wales had done well in the international competition that year. The woman in black brought in cups of tea on a small tray and they sat quietly together watching the match, again he sensed there was something very familiar about her.

They watched the match together without a word being spoken and she seemed relaxed, curled in an armchair not far away from him. There was an air of almost calm domesticity and he wondered if it might be a good time to ask some questions. A little apprehensively he decided to try. Breaking the long silence, he asked simply, "What is your name?"

"My name Akemi," she replied.

He dared to go further, "Why am I here?" he asked. She paused as if thinking before answering, "I paid look after you." His curiosity aroused he continued, "Who is paying you and why?" Her response to these questions left him with no further information, answering with her eyes closed, "It no matter, it not important, you no need know these things."

Again they sank into a long silence; he put his hand in his pocket his fingers feeling the smooth surface of the picture he'd picked up from the floor earlier. Dare he ask her what she knew about the person missing from the photograph? Tentatively, slowly he took it out of his pocket. "Who else was in this photo?" he asked the question with trepidation but was unprepared for the ferocity and unreserved anger of the response. With her eyelids closed and her voice raised she shouted accusingly, "You been in my things, you no go through my things." Then she snatched the photo from him, she placed her finger next to where he was standing in the photo and said, "You no remember her any more, she gone away, she evil one, she cause trouble for you." Although fearful of her reaction he could not help but ask, "Who was she?" Her reaction was to throw the photo onto the carpet and storm out of the room. Gabriel quickly rescued the photograph, thankful that it was still intact.

It wasn't long before she came back as if nothing had happened, her manner once again calm even bordering on friendly, she brought with her a mug of steaming liquid, which she said he must drink because it would help him sleep. Somewhat reluctantly he complied, not wishing to evoke any further tantrums. As he sipped the drink slowly she once again disappeared into the kitchen and returned with a small glass of water and a handful of various coloured pills which she laid out in a line in front of him. She told him that they were also to help him to sleep. At that moment all he wanted was to escape from the nightmare in which he'd become ensnared. He had one clue to the puzzle, the woman in black's name was Akemi but it still didn't mean anything to him. He knew he needed a plan, a plan to escape but that would have to wait until tomorrow. Drifting off to sleep, perchance to dream, was the best escape he could hope for right now and so he obediently swallowed the pills. He went to lie down and in the moments before sleep blotted out consciousness he recalled the previous night when in his dreams he'd vividly relived his time in Afghanistan. He hoped that in the refuge of unconsciousness his subconscious might recall what happened when he'd returned home to London.

4

An Indian summer

On his return from Afghanistan Gabriel had taken up the post in the London Civil Service and had already become increasingly disenchanted with the tedious ritual of his daily life. Travelling through central London to a small office in a large grey government building, he spent his days looking out onto a narrow street whilst going through the motions of compiling briefing notes for junior ministers. Britain was once again experiencing growing social inequality and massive unrest amongst the workers, the miners' strike resulting in a three day working week. Gabriel was instructed to be selective in the information he researched, it was to be used to justify the controversial ongoing industrial strategy policy. He became increasingly disillusioned and took the opportunity to embark upon a new career, accepting the post of International Politics lecturer at Oxford University.

He settled in Headington, a leafy suburb of Oxford, it wasn't long before a young man about his age joined the university department as another new lecturer. Having moved to Oxford from the North East, he was looking for somewhere to live and readily accepted Gabriel's offer to rent a room in his house. Gabriel was glad of the chance of the company, the house although small, had seemed big and empty during the time he'd spent there alone. The young man was Albert Westman, someone with whom Gabriel would share a lifelong friendship.

Gabriel and Albert enjoyed academic life; they were popular with students and were frequently invited to their parties. Gabriel particularly enjoyed the attention bestowed on him by the young female students. It was at one of these parties that he first met Franchesca, one of a small group standing in a corner of the room. She was beautiful, wearing a lovely fitted red dress that complemented her slim, perfect figure. She had long dark shiny hair, swarthy Mediterranean skin and delightful little dimples in her cheeks when she laughed. Albert said he had met her before at a party and that she was a post graduate student studying for a Master's degree in bio-chemistry. Picking up on Gabriel's obvious interest in the girl he offered to introduce him to her. Albert tactfully left them alone together and they talked for the rest of the evening. Franchesca told him that she came from Bolivia and she was the youngest of seven sisters. Her father had died when she was very young, so young that she could remember nothing about him. Her mother was from a rich Bolivian family and her grandparents had ensured that all the girls had received a first class education. She had come to Oxford to study as an undergraduate and was staying to complete her Master's degree. That night Gabriel walked her back to her shared student accommodation and to his surprise she agreed to meet him for a drink the next evening at seven o'clock.

The following day he was unable to concentrate on anything, constantly looking at his watch and counting the hours, the minutes until seven o'clock. He was completely captivated by Franchesca and arrived half an hour early at the pub, their designated meeting place. It was a warm June evening and Gabriel sat outside at a wooden picnic table; he waited and waited, growing more and more restless. Then she arrived, casually dressed in figure hugging jeans and a simple white tee shirt, a bright coloured bag resting on her shoulder. This was the beginning of a long and close friendship. It was a relationship which he tried unsuccessfully many times to progress beyond the level of friendship, but that first evening he was blissfully unaware that it was never to be.

Gabriel and Albert had a love of travel and unless Gabriel was lucky enough to get a date with Franchesca, he and Albert would spend the evenings in their local pub, drinking and dreaming of the exotic places they'd visit one day. As the end of the third semester at the university neared, an unexpected opportunity presented itself. An important part of the work at the university involved research which would lead to articles written and published in academic journals. Gabriel and Albert had collaborated producing articles as joint papers. Combining their joint interests they wrote papers on the international development of cities and the international development of railways and the relationship between them. One of their articles on the development of railways in India had recently been published.

One morning when Gabriel was walking from one lecture theatre to another, leather briefcase, books and papers strategically clasped under both arms, Albert came running up to him excitedly waving a letter and asking, "How do you fancy going to India this summer?" Proceeding to run by, saying, "late for tutorial, meet me in Gino's." Gino's was their favourite Italian restaurant where they often ate at the end of the day before moving on to spend the evening in the pub.

Gabriel's heart was racing in expectation as he sat at the gingham clothed table in Gino's looking out of the window anxiously waiting for Albert to appear. It wasn't long before he arrived, clutching the invitations he'd received in the post that morning. There were in fact two letters, both written on official headed notepaper. The first was an invitation to attend a conference at the University of Bombay. The second was from the Chief Public Relations Officer of Bombay Baroda and Central India Railway (BB&CI), and was a copy of a letter that had been sent to chief station masters in the city rail stations throughout India. It read, "This is to introduce, Mr. Gabriel Jones and Mr. Albert Westman who at our invitation will be travelling around India studying inter-city transportation systems and town planning. I should be grateful if you would render them whatever assistance is possible." They could not believe their luck and the next few weeks were spent reading travel guides and working out a route that would enable them to experience the famous tourist sites of India whilst visiting as many university departments and government offices as they could.

On a beautiful July morning they flew out of Heathrow and arrived on schedule in Santa Cruz airport, Bombay. The distinctive fragrance of India, a blend of camphor, incense, cows and spicy food, greeted them as they disembarked and walked the short distance across the tarmac from the aircraft to arrivals.

They made their way through the scantily furnished airport. There were many officials around, including policemen in their worn out uniforms, gaiter like socks and shorts. One of the policemen signalled to them to wait at a small desk with a sign above saying passport control. Albert took out his passport and showed it to the turbaned gentleman at the desk who gave it a cursory glance and handed it back to him. Being less organised than Albert, Gabriel was struggling to remember which of his many pockets contained his passport. With a sigh of relief he finally retrieved the illusive passport from his hand luggage. The official at the desk looked intently at each page, asked him to remove his sunglasses and scrutinised his face closely as if to convince himself that it matched the photograph on the inside of the passport, then he stood up and asked Gabriel to follow him to a small room just behind the desk. In a moment of panic Gabriel looked round for Albert and just managed to catch sight of him disappearing through the door marked exit. Once in the small room he was invited to take a seat, another Indian official entered, he also scrutinised the passport, the pair spoke quietly in their own particular dialect. One disappeared and a short while later returned accompanied by a smartly dressed European gentleman. "Hello Mr. Jones," he said, "I am Nicolai Peratrovska and I am an ambassador with the Russian embassy here in Bombay. On behalf of my country I wish to welcome you to India," he shook Gabriel's hand and asked, "How long do you intend to stay in India?"

"One month," Gabriel replied.

"What is your business here?" continued Peratrovska. Gabriel explained that he'd been invited to look at Southern India's developing transportation system. The man nodded and in a slightly sinister tone said, "If you find yourself in any trouble Mr Jones or encounter any problems during your stay in India do not hesitate to contact me at the embassy." Then he simply walked out through the door, the Indian official gave Gabriel a strange enquiring look and stamped his passport to show the date he'd arrived and the date he was expected to leave. Gabriel thanked him politely and walked away quickly, anxious to find Albert. He was not surprised by the incident, it had happened before when he'd travelled in Europe and only served to confirm his suspicions that he was still somehow of significance to the Russians.

Albert was waiting for him in the arrivals lounge. He jumped up as Gabriel walked towards him, he looked worried. "What was that all about?" he asked.

"Oh just Indian bureaucracy," Gabriel replied dismissively. He thought it better that Albert knew nothing about his past connections with Russia. Albert introduced him to the gentleman standing next to him; it was Sam Berkeley-Hall, the professor who'd invited them to attend the conference and had come personally to meet them at the airport. Gabriel had already formed a preconception of this man from the correspondence he'd seen between him and Albert. He expected him to be very upper class and he certainly was. He was English Public School educated, spoke with a very refined accent and was immaculately dressed in a white linen suit, shirt and light blue tie. He welcomed them, shook hands cordially and asked if they'd had a good journey and escorted them outside to a waiting car.

Unburdening themselves of luggage they sank gratefully into the leather upholstered seats of Sam's Jaguar. The car crawled through the city delicately weaving its way through the hoards of people wandering along the road seemingly undeterred by the cars and buses intermingling with the bicycles, the rickshaws and even animals. It was a maze of colour, women in multicoloured saris, men wearing long white sheets of cloth called dhoti and incongruously over the top of them a western branded tee shirt and very young scantily clad children with no apparent adult supervision running freely amid the dangers. They headed out of the city heading to Cobala, a district sprawling down the city's southernmost peninsula. They drove through a jumble of side streets into a street lined with large colonial style mansions finally arriving at 5, Corinthian Road. They were greeted at the door by two Indian young men dressed identically in long white robes with bright red and gold sashes and matching red turbans held at the front with little gold ornaments. They bowed as Sam got out of the car and immediately proceeded to empty the boot of the luggage and carry bags up the stairs to the large open front door. Gabriel watched in amazement as Sam explained that these were two of his servants Ashok and Bansi.

Sam introduced them to his wife Jenny an attractive woman casually dressed in cream trousers and a bright green open necked blouse, her dark blonde hair knotted in a bun that sat neatly against the nape of her neck. Together they gave a tour of the house, there were many rooms all lavishly and ornately furnished and with rotating blades suspended from the ceilings giving a welcome cool breeze to each room. They told their guests that their life in India was good; the Cobala district was home to many British families.

They climbed the stairs to the upper floor and Jenny pointed to a door leading to a room she said would be theirs for the duration of their stay in Cobala. At that moment Bansi, one of the servants, appeared with the suitcases, bowed as he passed and proceeded to place their suitcase inside the door, then moved past them again bowing as he left. Gabriel thought that this was something he'd never get used to. Sam sensing Gabriel's disquiet at the servility demonstrated by Bansi explained that it was perfectly normal for large houses to employ live-in servants, all the British had servants. It was good for the Indian economy rationalised Sam, many of the servants came from low castes and had travelled to find work in the city from the rural areas. Ashok and Bansi, Sam said, had travelled from Gujarat. The luxury of having servants meant that they had plenty of free time to enjoy their social life with the many British families who lived in the area. When the tour was completed, they all sat on a veranda looking down onto the large garden below, drinking masala tea served by Ashok from a large silver pot into tall glasses and reflecting on Sam's comment, Gabriel found himself agreeing that yes life was good here.

The next morning Gabriel woke early and armed with his camera ventured out to explore. Tea was being brewed on the pavement stalls; great urns of fresh milk being delivered from the countryside on carts, the tops plugged with straw; brightly uniformed children skipping their way to school, birds chirping in the banyan trees. He followed a sign to the Sassoon Docks and watched as the morning catch came in. The fishermen carrying the fish in baskets on their heads rushing to the market along the quay where colourfully clad Koli fisherwomen were sorting out the catch they had unloaded from the fishing boats. He was busy taking photographs as he did everywhere, when he was approached by a port official who pointed to a sign which clearly read, "Photography at the dock is forbidden without permission from the Bombay Port Trust."

Heading back to Corinthian Road, he wandered across the

Cobala Causeway which bisects the promontory and is the artery connecting Cobala's jumble of side streets and the European occupied wealthy area with its rambling gated mansions. Lost for a while in the back streets, he hurried by beggars, men, women and small children sitting on dirty bits of carpet on the dusty pavements. Once back in the area of Corinthian Road he entered a different world, one which had an unmistakeable English order about it – grand whitewashed buildings mingled with huge houses with prim names. A true reflection of the stark disparity between the very rich and the extremely poor living in close proximity in Bombay "the dream city" as Sam had described it.

Back at the house Gabriel found Sam, Jenny and Albert breakfasting in the appropriately named breakfast room, he joined them and tucked into a hearty morning meal. Sam had arranged a meeting with Harold Samuel, the Chief Public Relations Officer for the Bombay railway region. Harold, an ex army major, proved to be friendly and helpful and gave them a lot of important first hand information on the future development plans for the city. The meeting was followed by lunch with dignitaries from the local council for the area, at the nearby Taj Mahal Palace Hotel an iconic building in Bombay with its famous central floating staircase. Gabriel and Albert were extremely impressed by the attention paid to them and the hospitality given so generously by Sam and his well placed contacts in the city. After a series of lengthy drawn out goodbyes and exchange of addresses they left with Sam who had promised to show them some of the tourist attractions of the area that were within walking distance of the hotel.

"We are very close to the gateway of India," said Sam, pointing to the end of the wide road. "Look," he said, and as he spoke there came into view a beautifully architected colossal structure, Sam informed them that its construction began about 1911 on the spot where King George V and Queen Mary first landed in India. Sam led them to some steps behind the arch of the Gateway that leads to the Arabian Sea. Gabriel and Albert gasped as the breathtaking view of Bombay harbour span out before them, a vista known in India as the blue blanket, Sam told them.

A local boatman called out to them in his native language, Sam nodded and motioned to them to board the small boat which took them on a short trip to a green island home of The Elephant Caves. Arriving on the small quayside there were a few locals offering their services as guides, which Sam politely refused. They walked along a narrow road that led to steep stairs embedded in the rock. It was a long climb up to the top of the island to a place which seemed to be far away from the hustle and bustle of Bombay. There was something very calming about the island.

They joined a group of tourists to take the ferry back to the mainland, whilst on the ferry Sam met an Indian family, old friends that he hadn't seen for a while. The man was about Sam's age with his wife and two daughters. Sam introduced them as his good friend Ranjith Desai, his wife and two daughters. Sitting opposite them on a small wooden bench during the short journey back into the harbour Gabriel could not help smiling at the elder of the two daughters; she was exceptionally pretty, long black hair, chestnut skin and wearing a long dark blue sari, a blue veil trimmed with a gold braid framed her face. A strange feeling overcame came him. It was more than just an attraction: without knowing anything at all about this young girl he thought he would like to marry her. He later found out that her name was Jysonta and that it meant moonlight.

They were about to say goodbye to the family at the quayside when Ranjith announced in true Indian fashion that they were all cordially invited to dinner with him and his family that evening. Gabriel could not help noticing that Jysonta seemed particularly pleased. Sam graciously accepted her father's invitation. Gabriel's heart beat even faster as she turned to him and said, "I shall look forward to seeing you again later."

They returned to collect Jenny and change into appropriate clothing for their dinner at the Desai family home. Back at the house they experienced what Sam described as, "a much awaited summer rainstorm." They went out onto the veranda and watched as the sky darkened, the hills disappeared into a thick mist and a dense curtain of rain approached till it was right overhead. Thunder shook the house, huge raindrops splattered on the roof and the strong wind bent and twisted the tops of the fruit trees, in the garden orchard below.

They ventured out into the rain complete with umbrellas to go the short distance to Ranjith's house. Sam hailed a rickshaw and the four of them squeezed into the covered contraption drawn by a rickety cycle which circumvented the narrow streets and stopped outside the Desai home. Jysonta greeted them at the door, Gabriel was completely enchanted, she guided them into the sitting room where her parents, her young sister and a good looking man were seated. The man appeared to be a few years older than Jysonta, at first Gabriel thought he might be an elder brother but soon learnt she was engaged to be married to this man.

They sat down at the table to eat a delicious meal of delicately spiced chicken and rice which Mrs Desai proudly informed them was her speciality which she had personally prepared for them. Gabriel was surprised that Jysonta and future husband did not sit near to each other and that there was very little communication between them, it was as if they were strangers. In fact to his astonishment Jysonta appeared far more interested in talking to him about England, she told him that she wanted to be a pharmacist and that she had really wanted to study in England, but although her father had the means to pay for this, he was a very traditional man who believed it was his duty to see that she married into a good family whilst she was still young and settled down. She confided all this to him in a matter of fact way, she did not seem particularly unhappy that she had to forgo her dreams and conform to her father's wishes. It seemed she unquestioningly accepted that this was the way things were done. Abhi, her fiancé, she explained had been chosen for her because he was from a good Hindu family and had good prospects having recently qualified as a solicitor.

They left after a very pleasant evening at the Desai family home, whilst walking with the family in the dark of the late evening through the garden to the gate Gabriel managed to secretly squeeze Jysonta's hand and she offered no resistance. Now that he was fully aware of the situation he knew that he had to get over his strange infatuation with her. He decided that in the morning he would write a long letter to Franchesca.

* * *

The next day they left Bombay to travel the 150 miles to Poona. A taxi arrived at 9.30 to take them to the railway station, the driver got out and said unexpectedly, "Passports."

"Why?" asked Albert, the driver simply repeated "passports." They complied, he checked them carefully then scribbled some indecipherable hieroglyphics on a note pad. Seated finally in the back seat of the taxi, Gabriel thought the lack of any type of ornamentation was rather odd; Bombay taxis were renowned for their colourful and flamboyantly decorated interiors. He had been told that the taxi decor reflected the personality of the driver and often included Buddha like figures on the dashboard and colourful pendants hanging from the windscreen. This added to his suspicion that this particular taxi and driver had been hired by people wanting to keep track of his whereabouts whilst he was travelling in India. The driver could speak very little English and so there was no communication between them on the short journey. Albert having previously travelled in India thought the experience was odd, taxi drivers had never requested to see his passport before, he also commented on the uncustomary blandness of the cab. Gabriel agreed that it was all very strange, neglecting to add that he'd become accustomed to these strange random checks at unexpected points in his travels.

They arrived at Bori Bunder station, an impressive gothic style building that reminded them of London's St Pancras station.

They were looking forward to their journey on the Deccan Queen, India's first deluxe train, to run between the commercial capital Bombay and the cultural capital, Poona, it was one of the first intercity rail lines completed in India and also the first intercity rail line to be fully electrified. Gabriel's research at the university focussed on the innovation of the Indian railway network and this was his chance to see it for himself, and to take photographs to illustrate his lectures.

Then he saw Jysonta looking so beautiful in a blue sari, her bangled uncovered arms glinting in the sunlight, she was holding an umbrella. "You left this last night, I thought you might need it when the rains come," she said, then disappeared into the crowd as quickly as she had appeared. Gabriel was flattered to think that she had made two bus journeys to catch up with him at the station and he'd not even realised that he'd left the umbrella behind.

Harold was waiting for them on the station platform, he presented them with two tickets for second class travel on the Deccan Express, with typical Indian hospitality he said they were courtesy of the Bombay Baroda and Central India Railway (BB&CI), and he hoped they'd enjoy the experience on his railway of which he was very proud.

Waiting in anticipation on a crowded platform, a silver engine with scarlet mouldings crept into the station; an army of attendants appeared, swinging open carriage doors as they walked past the first class to the second class carriages. Making their way along a narrow corridor Gabriel and Albert entered a magnificent compartment with a silver wood and walnut panelled interior, distinctly colonial, with an aura of class, warmth and elegance. They placed their bags on the net rack that hung above the spacious seats draped with pristine white head rest covers bearing the BB&CI logo boldly embroidered in red and silver. Gabriel felt the elation of being pampered like royalty and sank contentedly into a seat next to the open sash window. Locals bearing trays congregated at the window trying to sell souvenirs.

A guard waved a green flag and slowly the magnificent train pulled away from the platform, young local children ran alongside, it was at that moment Gabriel saw, Nickolai standing amongst the others waving off their friends and loved ones. In his white linen suit and straw hut circled at the brim with a narrow black band, he was close to the end of the long platform and as they passed he raised his hand slightly tipping his hat towards the window, a gesture of farewell perhaps. Gabriel had grown used to the fact that his previous life would intrude into his present life whenever he least expected it, but nevertheless this never failed to disturb him.

Gabriel's spirits lifted once the train picked up speed and raced away from Bombay heading for Karjat, the station in the foothills just before the mighty Sahyadri Mountains. Stopping briefly at Lonavala they were surrounded once again by locals, many of them children, offering their wares through the open windows. The train passed through magnificent tunnels, emerging every now and then to see spectacular ravines covered with dense tropical forests. Khandala appeared lush after the pre-monsoon rains and monkeys from the bushes near the track bounded down, as the train slackened speed. It was amusing to see them eating bananas and bits of bread tossed out of the windows to them by the passengers. Then it seemed they left behind all the open spaces and the lovely countryside, a landscape innocent and untouched by civilization, as the Deccan Queen flowed through mud hut and tented slums juxtaposed between large concrete buildings to deliver them on time to Dadar station. They had arrived in Poona and took a short walk to the Hotel Gulmohr, in the heart of the city, close to the railway station. They were welcomed at the reception desk by a friendly young Asian man in western dress and shown to their rooms by a uniformed porter showing the gracious hospitality they had come to expect during their stay in India.

That first evening they explored downtown Poona looking for

nightlife entertainment but the narrow streets were unnaturally quiet. None of the cafes, night street traders selling tea and souvenirs, no rickshaws, none of the bustle that they had become used to in Bombay. All they encountered were poor beggars asleep on the pavements. They hurried back to the hotel, where a piano was playing in the forecourt and other hotel guests were gathered, they were mainly tourists of various nationalities. Gabriel and Albert joined a group of French doctors who were delegates attending a medical conference at the university. There were five of them altogether, Gabriel thought Cecile, one of two female delegates, might be interesting if he could get to know her, so strategically selected a chair close to her. A heated discussion was taking place on the merits of communism versus capitalism. Gabriel soon realised that Cecile had very strong opinions which she expressed with ardent intensity. Her anti socialist principles were the complete opposite of his ideals and so he decided to abstain from any involvement in their discussion. He made his excuses citing tiredness from the journey and the need for an early night and retired to his room and wrote a long letter to Franchesca.

Gabriel and Albert remained in Poona for rest of their stay in India. It was a beautiful old city surrounded by verdant hills and beautiful lakes with narrow winding roads, an old-world charm and many quaint characteristics, offering an interesting contrast to the new expanding city, sprawling slummed and unplanned inwards from the outskirts towards the old cultural centre.

Their days were full of pre arranged meetings with regional and local planning officers, and as is the way in India, these formal meetings led to many more informal meetings with officials anxious to give their visions for future plans for the development of their city and offering to pay handsomely if their ideas were to be expounded in any papers they might subsequently publish in international journals.

Their final day was free from meetings anxious to collect some souvenirs of the visit Gabriel headed out of the hotel wandering through side streets seeking out the local bazaars, assailed as usual by hordes of poor people. Eventually emerging from the maze of narrow streets he came upon the Phule Mandai market and was greeted by a spectacular burst of colours, vegetables and fruit glistening in the midday sun and an infectious energy of scantily clad vendors. Hidden away in the numerous lanes that surrounded the market he found old shops, some selling traditional clothing, others beads and bangles, others selling all kinds of leather goods. He entered one of the leather shops, instantly the intoxicating, overpowering smell of leather enveloped him. He moved between lines of leather bags suspended from the low ceiling and the sensation as they brushed his skin was one of pure sumptuous soft leather. He selected a soft dark brown leather ladies handbag from a hook above his head. It was intricately adorned with small flowers cut from lighter coloured leather. Somehow, he successfully bartered and finally paid a price which he thought was very reasonable for such a lovely quality bag and walked away happy with his present for Franchesca.

Early the next morning they boarded the Deccan Queen on a return journey to Bombay from where they were to catch a late evening flight to Heathrow. On their arrival at Bombay, Sam and Jenny met them off the train and drove them to the airport. Gabriel felt sad when he said goodbye to them, they had been very kind and hospitable. After the farewells Gabriel and Albert queued for boarding passes, passports in hand, Gabriel was watchful expecting at any moment to be summoned to a private room and questioned, but to his surprise it didn't happen this time and he passed through all the checks without any apparent problems. Nevertheless, Gabriel was aware of a man dressed in a white linen suit and straw hut circled at the brim with a narrow black band who appeared to be observing him closely as he made his way to the gate to board the aircraft.

5

The "Jeremy Bentham" connection

Gabriel felt someone shaking him and shouting, "Wake up, wake up, we have to go, we be late, wake up, wake up." He didn't want to wake up; he wanted to stay wrapped safely in his dreams. He didn't want to return to the reality of what his life had become, but he was being dragged forcibly back to the present by the woman in black. As he reluctantly let go of his slumber he remembered that her name was Akemi and again was struck by the familiarity of her movements as she laid out his clothes on the bed.

Gabriel sat up in bed, yet again his head felt heavy, as if he'd had too much to drink the night before. He held his head in his hands, Akemi was shouting, "Come on, we have to go, we have appointment, come on, get dressed, I make you food." She disappeared into the kitchen; Gabriel heard a kettle whistling, and the pleasant scent of bacon and warm toast. He dressed and joined Akemi already seated at the table upon where breakfast was shared out onto two identical plates. Taking the seat next to her Gabriel once again experienced that feeling of a familiar domesticity.

Akemi ate quickly and clearing away her plate she invited him to "hurry, hurry" adding "cab be here five minutes." Gabriel was about to dare to ask where they were going when there was a ring at the intercom. Akemi answered, grabbing her coat on the way, "We ready, we come now," she shouted into the intercom. She passed Gabriel a coat, unlocked the door which had been locked on the inside and led him down the flights of stairs and through the main door of the building to where the same car and the same driver that had delivered them to the flat yesterday was waiting for them. Akemi sat next to Gabriel in the back seat of the cab, he was listening for her to give instructions as to their destination but surprisingly she didn't speak and neither did the cab driver ask. Gabriel asked, "Where are we going?" she replied abruptly, "You'll see, it not far." Gabriel tried to recognise landmarks as they drove through busy streets but there was nothing that he recognised until in the distance rising above the other buildings he saw the outline of an ornate dome. They turned right into a narrow street, on the corner was a pub, its sign, "The Jeremy Bentham" swinging in the breeze. Gabriel was trembling with the excitement of knowing where he was. Akemi, noticing his agitated state asked, "What is it? Why your hands shaking?" He clasped his hands together trying belatedly to hide his excitement. He was not prepared to tell her that he knew this area well, that he'd spent many evenings with friends drinking in the Jeremy Bentham. Then the familiar Octagon Building of University College London came into view.

They drove straight past, meandering through street after street until they reached a large square occupied by a large rambling building with many smaller outbuildings. An ambulance screeched by, then its sirens suddenly silent, confirming Gabriel's thoughts that this was a hospital, he knew there were a few of them in this vicinity. He recalled that his friend Max was a doctor in a hospital somewhere around here but couldn't remember which one.

Gabriel had kept in touch with Max after his return from Afghanistan. Max had been a neurological surgeon at the University College Hospital and they had often met at the Jeremy Bentham. It was the closest pub to UCL where Gabriel had studied for his degree. The pub was always swarming with young undergraduates, but one particular summer evening it became very noisy, they couldn't hear each other speak above the noise and made the decision to move outside to the quiet of the beer garden.

Perhaps it was the pleasant warmth of that particular summer evening and the fact that they found themselves alone, secluded in the heavily scented garden both having drunk far more than usual that led to the conversation that followed between them. Max opened up first, he wanted to confess that some aspects of his work as a neurological specialist worried him. He went on to make Gabriel promise that he'd never repeat to anyone what he was about to divulge to him. He told him that he was involved in research into brain disorders and had been asked to take part in various experiments that involved trial drugs. He never elaborated on the nature of these experiments all that he would say was that the whole process that he had committed himself to, in order to further his career, was disturbing him.

Gabriel felt privileged that Max trusted him enough to share this concern with him and perhaps it was this that led Gabriel to tell him about parts of his life that he'd never spoken about to anyone. He told him that when he was younger he'd worked one summer as a translator in the Russian Embassy in London, that he'd travelled to Leningrad and that while he was there he'd seen certain things that he could never admit to having seen and overheard conversations that he should never have been party to. He explained that at that time he'd been rather naive and had entered into agreements that years later he regretted. He also told him about the photographs he'd taken of the people he'd met there and the places he'd seen. For a while they sat in silence relieved that they'd talked about these private things but aware even in their drunken state that the next morning they would regret that the conversation between them had ever taken place.

Gabriel's mind returned to the present as the taxi stopped outside a long low pre-fabricated building. "Come on, hurry, hurry

43

we'll be late," Akemi was shouting. At the reception desk, Akemi spoke in a low voice, almost a whisper to the young girl sitting there. The girl shuffled files, selecting one thick file and placing it at the forefront of the desk. Gabriel could see that it had his name clearly written on it as well as the word confidential stamped in large blue capital letters. They didn't wait very long before another girl came out of a side room and called, "Mr. Gabriel Jones."

Akemi went in first, Gabriel followed her into the room, a smartly dressed female sat on one side of a desk and gestured to them to take the small plastic seats opposite. "Good morning, Mr. Jones, how are you today?" her friendly tone cleverly disguising her firm, practical, purely professional attitude. Without waiting for his reply, she went on to introduce herself as Eleanor Kozlowski, a research assistant at the Institute and without a pause explained that today she was going to conduct some tests. Gabriel asked, "What tests? Why are you doing these tests?" Eleanor gave him a sympathetic smile and in a patronising voice answered, "This is a research institute and the tests are merely to see the effects of the medication you are taking."

Gabriel asked if she knew a doctor named Max who was a friend of his and who worked in a research unit in this area of London. "No one called Max works here," she replied dismissively. "Now Mr. Jones, can we get on with the tests? This is the first thing you have to do, it's a questionnaire, tick the appropriate answers, it will only take a few minutes." She placed two A4 sheets of paper in front of him and a pen. Picking up the pen Gabriel read the words Neurological Research Unit clearly written on it in small red letters. Reading the list of questions before him he realised it was a psychological personality test. His naturally analytical mind told him that it wasn't a very well designed questionnaire, a simple tick box system for yes and no questions and biased questions leading to a particular response. He decided to expose the stupidity of it by giving negative answers to every question and ticked the no box for all thirty five questions; it was completed in a matter of seconds. Not expecting him to complete it so quickly Eleanor looked up in surprised when he pushed the finished questionnaire across the desk towards her.

"That's fine," she said without looking at his answers and slipping the sheets into a file, "now follow me." Akemi remained seated as Gabriel was led into a small dark room, no bigger than a large cupboard. When Eleanor switched on a light, it reminded him of a room where you have eye tests but unlike an opticians there were was no white board with letters vertically decreasing in size line by line Instead there was a small blank screen. Eleanor told him to sit down and placed a contraption with wires attached onto his head telling him to relax whist she adjusted it around his ears. Then the light was switched off and the screen lit up. "I am going to show you some pictures of well known sites in the world, I know you have travelled widely and I just want to see if you can remember the names and where they are located, is that clear?" Gabriel replied, "Yes."

Four sequential images flashed onto the screen, each lasting just a few seconds, the Eiffel Tower, the Brandenburg Gate, the Tower of London, the Sydney Opera House. Then the screen went blank. "Now, Mr. Jones, can you tell me the names of the four landmarks in the correct order they appeared?"

"The Eiffel Tower, the Brandenburg Gate, the Tower of London and the Sydney Opera House," he replied immediately. "Well done," she said patronisingly. More pictures of various landmarks followed and each time he remembered them perfectly. Then she asked him to say the months of the year backwards, he thought it bizarre, but did as she asked. After a short pause she again asked him to repeat the names of the first four landmarks he'd been shown, which he did without hesitation.

"Now I am going to make things more difficult," she said, and onto the screen came a map, an outline of a large country with the blue of the Arctic ocean shown to the north and sea of

Japan to the east with dots representing cities but the names had been blanked out and replaced with numbers. Gabriel recognised it immediately, "Have you ever seen this map before?" she asked. His hands started to shake, he'd never expected to see that map again. He clasped his hands tightly together, fearful that she might detect his agitation. "No, never," he replied emphatically. She went on to ask, "Do you know which country it is?" He felt it pointless to deny the fact that he knew it was a map of the old Soviet Union, so he said, "This is a very old map, the Soviet Union no longer exists, it has been broken up into many separate countries." Somewhat impatiently she continued, "Yes, Mr Jones, I am fully aware of that, but do you know the names of any of the towns and cities marked on this map?" She pointed to each of them in turn. "No," he said again. He was not convinced that she believed him as she said dismissively, "That's all for today, but I'll be seeing you again soon," and opened the door leading to the room where Akemi was waiting. Gabriel noted that Eleanor spoke to Akemi in a whispered tone, wrote something on a small piece of paper and handed it to her.

Outside the building the same cab was waiting for them, it was parked in the exact place where they had left it, Gabriel felt sure that it hadn't moved from the spot and found it strange that a London cabbie would wait for the two hours and wondered who might be paying him for his time? Gabriel was relieved to get out of the building, but his mind was racing. Why after all this time were they still interested in him? Who were they? Convinced it was one of the security agencies, he had no way of knowing whether it was British security MI5 or the American CIA or was it still the Russians who were after him because of what he knew? The only person he'd ever confided in was Max, he knew the story of the map and how inadvertently he'd become aware of it. It was during one of his trips to Leningrad, he was in a government building for a pre-arranged meeting with an official where he was to collect some papers to take back to his contact in the UK. He was waiting in a huge room, with high lavishly decorated ceiling; like all the official buildings in Leningrad the ostentation of the interiors contrasted greatly with their grey concrete plain exteriors. Gabriel had always been a restless soul, unable to sit still for very long, he wandered around the room, a number of large doors led to other rooms, one was slightly ajar, he peeped cautiously into the room, facing him on a wall was the map, the exact same map Eleanor had displayed on the screen. It was only a brief look before an official tapped his shoulder and said in a very firm tone of voice, "Mr. Jones, you have not seen this map, you will never speak of it to anyone, do you understand."

"Yes, of course, I understand," he'd replied guiltily.

Gabriel had faithfully kept his word, he'd told no one until that drunken summer night, with Max. Somehow he knew it must all be connected, Max was involved in experimental research, Eleanor said that the place they'd just left was a research institute. Max knew he'd seen the map, Eleanor showed him the map and asked if he recognised it. He must try and find Max, he was the only one who could help him. He had to work out an escape plan, the cab was moving along a busy road, he saw a traffic signal ahead, it was green, the cab slowed down as they approached anticipating the light was about to change. The light went red, the cab pulled up and stopped, Gabriel glanced at Akemi, she had put on a pair of glasses and was intent on reading the piece of paper Eleanor had handed to her. Gabriel saw his chance, he opened the door, jumped out and he ran. He could hear Akemi behind him shouting, "Catch him, catch him." He turned and ran down a side street, her voice faded into the distance, then out of the side street and onto a busy main road crowded with people. He kept running and running until his legs became leaden and he was struggling to breathe. He'd reached a small green parkland area, it was secluded from the main road and there were a few brightly coloured ironwork benches, exhausted he slumped onto the first bench knowing that he was far enough away from Akemi to be safe. He knew he needed to work out the next stage of his plan which was to find Max. It had taken all his strength to get this far, he was heavily medicated and it was not surprising therefore that he fell asleep.

When he woke a six-foot policeman was looking down at him. "Are you Mr Gabriel Jones?" he asked.

"Yes," Gabriel replied, asking, "how do you know my name?"

"You have been reported as a missing person, you fit the description we've been given," he answered. Gabriel desperate to talk to someone who was prepared to listen, cried out, "Please, please, you've got to help me."

The policeman replied kindly, "Don't worry sir, we'll see you get home safely."

Gabriel shouted, "No, no you don't understand, I'm being kept a prisoner and being forced to take part in experimental drugs research, please you have to help me." The policeman looked at him in kind disbelief and led him to the main road where a police car was waiting. Gabriel got into the back seat, the policeman and his driver listened patiently whilst he continued desperately to explain what was happening to him. "Don't worry, everything will be OK," they reassured him.

To Gabriel's dismay they arrived at the block of flats where he'd spent the past night with Akemi, he protested as they led him up the stairs to Akemi who was waiting on the landing. "Oh, thank you, thank you, officer," she said. Then one answered a message that had come through on his radio system and said, "Sorry, we've got to go." They left quickly, Akemi shouting angrily at him, led him into the flat locking the door from the inside.

Gabriel had no energy left, he didn't want to even try to talk to her and he asked her to leave him alone because he was so very tired. Her anger was subsiding and her voice was calmer when she replied, "You go lie down now, but you need new medication first, I have it here."

"What is this new medication?" Gabriel asked. She told him

that the doctor had said it was very important, very important that she makes sure that he takes the tablets. She held out a tumbler of water and a handful of various coloured pills. Gabriel felt helpless; not having the strength to argue with her he swallowed the medication.

He knew that he had only a short time, perhaps half an hour at most before the drugs would take effect. He knew what to expect, first the mist would start to swirl around inside his head jumbling up his thoughts, followed by the blanket of fog that would erase them altogether until finally he would find himself travelling back in time.

Gabriel was determined to use the short space of lucidity remaining to try and recall everything he could about his conversations with Max, any little piece of information that might give him a clue as to how to find him. He remembered speaking to him on the telephone, he must have a number somewhere, he meticulously kept the phone numbers of everyone he knew, they were comforting symbols of the many friends he claimed to have, although in reality most were only casual acquaintances. They would be in his pocket size address book, he could visualise the book, he'd bought it many years ago whilst on holiday in Morocco, it had a brown leather cover and all the addresses and contact numbers were organised alphabetically, he carried it with him everywhere, but where was it now? When Akemi first brought him to this flat he recalled she was carrying a navy rucksack which he recognised as his bag, perhaps the pocket book was in there.

Jumbled half memories were stubbornly filtering through, as Gabriel tried desperately to resist the effects of the mind numbing drugs. He recalled that the last time he had seen Max he'd married, an athletic looking bronzed Australian girl. His mind was slowing as if being put on standby, seemingly disconnected images floating around in his head, Franchesca looking as lovely as always, a wedding scene of a couple shrouded in mist, a young man among the wedding guests who looked remarkably like him but taller. The images were becoming less and less clear and were soon replaced by the darkness as the deep chemically induced sleep once again enveloped him.

6

Lucas finds his father

When he returned from India Gabriel was looking forward to seeing Franchesca, he'd sent many postcards, the last one informing her of the date that he was returning to the UK. Once back in Oxford he waited a few days, hoping she'd contact him, but heard nothing, eventually late one afternoon he decided to make the call. Attempting to sound as casual as possible, he said, "Hi Franchesca, it's Gabriel."

"Hi there, how are you?" came her equally casual response, quickly going on to explain that it wasn't a good time to talk as she was already late for an appointment but she'd be in the pub later and they could catch up with each other there.

Gabriel made his way to their old meeting place, having carefully wrapped the handbag he'd bought for her in the Poona market. She was already there when he arrived, greeting him with a sisterly kiss on the cheek. He just had time to order drinks and bring them across to the table when they were joined by a man about Gabriel's age or perhaps slightly older. Franchesca introduced him as John; Gabriel was surprised that they seemed to know each other well. "Gabriel has just returned from India,"

51

Franchesca informed her companion. "Really, how interesting," he responded, whilst turning away from Gabriel and towards Franchesca. They were both smiling and appeared to be sharing a private joke from which Gabriel was excluded.

Listening to them talk so intently about trivia, the attraction between them soon became apparent to Gabriel. What on earth could Franchesca see in this non descript man.? To Gabriel he appeared to be a complete nonentity, a middle aged man with greying hair, his gaping shirt buttons revealing the signs of middle age spread. Gabriel instantly took a dislike to him, a judgement influenced not least by the severe pangs of intense jealousy he was experiencing.

The present he'd so carefully chosen for Franchesca was still in his briefcase. Gabriel could feel his emotions rising to the surface and knew he needed to move away from them before he embarrassed himself. He politely made an excuse and left them together saying that he needed to talk to a group of students sitting at the bar.

After that meeting Gabriel decided not to contact Franchesca but wait, believing that in time she would contact him. A few months had passed when to his complete astonishment Gabriel received an invitation to her wedding. It seemed her relationship with John had lasted in spite of Gabriel's reservations about their lack of suitability for each other. He immediately called her on the pretext of offering his congratulations but, as the conversation continued, he inevitably made a last desperate attempt to dissuade her but she ignored his concerns and simply laughed at him in her inimitable way.

The wedding was to be quite an informal affair taking place in an Oxford registry office with only a few close friends invited. Feeling rather downhearted Gabriel dressed appropriately in a light suit, crisp white shirt and obligatory silver tie. He was just about to leave to travel the few miles to the wedding when the postman arrived and a pile of letters pushed through the letterbox landed haphazardly on the mat inside the door. Most appeared to be the usual unrequested junk mail but amongst them Gabriel noticed a small envelop with his name neatly hand written. Retrieving this particular letter from the pile he saw the postmark stamped Swansea, South Wales, he paused for a second to wonder who might have taken the trouble to write to him. Opening the letter he found four neatly handwritten sheets of paper; Gabriel was totally unprepared for what he was about to read.

Dear Gabriel,

I have wanted to write to you for a long time but I was not sure whether you would want to hear from me or not. I have decided to do it anyway and you can decide, I will understand if you do not reply.

I am your son, Lucas, my mum has always spoke, well of you and has told me all about your relationship with her. I know that you were married to my mum and that the marriage broke up very soon after I was born. My mum explained that these things happened a lot in the 1960s and it was not that unusual.

I have only one real memory of you, I think I must have been about three or four years old and I can remember that you came to see me at my grandparents' house and I remember sitting on your knee. As you know my mum remarried and my stepfather has been very kind to me. I had a very happy childhood. When I was eighteen and looking to go to university, I deliberately applied to the Oxford college where my mum had told me you were working as a lecturer. I was accepted and studied there for three years, our paths did not cross because I was studying law and I know you were lecturing in another department. Nevertheless I did venture into your department and saw your photo on the wall amongst "the rogue gallery" of lecturers. I also got to know some of your students and without disclosing my identity I asked them about you. They told me you drank cold tea and so do I.

When I graduated I married the girl I had met at university and we moved to London where I completed my training whilst working for a law firm. I now work for a small family law firm in Swansea and we have a small cottage overlooking the sea on the beautiful Gower coast. I am also a father; I have two beautiful young boys.

I would very much like to get to know you although as I said earlier I completely understand that it might be difficult for you at this stage of your life.

Hoping to hear from you soon,
Lucas.

Gabriel was still standing by the door, having read and re-read the letter over and over again. He sat down still holding the letter. It was a mixture of emotions, disbelief that Lucas had felt the need to contact him and exhilaration at the thought of seeing his son again. It must have been thirty years ago when Gabriel had last seen Lucas and Gabriel clearly remembered that day. His estranged young wife and his son had been staying with her parents in Cardiff and Gabriel had made the journey from London to visit them. He was right, that day he sat on his knee in his grandparents' house was the last time Lucas had seen his father, the day that Gabriel had physically and emotionally said goodbye to him. It was the day that he'd agreed to the divorce and to the legal adoption of Lucas by the man his mum intended to marry once the divorce was complete.

Gabriel's relationship with Lucas's mum had been a whirlwind romance in the 1960s, she was a beautiful young girl, an art student at a London college. She was unlike any girl he'd ever known and he'd known many. She was highly strung, artistic and temperamental and he was completely infatuated with her. Only a few months after their first date they were married. Her family organised a traditional church wedding with all the traditional festivities and conventionalities associated with such an occasion. Gabriel remembered feeling slightly uncomfortable and overwhelmed with all the fuss and attention to detail involved in the event and being thankful when it was all over.

He was working in London and she continued to study for her degree in Fine Arts at a London college. For a short while they were blissfully happy until one day just a few months after the wedding, she announced that she was pregnant. The pregnancy was unplanned and neither of them was ready for such a huge commitment. Gabriel had always been a very self centred character and the responsibility of a child weighed heavily on him. His wife was very young with an indefinable, unworldly charm; it was what had attracted and endeared him to her. She had the enviable ability to completely dissociate herself from any harsh reality and escape into her own mystical creative artistic world. He worried about how either of them would cope with the demands of parenthood.

They grew apart during the pregnancy, partly because Gabriel spent his days at work and his nights at the pub determined that his life was not going to change because of the circumstances. Then Lucas was born and he could no longer pretend. He had to admit to himself that his life had changed. He tried to take on his new role of a father but in retrospect not very hard. In reality he knew he didn't want to be domesticated, to be tamed, he wanted his freedom. When his wife took Lucas and returned home to visit her parents, he made the decision, quite coldly, that he could not cope with marriage or with fatherhood.

Gabriel's reminiscences were interrupted by a phone ringing; it was Franchesca, concerned that he'd not yet arrived at the registry office. She urged him to hurry if he didn't want to miss her big day. He folded Lucas's letter carefully and tucked it into the inside pocket of his jacket and drove the few miles to the wedding venue.

"Where have you been, we've been waiting for you?" asked Franchesca accusingly, she glared at him and not waiting for an answer, turned, took John's arm, and walked into a room decked out with blue and white flowers. Gabriel thought Franchesca looked beautiful in a pale blue suit that complemented her tiny figure and a simple white flower placed at the side of her lovely long dark hair. As the ceremony progressed, he watched enviously wishing that it was he and not John standing by her side. When he heard Franchesca say the final words "I do" he knew that a part of him would always be in love with her. He comforted himself with the thought that in spite of the marriage he'd just witnessed he believed that this feeling was reciprocated and a part of Franchesca would always be in love with him.

Later at the pub on the river where the guests were all joyfully assembled after the wedding, Gabriel sought a quiet spot in the beer garden. Seated at a small table overlooking the river, pint of beer in hand, he drew Lucas's letter from his pocket and read it over and over again and was surprised by the range of emotions it stirred in him. He recalled the overwhelming feeling of love he'd felt when he'd held him for the first time and how he'd questioned this emotion in the sleepless nights that had followed. He felt anger that came from a deep sense of disappointment and regret that he'd missed Lucas's childhood, his adolescence, his graduation, his marriage. He wished he had been there for him during all those times. He could not help having a sense of pride in what Lucas had achieved. He was proud of his son and tried to convince himself that somehow he was at least partly responsible for this achievement because of course he was his son, he had his DNA.

Gabriel was still holding the letter when he heard Franchesca's voice, "So there you are, I've been looking for you everywhere, you look very thoughtful, what's that you're reading?" she asked. Franchesca had been a close friend for a long time but Gabriel had never told her that he had a son. There were many aspects of his past life that he did not share with other people however close they became. He was surprised that Franchesca had left the lively celebrations going on inside the pub and felt the need to come and find him but he couldn't find the words to try and explain things to her, he was speechless. Not knowing what else to do he handed her the letter, giving him a strange quizzical look she started to read it slowly and carefully. When she'd finished, she looked up at him and said quietly, "So you have a son," Gabriel was still struggling to find the right words to try and explain everything to her. Eventually, after a long silence he told her that it was a long time ago and it was a long story. Folding the letter and returning it to him she said, "There is so much that I don't know about you, you have so many secrets, sometimes I think I don't know who you really are. Do you want to meet him?" she asked.

Gabriel said, "Yes I do," the answer was spontaneous; from the very first reading of the letter he knew instinctively that he desperately wanted to meet his son. Then, so typical of the practical, pragmatic Franchesca he'd come to know, she said, "Well if you have made the decision, can you now please come and join the other guests and try to look as if you are happy for me." She took his hand pulled him up from the seat and led him back inside the pub.

Inside the atmosphere was one of merriment, a band upon a small stage playing lively music, couples dancing whilst others gathered together laughing, drinking and chatting, wholly immersing themselves in the festivity. Gabriel looked around for John and Franchesca and glimpsed them in the centre of the dance floor, arms wound around each other momentarily locked in their own private world. Was this to be a lifelong romance he wondered? At that moment Gabriel envied what they were sharing together and questioned whether he would ever have that experience. Perhaps as Franchesca had once observed in one of their many intimate conversations he was too much in love with himself to ever find romance, quoting a line from Oscar Wilde,

"Loving oneself is the beginning of a lifelong romance," she had said with a wistful look on her face.

The next day Gabriel wrote a brief letter to Lucas simply saying that he was pleased to hear from him and that he'd be very happy to meet him at a place and time that was suitable to them both. Lucas replied within days and it was agreed that they would meet in Gino's cafe. Gabriel knew it well having spent many pleasant hours there with his Oxford friends.

It was a lunchtime rendezvous; Gabriel planned to get there early and find a window seat from where he knew he'd be able to catch a glimpse of his son as he arrived. Lucas must have had the very same thought and was sitting in that very same seat when Gabriel arrived. Gabriel recognised him instantly; he could have been looking at a photograph of himself taken at that age. The resemblance was striking; there was no denying that this was his son. Lucas stood up smiled and greeted him with a friendly handshake; Gabriel was instantly won over by his infectious smile his apparent light heartedness and easy manner. All the nervous anticipation he'd felt about their reunion ebbed away.

They chatted easily as a pair getting to know each other would, it was mostly superficial chat in which they recounted significant chronological events in their lives. Lucas talked about his school days, his college days, his graduation, his marriage, his career and the birth of his children. Gabriel talked of his childhood growing up in Wales, about Lucas's grandparents both of whom had now passed away, about the various academic degrees he'd acquired over the years and tales of his adventures around the world. There was so much more Gabriel wanted to tell his son but thought it best to keep certain things private, fearful that Lucas might disapprove of his unconventional escapades. There was nothing extraordinary or unusual about Lucas's life so far, nothing that any father could disapprove of but Gabriel could not help feeling it was all rather unexciting and mundane and lacking in colour when compared to the daring exploits that had been a constant feature of his own life.

Gabriel still kept the sense of pride in his son but secretly wished that he had inherited his father's spirit of adventure.

Gabriel was grateful that his son did not seem to want to venture too deep into the complexity of the reasons as to why Gabriel had not been a part of his life or why he'd not tried to make contact with him. Lucas explained that his desire to know his biological father had grown in intensity since becoming a father himself. He was clearly very proud of his two young boys, showing the recent photographs of them and describing in great detail the characteristics of their individual personalities.

The time passed very quickly, Gabriel was surprised and a little sad when Lucas said it was time to catch his train back to South Wales. He drove him to Paddington station, waited till his train arrived and waved goodbye. It had been a very pleasant encounter and when they parted having agreed to keep in contact Gabriel felt as if he'd found a part of himself that he hadn't been aware he had lost.

7

Albert's visit

Gabriel had no idea of time, there were no clocks in the small flat but he assumed on waking that it must be morning, the bedroom door was open but the flat was unusually quiet, there were no sounds of movement and no pleasant aromas of breakfast cooking. His head still felt heavy but the intoxicating effect of the previous evening's cocktail of drugs thankfully was beginning to wane. He was feeling almost human again. Still wearing his boxer shorts and tee shirt and barefoot he crept into the living room, there was no sign of Akemi. Hopefully he tried the door that led out onto the landing but as expected it was locked.

In the kitchen the water in the kettle was still warm so he knew she hadn't been gone very long. It was the first time he'd been alone in the small kitchen, there was a small window in front of the sink, he leant over and peered out. He knew that he was on the top floor of an apartment block but from the window he could see that it was part of an L shaped block, below there were neatly laid out flower beds separated by paths leading to the main doors. He watched as a young girl with a small toddler and another child in a pushchair made their way along the path to the door; an elderly couple were leaving the flats, the man was walking slowly with the aid of a stick, they were walking arm in arm and stopped to talk to the young girl and her children. The normality of everyday life going on before his eyes was both comforting and disturbing. Why was he being held prisoner in a place where other people were busy living normal lives and were free to come and go as they pleased?

Gabriel turned away from the window and scratched his head; he could not shake off the niggling thought that he had forgotten something that was very important. It was something he'd recalled clearly the previous night before he fell asleep, a thought he'd desperately tried to imprint on his brain before the drugs had taken effect.

The kitchen faced a tiny entrance hall, there was a small telephone table and a coat stand cluttered with coats including his old red anorak. There were umbrellas, walking sticks of various heights, old telephone directories, boxed games and jigsaw puzzles. Under a mountain of plastic carrier bags branded with the names of various supermarkets were small suitcases and to his surprise something that he recognised only too well; it was his old, worn, brown leather holdall.

Gabriel was so happy to have found something that he recognised as belonging to him. His brown leather holdall, purchased in a Casablanca bazaar had accompanied him on many of his travels. He rescued it from where it was stacked haphazardly in a corner; it had a distinctive smell of old leather, the creases, scratches and scars testimony to its travels over the years. He hesitated before opening it, almost wanting to stroke it; at that moment it was so reassuring to be holding something so personal, something that held so many memories. Gently unzipping the bag he held it upside down tipping out its contents; pairs of socks, boxer shorts, tee shirts, a comb, anti-histamine tablets tumbled on to the floor. Remembering that the bag had an inside pocket must have triggered the niggling memory he'd been so anxious to recall.

It came in a sudden flash like a neon sign beaming out "address book," followed by a second flash "Max, telephone number."

The inside pocket, he called it his secret compartment, was where he'd always kept his passport, other travel documents and his address book regularly updated with details of people met on his travels. Hands shaking expectantly he unzipped the compartment but as quickly as they had been raised his hopes were dashed. There was no passport and no address book. Despondently he started to gather up the pile of clothes carelessly thrown onto the floor and felt a wallet tucked neatly into a shirt pocket, opening it revealed an Oyster card and various loyalty cards but there was no money and most worrying of all no bank debit and credit cards.

The door to the flat opened and Akemi entered laden with carrier bags. Gabriel wanted to ask her if she knew anything about the missing bank cards but her demeanour suggested she was tired, fraught and anxious. He decided to wait until there was a more opportune moment to raise the matter. There was little in the way of any meaningful conversation between them. Akemi explained that she'd had to go out to get provisions and busied herself cooking breakfast. Gabriel found the silence uncomfortable, he went back to the hallway and looked through the boxes of games and jigsaws, he felt that he needed to look as if he was absorbed in doing something which might serve to normalise the silence between them. Selecting a box with a picture of Big Ben and the Houses of Parliament, Gabriel took it over to a coffee table and emptied out the 500 pieces. He was systematically sorting the pieces by their colours when Akemi appeared holding a tray containing a boiled egg and some toast. She grunted disapprovingly when she saw the contents of the jigsaw on the table. He took the tray from her and placed it on his lap.

The phone rang in the hallway, Gabriel turning his head in the direction of the phone endeavouring to listen, heard her say, "not today, it not convenient today," her voice was getting louder, "he asleep, he no want see you," Gabriel knew that she was talking about him, then her tone softened and he heard her say a curt "goodbye."

"Who was that?" asked Gabriel.

"Some person called Albert," she answered, "He said he in London and he coming here to see you, he coming today."

Albert was one of Gabriel's oldest friends and he hadn't seen him for years. It was apparent that Akemi wasn't very happy about the impending visit, busily rushing around making an attempt to tidy and give the room an appearance of cosy domesticity. Gabriel was excited but also apprehensive and puzzled, how on earth did Albert know where he was? How had he found him? He started making plans, he needed to get Albert's help to escape from this place, but he had to be careful, Akemi would be listening to everything he said to him and watching everything he did, it was of course what they had employed her to do.

It was just after two o'clock when there was a knock at the door, Gabriel jumped up to answer but Akemi brushed past him pushing him out of her way, she took the key out of her trouser pocket and opened the door. A casually dressed tall gentleman with a shock of grey hair entered. Gabriel didn't recognise him, this wasn't the Albert he'd been expecting to see. Neither did he think the man recognised him, but he nevertheless held out his hand, saying politely, "Hello, long time no see, how are you mate?" Gabriel stared blankly at him whilst the man waited for an answer, "Not very good today," he replied. Ignoring the negativity of the response Albert went on to explain that he was spending a few days in London, he took a seat close to Gabriel and was chatting incessantly about his lovely wife, his successful children, his beautiful grandchildren. Gabriel pretended to listen whilst resisting the temptation to shout out, "enough about you and your happy mundane life. I want you to listen to my story." His opportunity came when Akemi, who since Albert's arrival was portraying herself as a long suffering, totally submissive, intensely

63

caring person, decided politely to offer Albert a cup of tea. As soon as she disappeared into the kitchen, Gabriel leant over to whisper in Albert's ear that he was being kept a prisoner and that he was part of a drug testing programme. Albert stared wide eyed a look of complete disbelief. Gabriel found the silence that followed disconcerting and immediately regretted having revealed his vulnerability to this guy.

Still not convinced that this person really was Albert, Gabriel decided to test him. "How's Franchesca," he asked. Albert looked surprised at the question and seemed to pause for a while before answering, "I don't know, haven't heard anything about her for ages, think someone told me she moved to Exeter." This was revealing and only served to feed Gabriel's suspicions, Gabriel knew Franchesca would never have left Oxford without telling him.

Gabriel continued, asking if he'd heard from Max?

"Max?" Albert repeated questioningly, suggesting that the name meant nothing to him. Then seconds later as if in a moment of enlightenment replied, "Oh Max. Yes, I remember, he was a friend of yours but I hardly knew him," commented Albert, hoping to deflect the conversation away from Max. Frustrated by his response. Gabriel persisted, saying firmly, "Max was a doctor, he worked in a London hospital, and he stayed with us in Oxford when we shared a house together."

"Sorry mate, don't know anything about him," Albert replied dismissively.

Gabriel had introduced Albert to Max, a decision that he came later to bitterly regret. The pair shared a schoolboyish sense of humour which Gabriel found irritating. Soon the pair came to realise that their mutual friend Gabriel provided a perfect target for their mischievous, light hearted pranks. They took pleasure in playing to Gabriel's fixation with his self image, casually dropping suggestions about the latest trendy wear on the market citing fictitious brand names. They knew Gabriel, ever keen to display his stylish accessories, would spend days combing the London boutiques in an effort to find them.

Perhaps it was inevitable that what they believed to be harmless schoolboy jokes would inevitably backfire on them and that Gabriel would react badly at seeing himself as an object of ridicule. Albert and Max met up with Gabriel one evening in the local pub where they found him surrounded by students, clearly the centre of attention, proudly displaying a host of valentine cards that he'd collected from his pigeon hole at the college that day. Unbeknown to Gabriel, it was Albert and Max who had sent the cards knowing that they would give his already over inflated ego a boost. But that evening they were unable to hide their hilarity as Gabriel was engaged in ostentatiously displaying the cards, believing as he did that they were a clear indication of his popularity with the women.

Gabriel knew he would never forgive either of them for belittling him and embarrassing him in front of his students. Gabriel was intensely jealous of the close friendship that the pair shared and would never forgive them for what he saw as their infidelity. Now Gabriel was finding it even more impossible to believe that Albert would not remember Max. His doubts over the authenticity of the person sitting beside him were ultimately confirmed.

Akemi came in carrying a tray with a pot of tea, cups and a plate of varied, expensive looking biscuits, kneeling subserviently on the floor she poured the tea into the cups. Gabriel noticed that she was wearing makeup and had brushed her hair; she was smiling and speaking to Albert in a soft, gentle, lilting voice. She seemed completely transformed, no longer the angry, uncommunicative person he'd come to know. Albert or whoever he was, appeared completely enchanted by her, chatting to her about how long he had known Gabriel and the happy times they'd spent together working in Oxford. Gabriel felt this was part of the process of disarming him, of getting him to accept who he said he was and the facts he was conveying to Akemi could easily have been researched by someone trying to pretend they knew him well.

Then casually Albert mentioned that he'd heard that Gabriel had taken up the offer to stay with his students' families in Syria and Jordan. By now Gabriel had become convinced the man was part of the conspiracy and under the pretext of being his old friend Albert Westerman, had been sent to get information from him. Gabriel knew how to handle such subterfuge, he'd been trained to survive interrogation and had never forgotten the techniques. Lie convincingly, overload with irrelevant information whilst appearing to be cooperative and telling them what you think they want to hear.

He decided to invent a series of adventures and misadventures that he would pretend to have experienced whilst visiting his students and travelling through Syria and Jordan a few years ago. Most of the detail was recalled from watching TV documentaries on the Iraq war and listening to the BBC World Service on the radio. Gabriel described people he'd met who he suspected had ulterior motives in the region, they included Americans working for the oil companies, French and Dutch aid workers, German medics and local people including both Sunni and Shia Muslims, their characters all based on people he'd encountered on his real travels in other parts of the world.

Gabriel paused for a second and noticed Akemi and the guy sitting next to him were watching him closely and listening intently, the attention he was getting incentivised him to continue with the fabrication. Enjoying the moment he went on to describe a chance meeting in an open air cafe in Tehran where an Iranian diplomat had told him of a plot to overthrow the current government in Iraq. Of course he couldn't remember the name of this man but he was very convinced that this intended coup would occur. They were still listening, so he continued adding even more colour to the story. He described the many conversations overheard between locals who had spoken of friends being recruited to join an unofficial group calling itself the Army of Islam. The feeling amongst the locals was that this army was growing day by day and their objective was to take over the whole of the region, they were recruiting in Syria, Libya, Egypt in fact they were reaching out throughout the world.

The man looked at him incredulously and said, "Really, how interesting." Akemi in her now friendly manner said, "Oh Gabriel, you are so lucky you have had such an interesting life." Gabriel agreed, he knew that he'd been lucky and life had been interesting up until now. He wondered if this might be an appropriate moment to bring up the matter of his missing passport. He decided to take a chance explaining that he had found his travel bag and his passport which he always kept in the bag was missing. He asked her directly if she had taken it out if the bag. Her face took on the familiar unpleasant look, her eyelids lowered as she replied, "No, no why would I take your passport, if it's gone it's because you hide it somewhere." She turned to Albert and said with a sigh of frustration, "He hides everything from me." To Gabriel's astonishment the guy nodded sympathetically obviously agreeing with her reaction. Glancing at his watch he got up and announced, "Sorry, must go, got a meeting in an hour, good to see you again mate." He shook Gabriel's hand, stooped to kiss Akemi lightly on the cheek, whispered something in her ear and then he was gone. Gabriel wondered why he would be attending a meeting if, as he had said, he was genuinely in London to spend time with his family. Perhaps, Gabriel thought, the meeting was to report back on him and if so hopefully he would feed back the misinformation he'd deliberately fed to him. This might give him the time he needed to uncover who was at the heart of this conspiracy against him. Gabriel felt empowered, knowing that he'd been able to exert some control over the situation. He knew he must have a plan because as soon as any opportunity presented itself he would get out of this flat, make a run for it, find his real friends, they were the only ones who could lead him to Max who he remained convinced was where this had all started.

The flat was eerily quiet, Gabriel looked round for Akemi and found her kneeling on the floor in her bedroom, in front of her was a small shoe box and she was busy going through its contents. She had her back to him and as he was wearing only socks on his feet she didn't hear Gabriel approach as he crept up behind her. Looking over her head he could see the box contained papers and pass books for various banks. Suddenly she became aware of his presence, jumped to her feet trying to hide the contents of the box. Gabriel snatched it out of her hand and its contents fell onto the bedroom floor. The pass books had his name on them and inside the books were his credit cards and debit cards. Accusingly he shouted, "What are you doing with these?"

"I need them, I need money," she shrieked, grabbing the cards and holding them tightly to her chest. Gabriel was shaking with anger he grabbed her wrists and tried to wrestle the cards away from her, she struggled free then ran out of the room into the hallway, grabbing a coat from the stand she went out of the door and he heard the key turn in the lock.

Looking out of the kitchen window Gabriel could see her running along the path that led from the apartment block to the main road. Alone again, he sat down and put his head in his hands, the earlier feeling of having some control over what was happening to him had soon faded and he was left once again with a feeling of complete helplessness.

The phone rang, Gabriel jumped up to answer. "Hello," he said optimistically, hoping unrealistically for a voice he might recognise. There was no reply just silence. "Hello who is that?" he asked again, but still there was no reply. Gabriel became aware of a noise in the background, a rhythmic mechanical noise, to his alarm he could see a tape revolving in a recorder beside the phone.

Akemi opened the lock on the door, she was accompanied by a young man strangely dressed in a green trousers and a green jacket and carrying a large bag. The man smiled at Gabriel, he appeared friendly but the fact that he'd arrived with her told him to be careful and not to trust him. He started to talk to Gabriel asking questions about how he was feeling. Gabriel tried to tell him that he was a prisoner in this flat and the woman was stealing his money but she constantly interrupted. In a high pitched hysterical voice, she told the man dressed in green that Gabriel was violent, hitting her and verbally abusing her. Gabriel tried to explain that he'd never been violent to anyone and that he had not hurt her but his voice was shaky and he started to stammer unable to get the words out properly. The young man took Gabriel's arm, led him to a chair, politely asking him to sit down; he opened his bag and took out some instruments placing them on the table in front of them. He selected a long hypodermic needle, Gabriel struggled trying to resist but the man holding the needle was far younger and stronger than him. He felt the needle in his arm and seconds later his hands stopped shaking his heart stopped pounding and he felt his anger subsiding. He immediately began to feel calmer but he didn't want to lose his anger. He had a right to be angry and the anger gave him strength, the strength he needed to fight what was happening to him but he could feel it ebbing away. The medication was taking effect, he was feeling calmer, he was floating back to a happier time capturing a distinct vision of cherry blossom trees surrounding a quiet deep blue lake, a snow capped mountain peak reflected in the water. Gabriel could picture himself with a pretty girl and riding on bicycles around a path that circled the lake.

8

Romance with a Geisha girl

It took Gabriel a long time to get over his infatuation with Franchesca, even though they remained friends and met every now and again. Once when they were alone together she explained the qualities John had that attracted her to him. She told Gabriel that John was simple, uncomplicated, unselfish, laughingly adding that these certainly were qualities that Gabriel did not possess.

A few years passed, years during which Gabriel continued to enjoy life at Oxford, impressing students with talks about his travels illustrated with the many slides of photographs taken on his journeys. He took any opportunity to travel, taking advantage of the many international conferences asking for papers to be submitted on the fashionable subject of 20th century developments in world transport. One such conference was to be held in Kyoto, Japan in the late summer of 1980 and he was ecstatic when he received an invitation to attend.

Arriving in Osaka airport on a warm Sunday evening, Gabriel's transit through the airport was thankfully uneventful. A beautiful high speed express train arrived on time and delivered him on time effortlessly to Kyoto. The pre-booked hotel was within walking distance of the station and he was greeted by a smartly dressed concierge at the top of the steps of the grand building.

On entry he was impressed by the high-vaulted ceilings and grand windows and the walls displaying scenes from the hotel's 100-year history. He found his room pleasantly decorated with dark wooden furniture, heavy pale blue velvet curtains and thick carpeting in a muted floral pattern of blue and white. There was a large comfortable bed with focused reading lights above. He tested the large flat-screen television to discover that channels in several languages were available. Venturing into the bathroom he found wooden blinds covering a wide floor-to-ceiling window, glass doors enclosing an alcove with a gleaming white soaking tub and a spacious shower. The toilet offered various rinsing and warming functions with a wall panel of controls. The white thick and fluffy terry robes with white slippers peeping from the pocket were draped on a hanger behind the door. Gabriel remembered his back-packing days and the tiny bare room in the Kabul hotel and realised how far his life had progressed since then.

That evening in the spacious lounge bar he met the other conference delegates staying at the hotel, he thought they were an interesting group, not surprisingly all were male and all keen academics intent on discussing the research they intended to present at the conference. All were so engrossed in their specific research that they were oblivious to everyday practicalities. Gabriel asked if anyone knew the location of the Kyoto International Conference Hall, the conference venue for the next day. He was greeted with silence. "Shall I try and find out?" he asked. A few looked up and nodded and one said, "Good thinking," before returning to their intense discussion.

The young Japanese receptionist at the desk informed Gabriel that the Conference Hall was at a place called Takaragaike, to the north of Kyoto. With an air of pride she explained that they could travel there by a new subway, the Karasuma Line, the first to be constructed in Kyoto. Before returning to the group with this information, Gabriel noticed amongst the tourist information displayed at the reception desk, a pamphlet bearing a picture of a Geisha girl, he picked it up and was about to read its contents when a young Japanese man approached, shook his hand and introduced himself as Hashimoto explaining that he could arrange for him and the group to be entertained by Geisha girls at a tea house if they were interested.

Gabriel returned to the group who seemed to have exhausted their attempts to sell the unique significance of their own research topic whilst paying a token begrudging respect to everyone else's ideas. They seemed pleased when he explained that tomorrow's journey to the conference centre would be a relatively short and straightforward one. Hashimoto had followed Gabriel across the room and was introducing himself personally to all the members of the group. The atmosphere changed almost immediately, the high minded, ivory tower, cloistered, mentality replaced now with almost a normal joie de vivre. Hashimoto had successfully persuaded the whole group to join him the next evening on a visit to a Japanese Geisha tea house. He had explained that tea houses, or Ochayas, didn't accept guests without references from other clients because of security which meant it was very difficult for foreign guests to gain entry. However, he explained, well reputed five star hotels have contacts in the tea houses and can make the necessary arrangements for their guests to visit.

The next evening when the group returned from the conference, as arranged, Hashimoto was waiting for them in the foyer. Once they were all gathered together he was careful to explain that whatever preconceived ideas they may have had, the Geisha women were trained very seriously as skilled entertainers. He told them that it was important that they understood that the girls under a training programme, starting from a young age, the skills they learned were many, ranging from cultural dances to classical music and the arts and serving tea and this process could take many years. They were in great demand being hired to attend parties and gatherings, traditionally at tea houses or at traditional Japanese restaurants.

Taxis waited outside the hotel to take the group a few streets from the hotel to a traditional tea house which looked surprisingly uninviting from the outside. At the door they were provided with soft soled slippers and asked to remove their shoes, then they were ushered upstairs to a room full of guests seated around low Japanese dinner tables. Most of the guests were men but there were also some women and quite a few foreigners.

The evening started punctually with the house master introducing them to their hostesses for the evening, some were white faced young girls and some older ladies who had non painted faces. The hostesses moved between the tables engaging in light conversation with guests and serving drinks. Then the performance began and it was mesmerising to watch as they danced flipping their fans in perfect unison and moving gracefully to the music.

When the performance was over, the Geishas dispersed to join the guests at their tables. Chiako was one of the hostesses assigned to Gabriel's table for the evening. He could not believe how beautiful she was, her face was painted white but her delicate features seemed to shine through, her hair was jet black assembled neatly in the traditional Japanese style. He was entranced, unable to take his eyes off her. When she sat next to him, he could not believe that he was in such close proximity to this beautiful girl. At first he sat in silence not knowing what was the appropriate thing to say but she soon made him feel at ease, she was so effortlessly natural and friendly. Gabriel really, really liked her, he knew he would always remember this as a once in a lifetime evening when the beautiful Chiako chose to sit next to him. Alas the night was drawing to a close and he didn't want it to end. As Chiako rose and bowed with hands neatly together in front of her as is customary, he whispered, "I really enjoyed talking to you, thank you, I will remember tonight." To his utter surprise she answered, "I like you too and I am sure I will see you again."

Although it wasn't very far away from the hotel, the master of the house insisted on booking taxis for the group and waited outside with them like a true gentleman until they arrived. Gabriel could not sleep for thinking about Chiako; what did she mean when she said that she knew she would see him again? It wasn't long before his question would be answered. The next evening on returning to the hotel from the conference centre, Gabriel went to collect his key from the reception desk and was handed a folded piece of paper. It read simply, "Will you please meet with me by the main entrance to Gyoen Park, near the Imperial Palace. I will be there at seven o'clock, I look forward to seeing you again." It was signed Chiako. Once again, the receptionist was happy to give Gabriel directions telling him that the Kyoto Imperial Palace was only a ten minute subway ride from Kyoto Station.

Gabriel's heart was racing, looking at his watch he saw it was just before six o'clock. After taking a shower in his luxurious bathroom, he relaxed, swathed in a fluffy white coat, laid back against plump sumptuously soft pillows before he dressed and left the hotel to take the short journey on the subway to be with the girl of his dreams. She was waiting for him at the park gate; she welcomed him with a lovely smile and said, "I'm so glad you came." She was casually dressed in western clothes but looking just as beautiful as when he first met her dressed in her traditional costume. As they walked through the park the conversation flowed effortlessly between them, she spoke English perfectly and had such a natural and totally disarming manner, Gabriel felt completely at ease in her company.

She told him that she was not yet a Geisha, she was still training but her training was almost complete, she was only twenty one years old which she explained was quite young to become a Geisha. "It shows how good I am," she said with a seductive smile. Gabriel asked her if she had always wanted to be a Geisha girl and she explained that she had had no choice, her family had made the decision when she was eight years old. Compared with other girls back home in her village she was lucky, she'd been schooled in culture, dance, arts, language and been to expensive restaurants and parties and met and interacted with important people. When Chiako slipped her hand into his as they walked and talked, it seemed perfectly natural, as if they were already a couple, just like the many other young lovers strolling in the park that evening.

Gabriel and Chiako spent every evening together during his short stay in Kyoto, sometimes walking in the park and sometimes sitting in a restaurant, but always completely at ease in each other's company. On Gabriel's last day in Kyoto Chiako had a day clear of her duties at the tea house and he opted to miss the final day of the conference, thinking it hardly likely that he would be missed. Chiako had planned to take him to a place where she'd told him she loved to go on the days she didn't work.

The place she loved so much was an enormous lake just over the hill from central Kyoto; Chiako told Gabriel it was Lake Biwa, Japan's largest lake. It was a beautiful day, clear blue sky dotted with small patches of light fluffy white clouds high above them, they were both so happy that day, they hired bicycles and rode along the side of the lake, the light breeze causing Chiako's long black hair to float behind her as she rode. Gabriel followed her as she turned off the main cycle track and through a lightly wooded area that led to a small beach on the lake. They sat on the beach right on the edge of the lake, removed their shoes and let the clear water gently lap over their bare feet. Gabriel lifted her long hair and placed his arm around her shoulder, she rested her head on his shoulder and murmured, "I don't want today to end, I can't imagine that I will ever feel this happy again." They were both silent for a long time, both lost in the moment. Chiako was the first to break the silence, "After today you will go home and I will never see you again." Gabriel looked at her and for the first time detected sadness in her smile and noticed moisture veiling her eyes, "I've never seen you look sad before," he said, brushing a tear from her cheek. "You must remember that I have been taught the art of composure and poise and I am well skilled in keeping my personal feelings hidden," she replied.

It was at that moment Gabriel realised this beautiful, simple relationship had changed and that everything was about to become far more complicated. He knew in his heart that he did not want to leave her, but at the same time his head was desperately trying to rationalise the situation. He reminded her that she had told him how good her life was in Japan and that soon she would be a fully qualified Geisha. Chiako was quick to point out that once she became a Geisha she would not be allowed any independence until the debts of her expensive training were settled and that repayment could take several years. She added sadly, if she was lucky she might find a good danna, a patron, a wealthy man, who would cover all her expenses and look after her but that he would be likely to want a relationship with her in return for these favours.

Gabriel was holding her tightly, he never wanted to let her go, he could not imagine that she would be expected to have a relationship with any man out of a sense of gratitude for paying her debts. The words he was about to utter were completely unplanned. "Chiako, marry me."

* * *

Gabriel returned to England and some months passed until Chiako obtained a tourist visa which permitted her to travel to the UK. On a damp cold November London morning Gabriel made the journey across London to Heathrow to meet her. He scanned the arrivals monitor and seeing that the plane due to arrive from Tokyo was delayed by up to two hours he settled down in an uncomfortable chair in the arrivals lounge. Having a long wait gave him time to think, until now he'd deliberately tried not to think of the consequences of the impetuous question he'd uttered that day at the lake.

On arrival back in England it had all seemed like a far off

romantic dream, they had corresponded and Chiako asked to visit him in England. Now she was on her way and he was as certain as he could be that he wanted Chiako to be part of his future, but had to admit to himself that it would be complicated. Would she settle in a new country? How would she relate to all his friends? He began to panic realising the enormity of the change he was about to make to his life. Did he honestly want his life to change? Gabriel knew himself well, he was restless, selfish, freedom loving. Could he ever settle down to a normal life? These questions he would ask himself over and over again in the coming months.

The monitor facing him had changed many times, recording arrivals from all over the world but the flight from Tokyo remained stubbornly delayed. An hour passed and at last flashed the message flight landed. He really was looking forward to seeing Chiako in spite of his doubts, the magic was still there.

There were constant announcements from the airport loud speakers, the white background noise of busy airports that Gabriel had learnt to ignore, until clearly he heard his name called. "Would Mr. Gabriel Jones please contact the immigration desk." Although this was a rarer occurrence of late he half expected that he was once again about to be interrogated by intelligence officers. As always he'd carefully observed the people in the airport lounge, but had seen no one who seemed interested in him or who appeared to be watching him. In trepidation he located the immigration desk and was escorted into an office by two officials, Chiako was sitting there looking uncomfortable, she stood up and moved towards him as if to embrace him but was immediately told to sit down by the official on the opposite side of the desk. Gabriel was also asked to sit down. "Mr Jones we would like to ask you some questions. Do you know Miss Chiako Araki?"

"Yes I do," he replied.

"In what capacity do you know this woman?"

"She's a friend," Gabriel answered. The official went on to

explain that she had been stopped by the immigration authorities because she only had a tourist visa, which permitted her to stay in the UK for one month, but when her luggage was searched they discovered a prospectus for an Oxford college containing an application form for a language course. "If she is intending to study in the UK she will need a student visa not a tourist visa," the official announced sternly. Gabriel glanced at Chiako, she seemed so small and vulnerable sitting in this cold room being interrogated by the immigration people whose manner was far from friendly. Gabriel's instinct was to protect her, but he had forgotten how good she was in any social interaction. Her response came quickly, "The prospectus belongs to my friend, who travelled with me from Kyoto, she has a student visa and she has been accepted at this college, she gave me the prospectus because it has the college address and telephone number, I have it so that I can contact her if I need to, before she is allocated her accommodation by the college. I have no intention of studying in the UK." She paused before dismissing them with, "I think that answers your concerns, may we leave now?" The official looked slightly taken aback unused to being faced with the confidence Chiako had demonstrated in the face of his authority. Gabriel smiled at her and thought, *Chiako you know how to charm.* They were allowed to leave after Gabriel had agreed to act as a guarantor for Chiako during her short stay in the UK.

It was early December, a week before Chiako's tourist visa expired, when they drove the hundred miles from Oxford to be married in Swansea Registry Office where they had applied for a special marriage licence. It was late evening as they approached the city, leaving the blandness of the motorway descending an impressive elevated viaduct to reveal the truly magnificent curving shoreline of Swansea Bay and the vast expanse of sea. That night as if specially for them it was beautifully bathed in moonlight and Chiako was intoxicated by the scene, "This really is an enchanting, magical city," she said dreamily, leaning her head on Gabriel's shoulder. The magic lasted as Chiako, dressed in a flattering red coat with a fur collar, her hands tucked into a fur muff, stood by Gabriel's side in the small registry office in Swansea Civic Centre and made her vows in perfect English. He placed the ring he'd bought the previous day in Oxford on her finger and the Registrar declared they were married.

They returned to Oxford after a week spent blissfully in Wales. At first life seemed not to have changed that much, Gabriel went to work at the university every day and Chiako had a meal prepared when he arrived home, they met with Gabriel's friends in the pub during the evenings, Chiako was accepted by them and seemed relaxed in their company. Gabriel could not help but notice that Franchesca seemed to make very little effort to get to know Chiako and sometimes was quite offhand with her. Secretly he thought she was jealous and took some pleasure from this thought. Chiako's student friend Yoko who had travelled with her from Kyoto was studying English at a local college and was her constant companion, they spent afternoons drinking tea together and every week travelled to London to go shopping. Gabriel was in the final year of a part-time evening course at London University and if they were still in London on those evenings Chiako and Yoko would make their way to the Jeremy Bentham pub to join him. It was here that he introduced Max to Yoko, who was clearly enchanted by her. The four of them spent days out together, sightseeing and picnicking Japanese style in the local parks. Chiako and Yoko enjoyed preparing the food for these outings. It was all neatly compartmentalised in bento boxes and included sandwiches cut into unusual shapes, rice noodle salad, hard boiled eggs, slithers of smoked salmon and bamboo shoots. Gabriel remembered these times with affection and assumed Chiako was happy with her new life but it seems she was not.

Chiako waited a few months before she told her parents about their marriage even though she knew this would be seen as disrespectful in her culture. When eventually she did tell them they were angry and refused to accept her marriage because it had not been approved by her family. It was seen as shameful to marry a western man without their agreement. Her parents felt that they had sacrificed so much to give her the opportunity to become a Geisha and her actions were disrespectful to them. Gabriel knew that these things troubled her but Chiako was adept at hiding her true feelings.

One late afternoon Gabriel drove home as usual to find the house empty, at first he thought that Chiako must have gone shopping in London with her friend but as time went on and darkness fell he began to worry. He decided to call Yoko, who told him in a very matter of fact way that she had been in London with Chiako that day, she had accompanied Chiako to the airport where she had boarded a flight home to Japan.

Gabriel never saw Chiako again, although they corresponded briefly for a while, her letters were always courteous and polite but revealed little of her true feelings about their marriage and the reasons for her sudden departure. A year had gone by when he received a letter from a Japanese attorney asking for his consent to a divorce by mutual agreement. The process seemed relatively simple, all that was needed was for his solicitor to certify that the Japanese divorce procedures were compatible with those of his home country and his signature on the forms and it was done, Gabriel was divorced. Surprisingly he did not feel sad, if he felt anything it was gratitude for the return of his freedom. He clearly remembered thinking that once again he would be free to do whatever he liked, whenever he liked and with whomever he liked. Walking jauntily along the river on his way to work on the morning that he received the final confirmation of the divorce, he repeated these words, over and over again, mantra style, it was as if a heavy yoke had been lifted off him.

9

A red gemstone and a scrap of paper

Gabriel could hear voices coming from the room next door as he lay on the bed fighting for breath. Two men in green uniform came into the room one holding a phone to his ear and taking instructions which he was relaying to his colleague. Gabriel was slipping in and out of consciousness but felt a cold liquid gel being applied to his chest and could see large plasters on his chest with wires that connected to a small yellow box. The next thing he felt was an oxygen mask being placed over his nose and mouth, he was grateful to still be alive and in spite of his fear as to what was happening he began to logically try to interpret this strange sequence of events. His initial thought was that he was experiencing an allergic type reaction to the previous nights injection and hoped he was about to be given some form of antidote.

Both men left the room and quickly returned carrying two large poles that looked like gigantic rolling pins. Draped over the poles was a blue thick plastic sheet. Gabriel could not believe what happened next. One of the men lifted his body so that he was lying on his side whilst simultaneously another man unfurled the plastic sheeting, exposing it as a flat sheet suspended between the two poles. They proceeded to lay the sheet next to him and together managed to roll Gabriel on to the sheet. Then one at each end, arms fully extended, they took the ends of the poles in their hands and lifted him up. Suspended in this hammock they carried him through the flat and carefully down the flights of stairs to the outside where an ambulance was waiting.

Gabriel was loaded into the ambulance an oxygen mask still covering his nose and mouth, one of the men got in beside him and the other hurriedly jumped into the driving seat and the ambulance was racing through the streets of London with a loud siren and flashing blue light. Gabriel was convinced something was seriously wrong with him, why else would they be going so fast. He was terrified that he was about to die. Yet amidst the panic rational thoughts and questions flew in and out of his mind. If he died nobody would ever know what had really happened to him. Perhaps a post-mortem would reveal he'd been poisoned and then surely somebody would have to investigate his death. But could the secret services cover it up? Had someone intentionally tried to murder him or was it an accidental overdose or an allergic reaction on his part to whatever drug he'd been given?. Gabriel could hear the beat of his heart resounding in his ears and it was getting faster and faster and then the beat stopped and everything went dark.

The next thing he remembered was lying in bed in a room very much like the one where he'd woken up days or maybe it was weeks ago when his living nightmare began. Sitting in the chair next to his bed was an attractive middle aged woman. When he turned to look at her she smiled and said simply, "Hello Gabriel." She took his hand in hers and his eyes were drawn to the unusual ring she was wearing. It was a silver ring with a red gemstone delicately carved into the shape of a rose. He recognised the ring and then recognised the woman sitting in the chair. "Alicia," he whispered, "Yes it's me," she answered. Gabriel was so happy to see her but he felt very weak, too weak to try and talk and still holding Alicia's hand he closed his eyes again.

Gabriel had first met Alicia in a London bar when she was out with a group of friends for the evening. He'd singled her out as being the prettiest one of the group, her long dark hair and swarthy appearance reminded him of Franchesca. The pub was busy but Gabriel managed to manoeuvre his way through the crowd and position himself close to Alicia. Appearing to accidently brush against her, he apologised profusely and with his inimitable flirtatious charm and boyish grin delivered his well used chat up line, "Haven't I seen you somewhere before?" Alicia smiled, replying, "I don't think so," but readily accepted when Gabriel offered to buy her a drink. They were soon engaged in conversation, Alicia revealing that she was from Peru and was working as an au pair for a Spanish family with young children. Alicia was attractive with a likeable easy going personality, but she was also very intuitive and although she liked Gabriel very much she knew that he was flirtatious by nature and refused to succumb to his charms. Perhaps this was why they had remained close friends although they had not been in contact with each other for a few years.

Gabriel opened his eyes wondering if this was yet another of his dreams where long forgotten memories came flooding back to him. She was still sitting there looking concerned and still gripping his hand tightly. There were so many questions he wanted to ask if only he could find the strength. He struggled but managed to whisper to her, asking how she had found him. She explained that she was employed at the hospital, she distributed meals to the patients and she'd recognised his name on a list she'd been given. She told him he'd been there for a few days and she'd delivered a meal to him every day but he'd not been conscious. Each day when her morning shift ended she'd come and sat in the chair next to him. When Gabriel managed to ask why he was there and what was wrong with him Alicia shook her head saying that she didn't know, that she had asked but because she was not a member of his family nobody would tell her anything.

Suddenly the room filled with people dressed in white coats, they were purposefully armed with clipboards and seemed to swarm around the bed. One man was considerably older than the rest and appeared to be in charge; he asked Alicia politely to leave and proceeded to address the others authoritatively. Gabriel tried to make out what he was saying but he was speaking very quickly with a trace of a foreign accent and using medical terminology he did not understand. Gabriel knew that he was talking about him but never looking directly at him or showing any recognition of him as a real person. The man began to select individuals within the group firing questions at them and if anyone failed to answer correctly he mocked them in a supercilious manner deliberately causing embarrassment. Gabriel deduced that they were medical students, that the older man was their mentor and that he was being used as a case study or experiment in some medical condition or procedure. Having no idea what the condition was or what the procedure might be, he hoped that they would eventually stop talking about him and start talking to him. A vain hope, the lecture and questioning concluded, they left as quickly as they had appeared. Silently and deferentially the students filed out behind their mentor. A few of the entourage of students looked back curiously at Gabriel as they left. He raised his hand signalling for them to come back and talk to him but they appeared to have been collectively programmed to show no response.

As soon as they had gone Alicia popped her head through the door, she was wearing a long black apron over her dress and her hair was tied back and covered with a net. She quickly explained that she was starting her next shift and would be back as soon as she could.

The door had been left open and Gabriel could see people dressed in everyday clothes walking by and looking purposeful as if they knew exactly where they were going. At first it was just one or two, then more people came, elderly couples arm in arm, young couples some with young children, older couples with teenagers, some carried bunches of flowers and some had baskets of fruit. He remembered Alicia had said she was preparing meals for patients, if there are patients here then this place is not a prison as I first thought, it must be a hospital and these people passing by my door must be visitors.

With this realisation came the secret hope that amongst these visitors would be one of the many friends he'd acquired over the years, surely amongst them someone would have taken the trouble to find out where he was and would make an effort to come and see him. However, there was no established pattern to any of these friendships; it wasn't as if they met regularly in a particular venue on a particular week night. If Gabriel was to be honest he would have had to admit that he saw his friends when it suited him, if he happened to be in a particular area he'd call in on them hoping to find a meal and a bed for the night. Others were casual associates that he'd encounter as and when he frequented various clubs and bars in London. So he asked himself that day, how would they ever realise that he was missing, being held captive and at this moment in time in a hospital where they might visit him?

Gabriel was too weak to feel any anger instead he was overcome by an intense depressive feeling of loneliness. He had never liked being alone having always suffered from an inability to be content with his own company. He needed to be surrounded by people, friends, acquaintances in fact anyone who appeared to like him, showed an interest in him and was happy to listen to him talk about his adventurous unconventional life. Such relationships he found easy, happy in the company of anyone who was happy to listen to him and felt themselves fortunate to have the pleasure of his company. By contrast close long lasting inter personal relationships demanded commitment and inevitably involved compromises that he'd never found it possible to give.

A tall gentleman of Afro-Caribbean appearance and wearing a white coat and a stethoscope came into the room. Gabriel presumed he was a doctor and thinking this was a chance to find out what was happening to him, asked simply why he was there and what had happened to him. The doctor's reply gave nothing away, simply saying, "Everything has gone well, the procedure was successful, the device has been successfully implanted." He continued to assure him that everything was OK and that he should be able to leave soon. A machine in his pocket emitted an ear-piercing beeping noise and he reacted immediately, giving Gabriel no opportunity to question him further, as he turned to leave he said, "Your minder is on her way to collect you now."

As usual Gabriel was left with no answers only more questions. What device had been implanted? He remembered that the Soviets had used small tracking and monitoring devices that could be discreetly hidden on a person; perhaps technology had now progressed to the point where these could actually be implanted in the body. Perhaps his captors expected that he would manage to escape and this was their way of tracking him. The doctor had used the word "minder" to Gabriel this seemed a strange choice of word to use and he assumed that he was referring to the woman in black, the woman he'd come to know as Akemi.

Soon she arrived and in her typically officious manner Akemi summoned Gabriel to get dressed quickly because it was important that they left as soon as possible adding that a car was waiting outside for them. Gabriel knew it was useless to ask questions or to show any resistance to what she demanded and obediently did as she asked. It was when he removed the gown he'd been wearing that he noticed a small incision just below the breast bone on the left side of my chest. Tentatively he touched it, observing his reaction Akemi told him that his heart had stopped in the ambulance and they had put something inside his heart to make it work. The clumsy way she tried to explain things to him left Gabriel feeling more frustrated than ever.

Akemi helped Gabriel to dress obviously anxious that they

should leave as soon as possible and then led him out of the room through what appeared to be a ward of patients with their visitors sitting in chairs near their beds. Then along a corridor, private rooms similar to the one he'd occupied led off the corridor and he could not help but notice that these patients did not have any visitors. Gabriel wondered if they like him were the guinea pigs for the experiments taking place in this establishment. Further along he passed a small kitchen and looked for Alicia but there was no sign of her. When they came to a desk Akemi stopped and collected a large carrier bag embellished with a green cross within a blue circle and the word "prescription".

Once outside, Gabriel saw Alicia standing at a nearby bus stop she was no longer dressed in her black trousers and long black apron but wearing a flowery summer dress, he'd forgotten how pretty she was. His heart started beating rapidly as he ran towards her, exhausted by the effort he flung himself into her outreached arms. Akemi was quick to follow him but her limp slowed her down and Gabriel managed to find a moment before she got too close to whisper to Alicia asking her to tell someone that he was being kept a prisoner by the women in black. Alicia quickly put her hand in her pocket and took out a small envelope which she crumpled in her hand. As Akemi approached shouting angrily at them, Alicia took Gabriel's hand in hers carefully concealing the crumpled piece of paper that she passed to him. Gabriel grasped it tightly locking it securely into his clenched fist. Akemi started to shout at Alicia, passers-by stopped wondering what was happening. Alicia was silent in the face of the verbal onslaught and Gabriel thought she actually looked frightened.

Not wishing to cause Alicia any further embarrassment or Akemi to realise that she had passed something to him Gabriel accompanied her as she firmly took his arm and guided him to the waiting black saloon. Gabriel knew that he was too weak and feeble to attempt an escape this time so focussed his mind on trying to memorise the route they were taking through London.

If he could identify landmarks then he would be able to work out which London hospital was responsible for the experiments that he'd become convinced they were performing on him. He was determined that one day he'd somehow manage to escape from this nightmare and expose this unlawful human experimentation and uncover the political conspiracy that lay behind his involvement in these experiments.

As Gabriel had expected they returned to the now familiar flat that he shared with Akemi. He was still holding the piece of paper Alicia had passed to him and anxious to find out what if anything was written on it. This tiny scrap of paper had gained a momentous significance in his mind, it had become a lifeline, a connection to the outside world, it felt as if freedom was waiting for him in his hand. Desperate to be left alone so that he could read it he told Akemi that he was exhausted and that he needed to sleep. Tipping out the contents of the carrier she had picked up at the hospital she insisted that he take medicine before he went to sleep. Gabriel was staggered by the amount of different boxes, tubes, syringes that splayed out onto the table. Akemi seemed confused as she sorted through the array as if she wasn't sure what she was looking for. Gabriel picked up one of the boxes and started to read the directions but Akemi snatched it from him, telling him that he must not touch the boxes and that only she knew the exact quantities of which drugs he needed. Gabriel did not have any confidence in her, he didn't think he needed all this medication and even if he did need it he didn't feel she was competent to know which of all this stuff he should take and when. Eventually extracting a number of different colour pills from the various boxes, she passed them to him with a glass of water, telling him to take them. Gabriel didn't want to take them but neither did he want her to notice his clenched hand and he wanted to be alone and so reluctantly he swallowed them.

Finally alone on the bed he gently unfurled the crumpled piece of paper. It was an envelope addressed to Alicia and it had her address in Edmonton, North London, clearly written on it, her quick thinking had given him a way of contacting her again. Immediately he memorised the address, repeating it over and over again as the wretched pills took his consciousness away.

10

A South American summer

Following their chance encounter in a London bar Gabriel and Alicia became good friends and although he found her attractive their friendship was not one that had involved any romantic attachment. One evening whilst having a casual drink in a pub with Alicia, she mentioned that she was going back home to see her parents in Peru. It was coming close to the end of the summer term and surprisingly Gabriel had no travel plans for the long vacation that lay ahead. The idea of travelling in South America appealed to Gabriel. Alicia had described in great detail the attractions of her native Peru the unspoilt beaches on the Pacific coast, the vibrant nightlife, and the lovely restaurants with their exquisite cuisine. On the spur of the moment Gabriel decided that South America was to be his vacation destination. That night Gabriel and Alicia agreed to meet up in Peru.

Gabriel had also become friendly with one of his post graduate students, a French girl called Cecile and when telling her of his plans she asked if she might join him on the adventure. Although not immediately attracted to her, he was flattered by the attention she gave him. He'd suspected that she might be infatuated with him and the way she immediately jumped at this opportunity to be his travelling companion confirmed this.

It was a warm July Monday morning when they set off from Heathrow bound for Barbados on a long nine hour flight. After lunch, served not long after take-off, Cecile rested her head on Gabriel's shoulder and slept for the rest of the journey. Whilst she slept he stared out of the window at the clouds below feeling disappointed to be deprived of human communication. Whenever he sat next to a stranger on a plane he always managed to engage them in conversation, it was what made the journey interesting as well as helping time pass quickly. He wondered as he listened to her heavy breathing if this was an omen of things to come on their travels together.

From Barbados they took a short connecting flight to Caracas arriving at Simon Bolivar airport in the early evening. Gabriel waited nervously as they approached customs having learnt to expect that he might be singled out for special treatment. There was a group of young people with light luggage in the line and Gabriel deliberately manoeuvred himself and Cecile into their midst hoping to inconspicuously blend into the group. Gabriel found himself standing next to a young man who smiled pleasantly and introduced himself as Tim. Gabriel and Tim chatted easily as they shuffled along in the queue heading to the custom checks. Gabriel learnt that Tim had recently completed his degree in Psychology and had accepted a placement to work with the VSO. He was intending to travel overland to Peru to take up the post as an English teacher at a boys' school. Gabriel immediately decided that Tim was an interesting guy and that he liked him, he was, however, unaware at this moment of how significant the chance meeting was to become as his journey through South America unfolded. To Gabriel's surprise and relief they were finally ushered through customs having shown passports and visas and having completed the other necessary formalities by answering straightforward questions about their proposed itinerary and the purpose of their visit.

Once out of the airport and into the heat of the evening and the chaos of the city, taxis swarmed like bees. Amidst the crowds emerging from the airport trolleys laden with luggage, Gabriel caught a glimpse of Tim standing on the kerbside. Taking Cecile by the hand he negotiated their way through the hoard until they reached him. "Hello again, fancy sharing a taxi?" he asked. Tim shook his head and explained that cab fares were extortionate. He pointed to a bus stop 300 yards away across the embankment from where he said they could get a bus to the Nuevo Circo bus terminal. From this early stage of his encounter with Tim Gabriel found himself following his guidance and judgement, as if instinctively he trusted him completely although he hardly knew him.

The three of them boarded the crowded bus managing to find two seats at the rear; Cecile agreed to sit on Gabriel's lap. Tim and Gabriel squeezed close together on the two small seats, laughed about the cramped conditions and joked about the perspiration and smell of body odour which reflected their already long journey in the heat. They were remarkably at ease in each other's company travelling the 25 km towards central Caracas along the highway through the coastal mountains.

Gabriel's admiration for Tim continued to grow as he confidently described his plan for the first leg of his journey across Venezuela into Columbia staying in the beautiful Columbian city of Palmino for a few days. From there he would head for the capital Bogota before stopping off in Ecuador for a few days and finally getting to Peru where he was due to take up his VSO post in a few weeks' time. He had clearly done all the research and had a clear itinerary including locations of major transport hubs and cheap hotels for stop over points. Gabriel on the other hand had no clear plan or itinerary, his decision to travel to South America had been made on the spur of the moment, knowing only that he wanted to see as many countries as he could in the time he was there. He was confident enough to think he'd find his way from one country to another and find places to stay as needed. Tim's attention to detail was impressive, he had maps with his route clearly outlined and details of detours he intended to take visiting modern architectural places of interest and ancient historical sites. Gabriel was about to suggest that they team up and travel together to Peru when Tim as if reading his thoughts said, "It would be good to have some company on the way, it can get quite lonely travelling so far on one's own." Needless to say Gabriel immediately jumped at the chance, "That would be great," they both laughed and shook hands, firmly cementing the agreement. Gabriel became aware of Cecile sitting motionless on his lap and realised it had been impolite not to consult her before making the decision. "OK with you?" he asked her, she nodded and answered briefly, "Yes, it's OK." She appeared to be completely indifferent and Gabriel was grateful that she did not raise any objections.

Gabriel really liked Tim, he was clearly level headed but also adventurous and fun loving and Gabriel welcomed the opportunity to share the journey with him, particularly as he was becoming increasingly irritated by Cecile who so far on their travels had been moody and generally uncommunicative. As the bus meandered its way along the highway heading to the city of Caracas Tim explained that staying in Venezuela wasn't an option for him. The collapse of oil prices and rapid price inflation meant that accommodation prices in Venezuela were way beyond his limited budget. He planned to head for Columbia and take the easiest and safest border crossing from San Antonio del Táchira in Venezuela to Cúcuta in Colombia.

The bus chugged into the chaotic Nuevo Circo bus terminal in central Caracas, there were long lines of people waiting to buy tickets, long queues waiting for the buses to arrive and when they did hoards of people pushing to get on. Eventually they got their tickets and pushed their way through the throng. Thankfully they boarded the bus to San Antonio, managing to find three seats close together.

Then they were on their way to the Venezuelan border town

of San Antonio del Táchira. In spite of the heat outside the air conditioned bus felt distinctly chilly and they rummaged through their luggage to find sweaters. Once out of the busy city and through the shanty towns of its suburbs the sun got lower and lower in the sky until the bright red glow dropped below the horizon and it was dark. Cecile as usual had shut her eyes and was asleep almost as soon as the bus left the terminal. Tim and Gabriel had chatted for a while until as darkness fell they too succumbed to sleep.

Some hours later whilst still dark they were awakened by the driver announcing they'd reached the border crossing. The bus stopped and the driver instructed them to disembark because they had to pass through the customs and immigration on either side of the Simon Bolivar Bridge. A queue had already formed and they made their way slowly towards the check point where a friendly official stamped their exit visas and wished them luck. They said cheerio to Venezuela and got back on the bus which drove slowly across the bridge past the Venezuelan flags marking their departure point from the country.

As they crossed into Columbia the bus stopped outside a building which Tim reliably informed them was the (DAS) the Security Service agency of Colombia which was also responsible for the immigration services. Gabriel aware that his political connections of the past had a way of catching up with him on these occasions was naturally nervous. Officials boarded the bus moving quickly past the other passengers who were all Columbian nationals until they reached them at the rear. Having showed their passports as requested they were ordered to get off the bus and to accompany them into the DAS building. It became obvious that this was no ordinary country, they were ushered into the building by men holding guns; the passport officials had obviously alerted the army. Cecile was visibly frightened and Gabriel protectively put his arm around her. She was trembling and he was apprehensive. Tim who undoubtedly possessed a maturity far beyond his years and sensing their nervousness tried to put them at ease saying, "Don't worry, trust me this is what happens here, just answer their questions and it'll be OK."

Once in the building they were separated and taken individually to small rooms and asked about their reasons for wanting to enter Columbia and then thoroughly searched. Finally they were given entry stamps into the country and escorted back to the waiting bus. Safely back on the bus they breathed sighs of relief, their relief tempered only by Cecile's realization that her expensive camera and money in Venezuelan bolivars had been taken from her rucksack during the search. Shortly they reached the border town of Cúcuta, Cecile still upset over the loss of her possessions complained that she was very tired and insisted they find somewhere to stay in the city. Tim had intended to take another bus to Pamplona which he said was only about an hour and a half away and was reluctant to change his plans. Gabriel did his best to dissuade Cecile but arguing with her proved pointless, her mind was made up. Sadly, Gabriel bid farewell to Tim but not before arranging to meet with him at his Pamplona hotel as soon as he could.

Tim had warned Gabriel to be careful in the city telling him that it was a border crossing and had a reputation for being a swelteringly hot, unattractive, crime ridden city. This was why he felt it made far more sense to spend the night in tranquil Pamplona. Then he told him about a hotel not far from the bus station called the Hotel Zulia which should be easy to find. It was the early hours of the morning but nevertheless it was hot and muggy as they walked through the drab, lifeless streets. Gabriel tried to have a conversation with Cecile but she was unresponsive other than to say she felt unwell and needed to sleep.

After some unnecessary detours they found the Hotel Zulia, the main doors were closed, when Gabriel rang a bell, a man appeared. He was obviously not pleased that they'd woken him. He quickly entered their names in the guest book and handed them a room key. The room was grubby with no air conditioning, windows with broken catches so they could not be opened and the shower did not work. Cecile was furious and started shouting at Gabriel who got very angry with her. He told Cecile that it was her selfishness that had led them to end up in this place because he'd really wanted to travel with Tim to Pamplona and find a hotel there.

Tired from the journey and tired of the argument that was leading nowhere Gabriel decided to undress and get into the uncomfortable looking bed that dominated the room and it wasn't long before Cecile did the same. Gabriel awoke at two o'clock in the afternoon and drew the curtains letting sunlight into the drab room, at the small sink he splashed cold water over his face and body immediately feeling refreshed. Cecile was stirring and not wanting to ruin the rest of the day he forced a polite, "Good morning, or rather afternoon," he could not be certain but thought she managed a smile in response. Gabriel sat on the bed drying his wet hair with one of the few towels from the defunct shower room. "This place is not good, let's check out, head back to the bus station and get to Pamplona." To his surprise there was no disagreement she simply agreed, replying, "OK I'll get dressed."

They had breakfast at tea time in a dirty little cafe at the end of the street and made their way directly to the bus station. Unsavoury characters were hanging around the station and Gabriel suspected they were professional con artists, fraudsters and tricksters who preyed on international travellers. Deliberately ignoring them, he walked on and managed to find a bus going to Pamplona that was leaving within the hour.

The journey lasted about two hours, Cecile still reluctant to engage in any meaningful conversation buried her head in a book appearing to read a South America travel guide, although Gabriel noticed that she didn't turn many pages. The bus was the most modern and the most comfortable one of their travels so far. Gabriel relaxed, laying his head back on the cushioned headrest and began to look forward to reaching Pamplona and seeing Tim again.

Leaving the drabness of Cúcuta behind, their journey opened out into open country with dramatic views of the mountain scenery as the bus weaved along its route towards Pamplona a small city nestled in the mountains of the Eastern Andes. They stopped briefly at a small roadside cafe on the side of a mountain and felt the coolness of the air a welcome relief after the sweltering temperatures of Cúcuta. On reaching the town the bus slowly negotiated its way through the narrow cobbled streets stopping to let off passengers along the way. It was at one of these impromptu stops that Gabriel spotted Tim wearing fashionable sunglasses and striding nonchalantly along the pavement. Jumping from his seat, Gabriel grabbed his suitcase from the overhead rack and calling Cecile to follow they joined the passengers leaving the bus. "Tim, Tim," Gabriel shouted, Tim responded immediately and walked towards him with his arms open wide and they greeted each other with a hug. "I knew you'd be here soon," said Tim, giving only a sideways glance to Cecile who had just caught up with them. Tim took the suitcases one in each hand and they walked together along the street to the nearby hotel, happy to be together again.

The hotel was a large two storey old colonial house and was located directly on the main square and proved to be far better than the one where they'd spent the previous night. The room was large and airy with windows that opened out into the square below and a lovely shower that worked. Cecile unpacked and looked happier than Gabriel had seen her so far. Perhaps now he hoped her attitude to their adventure together might improve. Cecile was whistling a tune and appeared happy enough to spend time settling into her new surroundings. She said she wanted to unpack and take a long awaited shower and didn't seem to mind when Gabriel announced that he was going to find Tim who'd said he'd be in the downstairs bar.

Gabriel found Tim relaxing in the small hotel bar, casually

dressed in light shorts showing his long bronzed legs, an open neck shirt and dark sun glasses, his long dark hair was brushed back from his face revealing small droplets of sweat on his brow. They wandered out into the busy square, it was early evening and locals having finished work for the day were meeting up in the many colourful bars and restaurants that were dotted around. Tim, keen to show his knowledge of the area, told Gabriel that this was the central plaza of the city and the large church on one side of the Plaza was the Santa Clara Cathedral. They sat at a small cafe next to the cathedral, perfectly relaxed drinking and watching the people passing by. They had been oblivious to the passing of time and all of a sudden it was dark. Gabriel was slightly concerned that he'd left Cecile alone all this time and told Tim he needed to get back to her. They headed back to the hotel together, Tim went into the bar and Gabriel went up to the room, where he found Cecile comfortably draped in blankets on the huge bed fast asleep.

The few days they spent in Pamplona passed pleasantly and quickly, Cecile and Tim did not relate well to each other at all and Cecile resented the time Gabriel spent with him but was reluctant to accompany them preferring she said to wander around on her own returning to the hotel to relax in the afternoons. So Tim and Gabriel spent the mornings wandering the corridors of the old covered market just off the main plaza with the many small shops.

On their last day they packed their rucksacks with fruit from the local market and headed off to the nearby Tama national park where they spent the day high up in the Andes. They were lying by a stream, fed by a waterfall cascading down the cliff face of a distant mountain, facing each other, resting on their elbows eating the juicy peaches they'd purchased in the market, the snow capped peaks above them and the rolling grass hills below. Bathing in the tranquillity of the moment Gabriel looked at Tim lying stretched out beside him, their eyes met and Gabriel was completely overcome by his emotions. It had become more than a friendship,

Gabriel knew that they were so totally compatible in every way, he began to question was it simply an affection he felt for Tim or was it something more? When they raised themselves up from the ground, they looked directly at each other and Gabriel suspected that Tim had experienced exactly the same emotion as he had but neither of them verbalised their feelings. They headed back down the mountain, both silent lost in their own thoughts.

The next day they left Pamplona and headed the short distance to Bucaramanga to catch a late morning train that would take them on the 340 mile journey south to Bogota. Tim and Gabriel had been strangely distant with each other since that day at the park. At Bucaramanga rail station they found that a recent landslide on the route meant that the train they were expecting to take was severely delayed. A ticket tout approached, offering the services of a minibus to take them as far as San Gil about two hours away from Bogota. As they hurried to load the bags into the minibus there was an embarrassingly awkward moment when Tim's hand touched Gabriel's. The chemistry between them was powerful but uncomfortable.

Some passengers were already on the bus, quite an interesting mix of nationalities, a Columbian family seated along the long back seat in their colourful ponchos and sombreros, a pair of young Australian backpackers and an elderly Spanish couple who were visiting relatives. There were a few seats left, Tim spread himself out taking two sears for himself, Gabriel felt this was a deliberate demonstration of the fact that he did not want to sit next to him on this trip. Cecile and Gabriel settled down for the journey on the seat behind him. The bus was about to leave when a young lad got on, the seat next to Tim was the only one left. Tim duly removed his coat, sweater and books allowing the young man to sit down.

The bus meandered its way through the busy city and onto the curvy roads that led up the mountainside finally leading to the highway leading to the Canon del Chicamocha with its spectacular breathtaking scenery. Crossing the mountains and river valleys the bus passed from one small town to the next picking up and letting off people along the way, the majority of these towns weren't on the maps but had pretty plazas and nice churches as well as people wearing traditional ponchos. They must have been travelling for about two hours, Tim had dropped off to sleep, his head leaning to one side and Gabriel was resisting the temptation to twirl his fingers through the dark curls that framed the nape of his neck when the driver announced that they'd arrived at the busy San Gil Inter City bus terminal

They alighted from the air conditioned bus into the heat of the busy bus terminal. Every few minutes a loud voice boomed out across the terminal announcing the arrival and departure times of the intercity buses in Spanish, German and English. The buses to Bogota were every hour and they'd just missed one. They wandered outside into a sunlit square a brightly decorated gringo cafe, advertising freshly pressed Columbian coffee looked inviting and was packed with local people. On entering they were greeted with the distinct smell of freshly ground coffee and a bubbly waitress wearing a long white apron. Tim left them to order the coffees saying he wanted to find out some information from the Tiende de Viajes just a few doors away from the cafe.

He returned looking excited, announcing, "Guys this is unbelievable." He explained that the assistant he'd spoken to had informed him that a flight from Bogota to Lima with Avianca, the Columbian national airline, was now cheaper than the 1000 miles long overland bus and train journeys that they had planned to make between these two cities. Tim went on to explain that the travel agent had told him that the recent air disasters had affected the demand for Avianca flights and because the planes had so many empty seats the airline was virtually giving them away. Gabriel remembered that these dramatic air crashes had made headline news in the UK.

After only a brief discussion they all agreed that this was too good an offer to miss and the three returned to the travel shop next door to buy the tickets.

By now the intercity bus to Bogota had arrived and was about to leave as they clambered aboard. The bus was modern by Columbian standards and far more comfortable than the minibus they'd travelled in earlier. Gabriel sank back enjoying the luxury of the padded seat and head rest. The full implications of their sudden decision to fly directly from Bogota to Lima washed over him. He took the tickets he'd bought from his travel wallet, it confirmed a flight from Bogota leaving at 11.45pm the following morning arriving in the late afternoon at Lima's Jorge Chávez Airport.

Gabriel had always known that he would bid farewell to Tim when they reached Lima where Tim would take up his teaching post. Then he and Cecile would take up Alicia's kind invitation to stay with her family. Yet it was only a few days ago that they'd sat together in the cafe on the Pamplona Plaza drinking coffee dreamily planning the next few weeks of their adventure, methodically tracing their route on a map, a route that led from Bogota to the border crossing at Ipiales to across the Rumichaca Bridge to Tulcán in Ecuador. Then on to Quito about five hours away. They had also planned to take a four-day rail journey on the famous Tren Crucero descending the Andes to the port of Guayaquil. Sadly, these dreams were never to be, tonight they would sleep in Bogota, spend one day in the city and just before midnight fly to Lima.

Gabriel knew that the cheap flight was as Tim had said too good an opportunity to miss but could not help but wonder whether he had also thought it was a perfect opportunity to put an end to what Gabriel had come to refer to in his head as "their affair." Cecile was already asleep beside him, her head resting on his shoulder. As he looked down at her he wished he could feel for her whatever it was he felt for Tim. Gabriel closed his eyes and floating by came visions of the women he'd become romantically involved with over the years, and there had been many of them.

He'd always fallen quickly in love and quickly out of love, forever searching for the ideal of perfect love and had come to question its existence. Did he after all have the potential to realise this perfect love or was he to be forever trapped by the conventional morality of his time? A morality fed by indoctrination as a child into the Catholic faith, when the threat of hell fire and damnation was implanted in such a way that it would last a lifetime.

It was late in the evening when they arrived in Bogota in a torrential rainstorm, the narrow streets were rapidly turning into streams the three of stood together trying to shelter from the downpour in a dirty hotel doorway just across the road from the huge bus terminus. "Taxi to the Dorantes Hotel La Candelaria?" said Tim who as usual was taking control of the situation.

It was a beautiful building much in need of attention but clean and friendly. Cecile was not impressed with the shared bathrooms down the hall, but returning from taking a shower was happy that at least the water was hot and minutes later was in bed fast asleep. Gabriel looked out of the window, it was a Saturday night and music was playing loudly in the street it was a perfect location if you wanted to party. He wandered down to the hotel foyer hoping to find Tim, he was there chatting happily with a party of young German backpackers. He looked pleased to see Gabriel and introduced him to his new friends. They were going to explore the neighbourhood bars and clubs and they invited them to join them.

It was a crazy night the streets were alive, it seemed Colombians loved to drink and loved to dance. They drifted in and out of bars and clubs resonating with the throb of live rock music and jazz. They mingled with local students, bohemians and artists; Gabriel always found a pretty young girl to dance with and took some pleasure in catching Tim's disapproving glance as he openly flirted. Reeling out of a bar, both of them rather the worse for alcohol, Tim took hold of Gabriel's arm firmly and in a reprimanding tone said, "Gabriel , take it easy, careful who you talk to, this area is notorious for drug dealers and some of those pretty Columbian girls are probably 'ladies of the night,' they'll lure you outside where their minders will rob you and beat you up. You'd better stay close to me." It was strange the way Gabriel accepted instinctively without question everything Tim said, he'd always been a very independent character often stubbornly pursuing his own objectives and ignoring the advice of others. Gabriel was older than Tim and assumed he had more life experience but he meekly and obediently accepted Tim's assessment of the situation that night.

Gabriel could remember moving along the street to another bar, sitting close to Tim drinking and talking but not what they talked about or how they got back to the hotel, or how he'd slept fully dressed in a strange bed before waking to a repeated knocking on the door. When he opened the door, Cecile was standing there with a look of disgust on her face shouting, "What are you doing in here? This is Tim's room, I was worried about you because you didn't come back last night, and I came to find Tim to see if he knew where you were." Luckily, hearing Cecile's loud angry voice, Tim came out of the shower room along the hall carrying a towel and wash bag. "Calm down Cecile, we both got pissed and crashed out in my room, it's as simple as that," explained Tim. "Oh really," she retorted, waving her arms dismissively and returned to her room along the hallway.

"Was it really as simple as that?" Gabriel asked. Tim gave him a look that said it all and Gabriel made his way back to the room he shared with Cecile. They packed in stony silence, joined Tim in the foyer and made their way to the airport to catch the pre-booked flight to Lima.

It was an uneventful flight with the aircraft only half occupied they were able to take advantage of the extra space and spread out across the spare seats. They all welcomed the opportunity to close their eyes and sleep, or at least pretend to sleep, as this conveniently avoided the need for any awkward communication between the three of them.

On arrival at the airport Gabriel was pleasantly surprised to see Alicia waiting for him, she extended her arms out to welcome him and they hugged. Tim was standing impatiently behind them waiting to say goodbye, he shook hands with Gabriel politely and they agreed to keep in touch and then he was gone.

Gabriel turned back to Alicia, intoxicated by her seductive perfume and thinking how pretty she looked with a white rose attached delicately to one side of her long dark hair. At that moment the heavy burden of guilt and disquiet he'd felt about his unusual attraction to Tim dissipated into the warm Peruvian air, replaced with an overwhelming infatuation with Alicia. Perhaps after all it was in Lima that he might finally realise his dream of finding the elusive perfect love.

11

Denial

Gabriel knew the moment he opened his eyes that he'd returned to the nightmare that was the reality of his waking life. Whilst asleep he escaped into the past when everything in his life had been good. In daylight hours he was consumed by dark thoughts of a looming bleak future. His escape plan had kept him alert and focussed but his hopes of ever achieving his goal were slowly ebbing away. Gabriel knew he was on a new journey, a journey for which he was unprepared, he had no maps, no itinerary and no way of knowing where he was going or how he was going to get there. The weakness of his body was overtaking his natural instinct for survival; an increasing fragility that he remained convinced was the consequence of the deliberate abuse of experimental drugs.

The debilitating weakness left him ever more dependent on Akemi; his hands would suddenly start shaking involuntarily when he tried to manage the buttons on his clothing, so each morning she would help him to dress. His hands would start shaking when he tried to eat, so Akemi would chop his food into small pieces making it easier for him to eat. Gabriel was becoming increasingly resentful of his dependence on this woman. There were times when he thought she was a kind person because of the uncomplaining way in which she went about the practical chores of shopping, cooking, cleaning and generally caring for his basic needs but he questioned her motives. She continued to forcefully insist that he took medication at regular intervals throughout the day; if he refused she would put it into his mouth holding it shut until she was convinced he'd swallowed it. Gabriel learnt to place the pills under his tongue and make a swallowing sound, when she moved away he'd spit them out and hide them under a cushion on the chair. When Akemi discovered this ploy, she became very angry, shouting and waving her arms in exasperation and threatening to leave him if he ever did it again. When Gabriel retorted excitedly, "Yes, yes, please go," her response was frightening, "You cannot look after yourself, if I go, who'll look after you? You need full time care, you have never had to look after yourself – you've never cooked a meal or done any of the normal things that people do every day – like shopping, cleaning. You have always played at life, you never bothered with such mundane things."

This was a threat that she would use time after time whenever he refused to do as she asked. Aware of how physically weak and frail he'd become Gabriel knew that he'd reached a stage in his life when he could not care for himself. He hated his dependence on Akemi, she knew this and exploited it to her advantage. He was scared when she lost her temper, knowing that he would not be able to defend himself if she was to attack him and there were many times when he thought she might.

Gabriel tried to keep track of time passing, the tree outside the bedroom window told him when the seasons changed as the green shoots of spring turned to the green foliage of summer then the beautiful russet brown of autumn before shedding its leaves for the darkness and cold of winter. All the days were the same with nothing to differentiate one from another. He'd wake in the morning, be given medicine, wash and dress, eat breakfast, be given more pills, sit on a chair watching pre-recorded video tapes whilst Akemi went shopping being sure to lock the door behind her. After a few hours when she returned he would be forced to take more medicine, then eat again, then sleep till evening, sit once again in the same chair in front of a television staring at the shapes passing across the screen but not really seeing anything. Gabriel was locked into his own world and nothing could invite him out of the dark place he was forced to inhabit.

Only occasionally would the telephone ring and when it did Akemi would either have a brief terse conversation in broken English or a long friendly conversations in her native Japanese. One day when the phone rang, Akemi spoke for a short time and then to Gabriel's complete amazement she handed him the receiver and said "It's Alicia, she wants to speak to you." He felt elated; he could sense the blood flowing in his veins and his heart pounding with excitement when he heard her melodic Spanish voice asking, "How are you Gabriel?"

"Alicia, Alicia, is it really you, where are you? How do you know I am here?" The questions kept coming. "Yes it is me and I know you are not very well, Can I come and see you tomorrow it's my day off from work?"

"Yes, yes, please come," he responded immediately, at which point Akemi took the phone out of his hand. He heard her say brusquely, "You come tomorrow morning, that OK," before replacing the receiver. "How does she know I'm here?" Gabriel asked. Akemi looked angry and at first she did not answer, she went into the kitchen and he could hear her preparing dinner.

It was later over dinner that Akemi explained that when making his bed, she'd found a piece of paper that he'd hidden under his mattress, the piece of paper with Alicia's name and telephone number that she had pressed into his hand outside the hospital. She had decided to call her and ask if she could spare some time to help care for him.

Akemi began to tell him things she had never said before, she said she was tired of caring for him, that he was too demanding, too selfish and that she had no life of her own. She desperately needed a rest away from him and she was hoping Alicia would be able to help her to care for him and give her the opportunity to have some time to herself. For the first time Gabriel began to feel sorry for her, but this empathy did not last long. He had always known that he was selfish and demanding but this time it was not his fault, if anyone's fault it was hers because for whatever reason she was forcing his dependence on her with the cocktail of drugs that she insisted on pumping into him at regular intervals throughout the day. He could not muster the energy to argue with her, they argued every day when she insisted he take the medication and as yet he'd never managed to succeed in winning these arguments.

Gabriel decided to retreat to the silence of the bedroom, it had been a long time since he'd looked forward to anything and now he was looking forward so much to seeing Alicia again. He needed to think how he could explain the bizarre situation in which he'd become entangled and how he could persuade her to help him to escape from it. He felt at last that he'd been thrown a lifeline and was determined to take it.

Alicia arrived promptly at 10am the next morning, Gabriel had a picture of her in his head, a picture of her as she was when he fell in love with her in the Lima airport, she didn't look the same but he knew it was Alicia. She had aged, matured but age had been kind to her she was still a very attractive woman with the same beautiful brown eyes and the sweet accented voice which sounded so comforting after Akemi's shrill tones. Akemi was ready to leave almost as soon as Alicia arrived. She gave a few curt instructions about the location of food and drink items and handed her a sheet of paper detailing the exact times when he needed to be given medication. Then she was gone, this time not locking the door behind her.

Alicia sat close to Gabriel holding his hands, "Oh Gabriel, you look so frail," her brown eyes filling with tears. Gabriel had a plan, there was no time for emotions, he had to convince Alicia to help him to escape and to insist they leave today before Akemi returned. He told her Akemi was slowly killing him and that she had the numbers of his bank cards and was stealing his money. Alicia looked at him sympathetically explaining that Akemi had told her that he'd say such things and it was because he was suffering with paranoia. Gabriel shook his head protesting, saying it was all lies, a story Akemi had made up so that she could keep him prisoner and steal from him. "You must help me," he pleaded.

Alicia took both his hands in hers and looked at him intently before saying, "I want you to listen to the story I am about to tell you, it is the story of events in your life that you have chosen to forget, events that have led you to where you are now."

Gabriel was agitated, every second was precious this was his chance to escape and he did not want to delay but he trusted Alicia and was interested in what she might be about to tell him. Alicia proceeded in her soft lilting Spanish accent which Gabriel found refreshingly comforting to recount a story. She told him that it was a love story about a very young Japanese girl called Kimiko. Gabriel reacted immediately at the sound of the name, shaking his head and cupping his hands over his ears as if the name had stirred long repressed memories within him, memories that were deeply buried somewhere in the darkness of his mind.

Alicia continued to tell the story. It was about five years ago, she told him, when Gabriel first met Kimiko who was a post graduate student studying architecture at a London university. Gabriel had moved to London a few years earlier and had acquired an apartment in the fashionable west side of the city. The pair became inseparable, living together in Gabriel's London apartment; friends observed that they shared something very special. When Kimiko graduated, Gabriel decided to leave his comfortable life in England and move to Japan and live with Kimiko in Kyoto. For a while all was well, they planned to marry and buy a house in a quiet suburb of the city. Kimiko's traditional Japanese family did not approve of her marrying a foreigner or of the significant age difference between them but Kimiko was prepared to go against their wishes.

They shared many personality traits; it was a true pair bonding. Both dreamt of finding a perfect love but at 21 years old Kimiko was at the beginning of this unpredictable mission whilst Gabriel at 68 years old believed that after all his previous liaisons he had finally found the one he wanted to share his life and who would love and care for him as long as it lasted. Gabriel's friends had tried to warn him of the dangers inherent in the relationship, warnings he had not heeded.

It was when they were planning their wedding that Kimiko raised the issue of children, a natural question to raise given her age but not one Gabriel wanted to face. Their relationship cooled, Kimiko spent more and more time at work returning late in the evenings. Nevertheless Gabriel remained convinced they would work it out and always be together until Kimiko announced that she had met someone else, a young architect at the prestigious firm where she had worked since their return to Japan. Gabriel's heart was broken and before long he'd returned home to London where he'd been admitted to hospital having suffered a nervous breakdown.

Gabriel who had been listening attentively suddenly became agitated, he got up and ran into the bedroom where he retrieved the photo he'd hidden, the torn photo he'd found taken outside a traditional Japanese house, an image from which someone had been deliberately removed. His hands shaking he held it in front of Alicia, and shouted angrily, "I remember now, this was our home in Kyoto, it was Kimiko beside me in this photo." He sat down next to Alicia, his eyes filled with tears and holding the photo close to his chest he lowered his head and started to rhythmically rock himself gently back and forth. Alicia put her arms around him hoping to offer some comfort but he quickly brushed her away. He became aggressive and unpredictable moving from one room to another, picking up papers and throwing them across the room whilst shouting, "You're lying, you're part of this conspiracy, I know you're lying." Alarmed by his sudden mood change Alicia went into the kitchen offering to make them both a cup of tea. She stood in the kitchen waiting for the kettle to boil regretting that she had rekindled Gabriel's painful memories by Kimiko. As she systematically prepared a tray selecting two matching cups and sugar bowl and milk jug she could hear Gabriel sobbing loudly in the next room. Slowly carrying the tray into the room she felt at a loss as to what words of comfort or understanding she would be able to offer him. She placed the tray on the small table and sat beside him. He had stopped crying but his eyes were still moist with tears when he turned towards her saying, "I know you're lying, Kimiko is dead, I was with her when she died." He immediately turned away from her and sat staring at the torn photograph, alone in his personal traumatised world, a world in which Alicia mistakenly believed she had no part to play other than to sit silently by him and hold his hand which she was thankful that he didn't reject when it was offered.

When Akemi returned Gabriel and Alicia were still sitting beside each other, two untouched cups of cold tea on the table before them. It was a mid winter afternoon and the light was fading, with a flick of a light switch Akemi swathed the room in a bright fluorescent light finally lifting the tension that had weighed heavily on Alicia. Alicia rose and and went into the kitchen where Akemi was busy unloading provisions from the carrier bags which she had struggled to carry up the stairs. Gabriel remained sitting at the window transfixed staring out into the darkness of the encroaching evening. The strength and intensity of the emotional outburst he had expressed when Alicia had spoken about Kimiko had shocked him. He knew there were deeply buried memories and wasn't sure whether he was incapable of remembering or whether he was deliberately protecting himself from the unbearable pain that he knew recalling them would bring. That afternoon during the hours he'd spent gazing out of the window he had dared to try to open the box containing the memories of Kimiko. Memories that he'd locked away in a far corner of his mind. He felt safe with Alicia next to him holding his hand; she offered a safe pair of arms waiting to catch him if a torrent of repressed emotions burst to the surface. Alicia who had felt so helpless at the time would have been happy to know that she had after all played a role that afternoon. Gabriel knew that Alicia unlike Akemi would not get angry and abusive; she wouldn't tell him that he was a lunatic and she wouldn't force him to take sedatives that would numb the anguish but deprive him of the indulgence of grieving for his loss.

Looking at the photograph of himself outside their Kyoto home Gabriel tried to imagine Kimiko standing next to him. Slowly he focussed on trying to reconstruct her face, starting with her deep brown eyes that had glowed with love lights when they'd first met, something Gabriel had read about in books but had never experienced. From there he tried to imagine her hair style, he remembered the deep brown colour and could almost feel its texture. It was as if he was drawing a picture slowly joining the dots together. Still staring at the photograph he saw a blurred image which gradually came into focus. Kimiko was there her outline superimposed over the original photo, the house had receded into the background and Kimiko had replaced Gabriel in the photo. Her long hair reaching to her shoulders, dressed in a long white dress and holding her hands out to him as if calling him towards her. Gabriel thought it was her ghost and closed his eyes immediately afraid of what he'd resurrected from the recesses of his mind.

As Alicia helped Akemi to unload the shopping she confessed that she'd spoken to Gabriel about Kimiko and described Gabriel's dramatic reactions to what she'd told him. Akemi grew angry, she moved closer to Alicia, lowered her eyelids and pointed her finger at her saying, "Never, never mention that woman's name to him ever again, do you hear me." Alicia remained in no doubt that somehow she had inadvertently crossed a line and Akemi was not happy about it and Alicia decided that the best thing to do in the circumstances was to make her apologies and leave. She collected her coat before going over to Gabriel, kissing him lightly on the forehead; she couldn't be sure that he would hear her but whispered, "I'll pray for you and come and see you again soon." To her surprise he turned away from the window, looked at her and squeezed her hand gently. Akemi stood at the sink in the kitchen and did not respond when Alicia said politely, "Goodbye, I'm going now and I'm very sorry for any distress I've caused."

Gabriel knew Akemi was angry by the way she slammed the dinner plates down on the table and shouted at him to get to the table before his food went cold. He knew Alicia would have told her about his outburst and he sat down obediently eating the tea she had prepared for him. Neither seemed inclined to speak about what had happened and Gabriel was almost grateful when Akemi laid out a line of pills on the table accompanied by a glass of water. Already frail and weak, the surge of emotions and the mental energy that he'd used had left him exhausted; he wanted to slip once again into another world and to forget.

12

The burglary and an escape

Gabriel tumbled out of bed and glanced at his reflection in the full length mirror attached to his bedroom wall. His hair was ruffled and he was unshaven but fully dressed in a pair of light casual trousers and an open necked shirt. Puzzled as to how and why he had slept through the night in his everyday clothes he made his way into the living room.

The room was littered with papers, books and CD cases were strewn haphazardly, drawers had been removed from cupboards and emptied onto the floor, Gabriel called out for Akemi but she wasn't there and the entrance door to the flat was partly open. He nervously negotiated his way through the disarray and peered tentatively out of the door. Looking over the banister to the stairs below Gabriel glimpsed the outline of a slightly built man or boy with a hooded jacket running down the last flight of stairs and disappearing out of the main door. He went back into the flat and looked out of the window from where he could see the same person running towards the main road.

He sat down for a moment staring in disbelief at the chaos in the room and trying to work out what he should do. It was clear the flat had been burgled but nothing seemed to be missing. Whoever it was had been looking for something and had clearly ransacked the place. Gabriel had always hidden any documents that might reveal the indiscretions of his past life but he no longer had any recollection of where he had hidden them. But he didn't have the time to worry about these things, the door was open and Akemi was not there, it was the perfect chance to escape from her; it was the opportunity he had been waiting for.

In the excitement of the moment he forgot to put on his shoes and ran quickly down the stairs and out of the door. It was a cold October morning and Gabriel had no coat and no shoes but undeterred he headed for the main road where he'd remembered seeing a bus stop. Many times he'd imagined finding a bus to take him to the pubs where his friends hung out. He could see the bus stop ahead and a red London transport bus in the distance.

In his haste he didn't notice the broken paving stone and fell awkwardly using his right arm to break the fall. He cried out, "Help me," to an elderly lady waiting at the bus stop. She came to his aid and with her help he managed to pull himself up from the ground. The bus had arrived at the stop and pulled up right beside Gabriel and the kindly old lady who'd helped him. Gabriel had cut his cheek bone when he fell and blood was streaming down his face, he was agitated and trembling. The bus driver stared at the dishevelled unshaven man wearing no shoes and asked what had happened to him. Shaken by the fall, Gabriel struggled to get his breath as he tried to explain that the flat where he was staying had been burgled. The bus driver, aware of the traffic congestion ahead and of his passengers anxious to be delivered to their destinations, was reluctant to get involved. It was one of those passengers who acted responsibly and called an ambulance. The elderly lady agreed to take Gabriel into her house which was only a few yards from the bus stop and wait with him for the ambulance to arrive.

Once inside the house the lady introduced herself as Mabel

and told Gabriel that she recognised him. She had seen him many times walking along the street arm in arm with a Japanese lady and had thought they seemed a very nice couple. Gabriel wanted desperately to tell her that they were not a couple and that the Japanese women was certainly not a nice person but his breathing had become so laboured that it was difficult for him to speak. Mabel made him a cup of hot tea explaining that she had added sugar because it would help him to overcome the shock of his fall. Gabriel's hands were shaking as he tried to crook his finger into handle of the porcelain cup decorated with sprigs of lavender. Gabriel thought it looked expensive and was afraid of breaking it. Fortunately Mabel seeing his shaking hands picked up the cup and put it to his lips. Gabriel felt tears well up in his eyes, it had been a long time since anyone had showed him such kindness and when he had taken a sip of the tea he managed to utter a muffled, "Thank you."

When the ambulance arrived, the paramedics did all the usual medical checks; they were concerned about his shortness of breath and suspected that he'd fractured his wrist when he fell. It was decided that he should be taken to the local hospital. Gabriel insisted on walking to the ambulance determined to demonstrate that he could be self reliant. He resented his dependence on Akemi, he blamed her for his increasing debility and now that at last he was free from her and the medication she forced upon him he was determined to regain his independence. He sat quietly in the ambulance reflecting on the strange events of the day so far. Someone had been in the flat searching for something. Gabriel still had a nagging suspicion that there might be something hidden in the flat that might incriminate him and wished he could remember exactly what was in the documents, he could only remember that somewhere there was a paper trail of his past naive involvements with dubious government officials.

Once at the hospital the paramedics helped him out of the ambulance and walked with him to the admissions and found him a chair. They spoke briefly to the lady seated at the desk, then smiled kindly at him, shook his hand and wished him good luck.

Gabriel began to take in his surroundings; he was seated in what seemed to be a long narrow corridor with a lot of doors. The admissions desk was at one end and above the desk was a white board with a long list of names Gabriel watched as his name was added. There were a lot of people quietly waiting in the corridor. Sitting directly opposite him was an elderly Asian gentleman, he had a long white beard and his hair was hidden under a neat black turban. He smiled at Gabriel who was feeling more relaxed, his breathing had become more regular and he had stopped shaking but realised that his wrist was swollen and very painful. Gabriel stood up and walked to the desk hoping that he could persuade the young girl to take pity on him and push his name up the list so that he could be seen sooner. He was impatient, he wanted to get his arm treated and get out of the hospital. Once outside he planned to get a bus or a tube train and go to one of the many pubs that he remembered his friends frequented. To his surprise his charm that he had always relied upon to get his way with young impressionable females failed miserably. The young girl paid no attention to his pleas and dismissed him saying, "Sorry Mr Jones but you will have to wait." Gabriel returned to his seat but soon thought of another tactic to get seen more quickly. He began to breathe heavily and loudly and found that his heart rate started to increase and he actually did start to become short of breath. The bearded man with the black turban asked if he was OK, Gabriel didn't reply but continued to gasp for breath. The man was himself elderly and had difficulty in walking but he managed with the aid of his walking frame to reach the reception desk. He pointed to Gabriel and the girl reacted immediately, summoning a nurse to attend to him. Within seconds Gabriel was given an oxygen mask, helped into a wheelchair and moved to a cubicle where two doctors were waiting. Gabriel thought they both looked very young and suspected that they were medical students.

The doctors helped Gabriel onto a bed and he lay back pleased that he had managed to cleverly jump the long queue of people waiting in the corridor. The young doctors were preparing to do the usual tests, one holding a thermometer; the other uncurled a stethoscope from around his neck. Gabriel forgot to exaggerate his breathing and started speaking quickly to explain that he needed protection from a women who was trying to kill him and that morning there had been a burglary in the flat where he was being kept prisoner. The doctors stopped and listened. Knowing that he had their full attention Gabriel continued, telling them that the women bullied him and forced him to take medication that he suspected were experimental drugs. The doctors looked at each other and Gabriel heard one suggest that they needed to get a psyche report. Alarmed, Gabriel sat up in the bed and shouted angrily, "I am not mad, you must believe me." The young doctors quickly drew back the curtains that encircled the cubicle and signalled to a male nurse. After a brief conversation with the nurse the doctors left Gabriel in his care.

* * *

When Akemi woke that morning to find the living room in a state of disarray she immediately suspected that Gabriel had got up during the night and had been searching for documents that he had hidden somewhere. She knew that he was obsessed with finding these documents, he'd often referred to them, she'd opened boxes and files and helped him to look for them but they had never found them. She had asked him why the documents were important but he'd always refused to tell her. She checked his bedroom to be sure he was still there. Her suspicions that he was responsible for the chaos she had seen in the living room were confirmed on seeing him sleeping soundly but fully dressed. She had started tidying the room anxious that everything should be put back in order before Gabriel woke for his breakfast when she was distracted by a knock at the door. Akemi recognised the young man standing at the door; he'd recently introduced himself when he and his young family had moved into the flat directly below. He apologised for disturbing her and asked if she could show him how to operate the heating system in his flat, it was a chilly October morning and it was the first time he'd needed to use it. Akemi agreed to help and accompanied him down a flight of stairs to his flat forgetting to lock the door to her own flat. It took a while for her to remember how the complicated system worked and then to demonstrate the sequence of manoeuvres necessary to kick start the heating. The neighbour expressed his gratitude for her help and then insisted on introducing her to his pretty young wife and two little boys colourfully clad in identical cartoon character pyjamas.

As soon as she got back upstairs she panicked on seeing the door to the flat open, her worst fears were realised when she looked into Gabriel's bedroom and saw that he'd gone. Frantically grabbing her coat and her walking stick she made her way onto the street below. She looked up and down the street, there were so many people at this time of the morning, school uniformed teenagers running, city workers smartly dressed heading towards the tube station. She thought she'd little hope of finding Gabriel amongst these fast moving crowds of people that typified the London morning rush hour. Nevertheless she continued searching looking through the windows of the cafes, scanning the lines of queues at the bus stops. Eventually any hope she had of finding him faded and she headed to the nearby local police station.

Akemi had a deeply ingrained cultural respect for authority and would deferentially comply with any suggestions or instructions given to her by anyone holding a position of power. It was thus a natural reaction for her in this situation to seek help from the police. She spoke to an officer explaining she wanted to report a missing person but to her surprise he was dismissive, simply telling her to calm down, go home and wait for the person to turn up. "No, no he very sick man and he not had medication," Akemi insisted. The officer still reluctant to help advised her to come back the following morning if he had not returned, eventually asking for the name of the person she wished to report missing. Akemi was close to tears when she said, "His name Gabriel Jones." As soon as he heard the name the officer's attitude changed. He stood up quickly, told Akemi to wait a moment while he spoke to a colleague, he soon returned and asking her to follow him and escorted her to an interview room.

He left her in the room which was small and cold, she waited feeling anxious and nervous but believing still that they would see that the situation was serious and help her. It was a while before a plain clothes officer entered and took a seat opposite her, he immediately started firing questions. He asked her how long she had known Mr. Jones and what was the nature of their relationship and of their financial arrangements. Then she was asked to describe the events of that morning immediately prior to Mr. Jones's disappearance. Akemi didn't understand why she was being asked these questions. The man was looking at her accusingly and was speaking quickly, Akemi becoming increasingly apprehensive and confused, she wasn't sure exactly what he was saying and was struggling to find the English words she needed to reply. She suspected that she was not giving the answers he wanted when he shook his head in exasperation, picked up the piece of paper where he'd jotted down notes and brusquely said, "Right, you come with me." Akemi was scared as she followed him out of the building and into the car park; he opened the door of a marked police car indicating for her to get into the back seat. She was driven out of the station along the main Broadway where earlier she had searched for Gabriel arriving a few moments later at the entrance to the apartment block where she lived. Two more plain clothes policemen were already there waiting outside the main door, they showed their warrant cards and asked her to accompany them upstairs to her flat. Akemi was alarmed to see the door to the flat adorned with blue tape with the words "Crime Scene Do Not Enter". One of the men raised the tape so indicating to her to enter the flat and asked her to tell them what if anything had been stolen.

"No, no you no understand," she cried, "It not burglary, it Gabriel who do this, he mad man, he need his medication, I have to find him." Seeing that Akemi was obviously upset and that her actions were becoming increasingly erratic, one of the police attempted to take control of what he felt was becoming a bizarre situation. He took her arm and tried to reassure her telling her that they had been informed that Gabriel was safe and that he had been taken to the local hospital.

"I must go there; I need to get his pills," she shouted, pushing past them and kicking her way through the carpet of strewn papers covering the floor towards a locked cupboard. "Here, look," she screamed pushing a drug prescription in front of them, then proceeding to throw boxes of pills haphazardly into a carrier bag and storming into the bathroom throwing toiletries and towels into the bag.

The two policemen were quick to understand that this was not a usual run of the mill burglary investigation and more likely a domestic disturbance. They nodded to each other, demonstrating a tacit understanding that their job here was done and there was nothing more they could do other than to let her go on her way.

13

A new friend and a notebook

It was evening by the time Akemi reached the hospital; the police had given her the name of the ward where she would find Gabriel, "Murphy Ward." The bus journey had taken over an hour and during that time she'd relived the events of the day. She struggled with the English language and her thoughts as always were in her native Japanese language. In stressful situations she found the sudden transition to speaking and reading English even more difficult than usual.

She had assumed that the bus had stopped at the main entrance which would lead to a reception desk and someone in authority who would direct her to the ward. But there was no desk and no one to ask and she was confronted by the array of signs and arrows pointing in all directions. She was tired and flustered, clutching the bag of medicines and everyday essentials that she had brought for Gabriel she impetuously chose one of the corridors. The corridor led her to another and another, she felt lost in a maze and was becoming more and more distraught. Turning one corner she saw a porter pushing a trolley and limping closer to him she shouted, "Murphy Ward, Murphy

Ward." The porter stopped and pointed to an elevator, without a word of thanks Akemi took the elevator which opened directly outside Murphy Ward.

She pushed open the doors to the ward, saw an area identified as the "Nurses' Station" but to her dismay there was no one there. Seeing a group of seven or eight nurses gathered together in a corner talking, her frustration spilled over into a hysterical outburst. She approached them shouting that it was very important that she see Gabriel Jones. She was calmly but firmly escorted to a nearby waiting room, the accompanying nurse explaining that they were in the process of a shift changeover. Reluctantly she sat and waited.

The doctor who had cared for Gabriel was handing over responsibility to his colleague, a young Egyptian called Malik who would care for Gabriel throughout the night. He explained that Gabriel had been very agitated when he arrived at the hospital but he had calmed down and was now resting peacefully. Pointing to the room where Akemi had been instructed to wait he added that there were serious ongoing safeguarding issues and that the woman in there could not be allowed near him until these issues were resolved. He read out the notes that the doctor had made when Gabriel had been admitted. "Patient delivered to hospital by ambulance with minor injury to hand and shortness of breath following an argument with carer, likely panic attack. Patient admitted to Murphy Ward due to safeguarding issues, patient states a Japanese woman has been abusing him by giving him extra medications, bullying him and hitting him. He says she has been trying to make him sign over his house to her."

Malik had not anticipated that his first job of the evening would be to ensure that the angry female in the waiting room would be denied access to his patient because of safeguarding concerns. As expected Akemi reacted badly, shouting at him that she must see Gabriel because only she had the medication he needed. Malik's attempts to reassure her that the hospital would provide him with any medication that they thought he needed fell on deaf ears. When she continued shouting at him and trying to push her way into the ward Malik felt he had little choice other than to call the hospital security guard. Akemi still angrily protesting was forced to leave the hospital with clear instructions not to return.

Meanwhile Gabriel sitting in a chair next to his hospital bed having just been given a cup of tea and offered biscuits was feeling more relaxed than he had felt for a long time. He'd received a lot of attention that day he had spoken to doctors, psychiatrists and hospital almoners. He had repeatedly and consistently told them all about his strange situation, about his imprisonment in a flat, about the woman pretending to care for him who was using his credit cards to steal his money and who was giving him drugs to dull his consciousness. The interest that they all showed in his story led him to think that perhaps this hospital was a safe place to be and that perhaps he could trust these people. When he heard Akemi's shrill high pitched voice in the corridor and heard Malik being told that she was not allowed to see him he knew they had believed his story.

Later that night when the other patients in the ward were asleep, Gabriel lay awake. His mind seemed clearer than usual and he was mindful to try to unravel all the varied complex strands of his life over the years that might help to uncover the mystery of what had happened to him. He started by making a mental list of close friends, methodically he listed them alphabetically and as he recalled each name he rated them numerically in terms of the extent to which he thought they were reliable and trustworthy. When Malik came by to check on him Gabriel asked for a pen and paper which Malik quickly found for him. Gabriel tried to write down the list he had in his head but became frustrated when his hand started shaking and found it impossible to hold the pen still. Malik quickly glanced around the small ward, all was quiet, he sat down beside Gabriel and kindly offered to help. Gabriel dictated the names and their corresponding ratings alongside whilst Malik neatly noted them down. When Malik out of curiosity asked to what the names and numbers referred, Gabriel replied that it was his way of working out something that was troubling him. Malik by nature was a very caring individual and asked Gabriel if he thought that talking to him about his concerns might help. Gabriel looked directly at Malik and sensing his sincerity was tempted to tell him his story but the secrets he had so securely locked away for so long had become too deeply buried to be entrusted to anyone. He told him only that there was a conspiracy against him and that those involved were dangerous people who would stop at nothing to get the information they wanted from him. Malik smiled in response, he found Gabriel interesting and mysterious and a welcome relief from the boredom of a long quiet night on the ward.

Gabriel was told that he would have to remain in the hospital for a few days for his physical and mental health to be observed and assessed. He found most of the doctors were competent and friendly, assuring him that his wrist was fractured but healing well and trying to relieve his anxieties telling him that overall his physical health was good considering his age. Gabriel looked forward to the evenings when the shifts changed and Malik reported for duty. Gabriel questioned why he had warmed so quickly to Malik, after all it had been a long time since he'd allowed himself to trust anyone. He slept through most of the daylight hours preferring to spend his waking hours talking to Malik.

When Malik's country had been thrown into political turmoil, he had been one of the many educated young people who had supported the opposition to Mubarak and when the Muslim Brotherhood took power he knew he would suffer for his political beliefs. He decided to join his elder brother, a qualified paediatrician working in London and soon found a placement as a trainee junior doctor at the same hospital. Malik had a swarthy complexion, broad infectious smile and kind eyes and enjoyed listening to Gabriel reminisce about his adventures and travels.

Gabriel revealed he had spent time in Egypt and Malik was impressed by his apparent insight into the complex social and political problems that were currently afflicting his country and the Middle East region.

Having been awake throughout the night Gabriel was disoriented and suspicious when he was awakened early one morning, placed in a wheelchair and transported across the hospital to see a specialist doctor. Gabriel took an instinct dislike to Dr Chang, he was unlike any of the other doctors he had seen at this hospital, a place where until this moment he had felt safe. Dr. Chang was distant, cold and spoke abruptly, deliberately avoiding eye contact, focussing instead on a computer screen. Almost as soon as Gabriel entered the room the doctor proceeded without any explanation to fire questions at him, they came quickly one after the other. Gabriel realised the doctor was simply reading the questions off the computer and ticking boxes alongside in response to his answers. He thought the questions were inane, why should he be asked if he could repeat the months of the year backwards from December? Why should he have to demonstrate his understanding of metric measurement when he was of an age that had always worked with the imperial system? Why should he know the capital city of a country that hadn't existed when he was a boy? When Gabriel raised this issue with the doctor he dismissed his argument as irrelevant and continued reading out the prescribed questions.

Unexpectedly the door swung open and, uninvited, two men strode purposefully into the room, the doctor looked up from the screen but did not seem surprised at their abrupt entry. Gabriel was grateful that the question and answer ritual had been interrupted. Looking at the two men he soon realised that they were not doctors. They were both tall and heavily built one was wearing tinted glasses and had dark hair with traces of grey the other was holding a black briefcase. Gabriel had an intense feeling of "déjà vu" a strong recollection that he had seen them both before. When

Dr. Chang stood up and accompanied them to a far corner of the room and a muffled conversation ensued, Gabriel remembered where he had seen these men before. It was in the strange hospital with barred windows where his nightmare had begun. His heart was pounding all his old fears fast returning, his inclination was to run but as he raised himself up from the chair his legs buckled beneath him, he stumbled and fell. He felt a pair of strong hands beneath his armpits firmly raising him up; he turned to look directly into the sinister face of the man wearing the dark tinted lenses. Gabriel was frightened, he looked around for the doctor but he had left, realising he was alone with these men he was gripped by fear, in a shaky trembling voice he screamed, "Who are you, what is it that you want from me?" Their response was to laugh mockingly at him, the tallest of the pair informing him in a patronising manner that they only wanted to protect him and that soon he would be returned to his minder at the safe house.

On hearing this Gabriel was panic stricken, over the past few days he had come to believe that he had finally escaped from Akemi and imprisonment. He started screaming and shouting, repeating over and over, "No, no, I won't go back to that place and that woman." Forcefully he was made to sit down and felt hands firmly pressing down on his shoulders ensuring that he could not raise his frail frame from the chair. When a doctor appeared, Gabriel cried, "Help me, please help me," the stone faced doctor ignoring his plea, produced a needle and syringe, rolled up Gabriel's shirt sleeve and injected him.

* * *

Malik arrived to start his evening shift joining his colleagues for the routine debriefing when the matron ran through the state of each patient on the ward before handing over their care to the night staff. Malik listened carefully, the briefing that night was short and to the point. He heard that most patients' conditions were unchanged, that one new patient had been admitted and that Mr Gabriel Jones had been discharged. This was something that Malik was not expecting to hear and although very aware he was not supposed to interrupt the matron, he could not resist uttering, "But he was so very frail and vulnerable." Matron gave him a look of disapproval and replied sharply, "Malik, he was assessed today by a specialist and it was decided that he was fit enough to be discharged."

It had been a long and busy day and matron was anxious to complete the handover and head home. As she started to walk away, Malik followed her, anxious to find out more about what had happened to Gabriel during the day. "How could he be discharged when there were serious safeguarding issues and his so called carer was under investigation?" Malik demanded. Matron dismissed him saying, "It was all sorted out before he was discharged." Malik persisted to ask questions, matron turned towards him and said firmly, "Malik it is not your place to question these decisions, I suggest you go back to your ward." Malik knew that he had been fortunate to come to England and to have a job that he loved, so reluctantly but dutifully returned to his ward.

Malik completed his rounds on the ward and when the lights dimmed and his patients were peacefully resting, he sat at his work station and looked across to the empty bed. As the night wore on he became increasingly concerned about Gabriel, he knew that he was weak and frail and that he genuinely believed the woman who was supposed to be his carer was abusing him. He decided to look for Gabriel's medical records on the computer which he knew should contain the reasons for his discharge and notes on any follow up care he might need. On entering the name Gabriel Jones, a message saying restricted access appeared. Malik thought this strange, it was possible for a patient to make such a request but he thought it unlikely that Gabriel would do this.

Later that evening a senior doctor who had also treated Gabriel was passing through and Malik spoke to him about his concerns. The colleague was equally surprised that Gabriel had been discharged. Looking quickly around the ward and seeing that all was quiet he sat alongside Malik at the work station and said that he had the authority to bypass the restricted access message. When Gabriel's records ultimately appeared on the screen, they were surprised by the brevity of information displayed. They showed simply a record of the date of admission, the reasons for the admission and a summary of the discharge notes which included a consultant psychiatrist report dated that day. The report stated, "The patient has an incurable condition and has made a very limited response to the medications that can help the condition. He has chronic psychotic symptoms and these often lead to rages towards his partner who he thinks is stealing from him. He scores poorly on standard tests of cognitive function which demonstrates his cognitive abilities have declined markedly. There are no concerns over his care; he is very well supported by his partner."

Malik looked up and shaking his head said to the doctor beside him, "I don't believe this, I have spent many hours talking to Gabriel, he's a very intelligent man and capable of rational thoughts, he talked to me about growing up in Wales, about his travels around the world." The senior doctor explained that this was not untypical of someone with the condition described in the report. With a sympathetic look he advised him not to get too close to his patients and emphasised the need to accept the decisions made by the experts. Malik continued to question the report saying it was wrong to call the woman looking after him his partner. The doctor rose to leave and placing his hand comfortingly on Malik's shoulder said, "Let it go, Malik."

But Malik couldn't let it go; his intuition was telling him that there was something wrong. From the conversations he'd had with Gabriel, Malik was convinced that he had been logically trying to work out a plan to escape from a bad situation. Malik wondered what had happened to the notebook in which he'd helped Gabriel to compile a list of names. Malik had an uncanny insight into the way Gabriel's mind worked, perhaps he thought, Gabriel might have left it somewhere on the ward in the hope that he'd find it. He looked across again at bed six where Gabriel had spent the last few days, it had been disinfected and made up with clean bedding in readiness for the next admission and Malik presumed that anything left in the adjacent locker would have been cleared away.

The night passed slowly and Malik was grateful when morning came and he could busy himself with his routine tasks on the ward. At eight o'clock he assembled to greet the day staff and hand over his patients to their care, among them was Lola a young Philippine nurse who had been responsible for Gabriel's care during the day time. As Malik was about to leave, Lola followed him saying that she had something for him. She opened her handbag and gave him Gabriel's notebook, she told him that he'd given it to her before he'd been taken away to see a psychiatrist. She said Gabriel had told her that he would not be coming back and that he was frightened, he'd made her promise that she would give the notebook to Malik who would know what to do with it.

With the notebook safely in his pocket Malik walked to the nearby cafe where every morning after his night shift ended he relaxed with a cup of coffee. Sitting quietly alone sipping his coffee he opened the notebook and stared at the lists of names and the numbers and symbols alongside them. Somehow he had known that Gabriel would leave the notebook for him. It was heart warming to know that he'd managed to gain the trust of a kind, gentle man at a time when he was so vulnerable and so alone. Malik spent a long time staring at the names in the book and the numbers and symbols Gabriel had asked him to assign to each of them. There were no addresses and no contact numbers. He was at a loss as to know what to do, what did it all mean? It was a code that he had no way of deciphering. Why had Gabriel explicitly told Lola that he'd know what to do with it?

14

An unwelcome return to prison

Sat by the window in Akemi's flat Gabriel stared sadly at the world outside, it was winter, the leaves had fallen off the trees, people hurried by wrapped in their warm coats and small white flakes of snow glistened as they landed on the grass. It was a tantalising glimpse of everyday life being acted out in the streets below, dark depressing clouds weighed heavily upon him as he reluctantly began to accept that it was a world in which he no longer had any part to play. Being heavily sedated when he was transported from the hospital he'd no memory of the journey and no way of knowing how long he had been back in the flat. It could have been days or even weeks, for Gabriel all days were the same, each one slowly and meaninglessly drifting monotonously into the next.

Since his return he'd found Akemi to be unusually attentive constantly checking that he was all right and telling him to be careful whenever he moved from one room to another. He suspected that someone, most likely someone she presumed had authority, had told her to try and show more kindness towards him. One day, sitting quietly wrapped in his own private world, he happened to look around the room noticing that it was clean, tidy and organised. Then suddenly it was transformed into a chaotic scene littered with papers and books and photographs. The vision triggered a vague niggling memory of waking up one morning and seeing the room in such disarray and he remembered the burglary. He mentioned this to Akemi but she'd immediately denied that it had ever happened and told him it was just another figment of his overactive imagination. As time went on he began to think that perhaps a burglary that he thought he'd remembered and all the events that followed, the time he had spent in the hospital, the kind Egyptian doctor whom he had innately trusted had after all been one of his many dreams.

That morning the phone had rung many times, this at first he did not think was unusual because Akemi often had long phone conversations. He assumed they were conversations with her friends, because she spoke in a friendly, relaxed way and always in her native Japanese. But there was something unusual about her response to the calls that morning, the conversations were short and abrupt and she spoke in English. He listened but found it difficult to understand what she was saying and she seemed keen to end every call quickly as if she was reluctant to talk to whoever was on the other end of the phone. As the day went on the succession of calls continued and each time the phone rang Akemi became visibly more and more agitated. After one of the calls she became very angry with Gabriel, accusing him of having told lies about her and inviting all these annoying calls from strange people who were pretending to be his friends. Gabriel desperately wanted to ask her who had called, hoping that she might give him a name that he recognised, someone who was a real friend, but he was frightened of her when she got this angry and she really was angry, shouting that he had no friends and that she was the only one who was caring for him. Gabriel could feel his hands beginning to tremble so he said nothing and sat quietly looking out of the window.

It wasn't long before he heard the door slam and the key turn in the lock, Akemi had gone out, this was usually what happened after an outburst and when she returned she would be calmer and act as if the outburst had never happened. Gabriel was glad to be left in peace and hoped the phone would ring again and that he'd have enough strength in his trembling hands to be able to pick it up and answer. Time ticked by, the phone never rang and a heavy, eerie silence hung over the room.

As time passed Gabriel became calmer, his hands stopped shaking and he managed to raise himself up from the chair by the window and slowly, falteringly, began to shuffle around the small flat. He looked in anticipation towards the telephone and realised with disbelief that the receiver had been removed. There could only be one explanation, Akemi must have had taken it with her so that he could not answer if anyone tried to call. Now he firmly believed that somebody was trying to contact him and was deliberately being prevented from doing so. He was furious and could feel the familiar rising waves of anxiety being fed by his frustration and anger.

Distracted by the sound of a choir singing somewhere outside he turned to the window. He was surprised to see below a small group of people waving tambourines, singing and wearing the distinctive red and black uniforms of the Salvation Army. Daylight was fading and Gabriel saw that some of the trees were decorated with twinkling lights and as he listened to the choir chanting the soothing lilting tune of "Silent night" he realised that it was Christmas. He opened the window and shouted down to the singers below, "Merry Christmas, Merry Christmas." When they shouted back, "A Merry Christmas to you too, Sir", he was overcome with emotion, his tears flowed and in desperation he shouted down to them, "Help, help, please, please help me."

The choir stopped singing and anxious faces stared up at the window, Gabriel shouted again, "Help, help." A woman had stopped in front of the assembled group and was waving her arms and saying something to them, when she turned to point up at him standing by the open window he could see that it was Akemi.

Slowly the choir started to walk away, a young boy remained standing staring at the window where Gabriel was frantically waving, he cupped his hands together and shouted "Don't worry, everything will be OK, Merry Christmas to you," then he ran to catch up with the rest of the singers who by now had moved on and were almost out of sight.

Moments later Gabriel heard the key in the lock and Akemi entered, her face glowing red from the cold winter wind. As well as the familiar bags of shopping that she always brought back from her daily excursions into the outside world, Gabriel noticed that she was carrying a pile of letters. Gabriel thought it unusual that there were so many of them and that there were many different coloured envelopes, some were red some silver, some gold. She handed over the pile to Gabriel saying curtly, "These for you." Gabriel held on, the stack for a little while although his hands were trembling. Of course, he thought, the carol singers, the lights on the trees outside and the snow, of course it must be Christmas and these are Christmas cards. He tried but his shaky hands meant it was too difficult to open them. So one by one he sifted through them, trying to recognise the writing and looking at the post marks and postage stamps for clues as to the senders. There were so many, he counted over fifty envelopes and the stamps revealed that they had come from all corners of the world, from Melbourne in Australia, Peru in South America as well as from Malaysia, Taiwan and Japan. He suspected that some were from his many students he had taught over the years and others from the many friends he had encountered on his travels. Akemi had unpacked the shopping and made a pot of tea which she brought to the table and sat down next to Gabriel. Her earlier dark mood had passed and she asked Gabriel if he would like her to open the envelopes. One by one she presented him with cards displaying winter scenes and Christmas festive symbols, some simply had a signature but many had personal messages thanking him for his help and support over the years and for his inspiration that had led to their personal achievements. So many cards from so many young people who were now pursuing professional careers as architects, teachers, lawyers, doctors in many different parts of the world. He was overcome with emotion simply knowing that he was remembered by people who thought he was important to them, it made him feel that after all his life had had some meaning and that it had not always been so dark and so bleak as it was now.

* * *

Malik had sat for a long while that morning in the cafe staring at Gabriel's notebook and trying to figure out what it all meant and how he could help. Gabriel had told him that the list he had asked him to compile for him recorded the names of all the people he thought were his trusted friends and with whom he had entrusted some of his secrets. Now he suspected that one or more of them may have betrayed these confidences. The symbol he had instructed him to place alongside each name, he'd explained, signified the likelihood of that person's betrayal of him. Malik tried to understand the meaning of Gabriel's code – did the tick in a circle or the cross in the square mean that person was trustworthy or not – and finally decided that it was a hopeless task.

Eventually almost out of desperation and with little hope of success he accessed his social media account and typed in all the names on Gabriel's list. He added a short message asking if any of the people on the list were friends or acquaintances of Gabriel Jones and if they were would they please contact him. He knew it was a shot in the dark but nevertheless Malik bought another coffee and sat patiently and expectantly waiting for a reply to his message but no one replied that morning.

It was the next day after another long night shift when Malik returned to the cafe and opened his laptop to find a reply. It read, "Hi Malik, I am an old friend of Gabriel Jones, but have not had any contact with him for a few years. I heard he had some sort of breakdown and didn't want any contact with anyone. I think the situation with his carer is a bit odd and I'm reluctant to get involved until I know more about what has happened to him. I see from your blog that you live and work in London and you are obviously concerned about Gabriel perhaps we could meet to talk about him." Sasha. Malik, excited that something had come of his initiative, replied immediately.

A few days later, Malik and Sasha met in an Italian coffee bar on the Portobello Road, a venue suggested by Sasha as it was close to where she lived. Malik had no idea of what to expect and was pleasantly surprised by the well spoken, smartly dressed lady who shook his hand warmly and introduced herself as Sasha. She had long dark hair with subtle hints of grey neatly draped into a pleat at the back and held with an ornate clasp. Malik found it difficult to guess her age, she was obviously of mature years but considerably younger than Gabriel, he thought. When Malik in the course of introducing himself mentioned his Egyptian nationality, her face lit up with genuine delight, it was as if she'd discovered a long lost relative. It seemed that she too had grown up in Cairo where her father had been a British Ambassador who'd married an Egyptian lady, Sasha's mother. After chatting for a while about their mutual interest in a country for which they both held a deep affection Sasha proceeded to tell Malik everything she knew about Gabriel.

They had first met about twenty years ago when Sasha and some friends happened to wander into a central London bar. The bar was popular with young professionals of all different nationalities and typical of the cosmopolitan easy going London scene of the day. She described the clear memory she still had of that first meeting, she remembered Gabriel standing at the bar holding a pint of beer and surrounded by a group of people, clearly the centre of attention and enjoying every minute of it. Sasha and her friends found themselves drawn easily into the group, with Gabriel as usual, taking the initiative of asking their names and introducing everyone. Sasha seemed keen to point out to Malik that she'd never been tempted into a romantic liaison with Gabriel. After a momentary infatuation with him when they first met she soon realised he had a lovable but flirtatious personality and decided that they would always be just very good friends.

Gabriel had many friends and acquaintances and was instrumental in introducing them to each other. These introductions had frequently resulted in long term liaisons and relationships. Gabriel's mate Alec married Yumiko after Gabriel introduced them to each other. Pete and Ollie met as a result of a meeting arranged by Gabriel who recognised they were alike and thought they would be happy spending time together. Malik recognised some of the names as being those on Gabriel's list.

Malik felt at ease with Sasha and to him it was clear that she genuinely had a deep affection for Gabriel and that their long term friendship was important to her. He decided to show her Gabriel's list of names and explain the concern Gabriel had expressed to him that one or more of the people named had betrayed him in some way. Sasha said she recognised many of the names as mutual friends, although some of them had since moved away from London she had continued to keep in close touch with them. She looked puzzled and was finding it difficult to believe that Gabriel had suspicious thoughts about any of the people on the list, they were all loyal trustworthy people and all were very fond of Gabriel. Malik asked her what she thought the symbols next to each of the names meant. Smiling she admitted that she knew that the symbols would have some significance to Gabriel but she had no way of knowing what the significance of them might be.

Still smiling Sasha explained that this was typical of the Gabriel they all loved and knew. He loved puzzles and had told her that when he was young he'd applied to GCHQ but had been rejected because of his tenuous connection with the Communist party. It seemed as a teenager he'd joined the party in order to get cheap pints at the Swansea Labour Club.

Sasha told Malik that there had been twelve of them who had met regularly and they jokingly referred to themselves as the dirty dozen. Gabriel had been instrumental in getting them to participate in what became affectionately known as "Gabriel's mystery tours", Gabriel would set them a challenge to decipher a series of cryptic clues, each clue leading them to a London pub or bar with the final clue leading to a specific City bar that he'd chosen for their venue that evening. The winning team were treated to beers all round. Sasha said she often looked back on these happy fun loving times.

Sasha then admitted to Malik that neither she nor any of their friends as far as she knew had been in contact with Gabriel for a few years because he had cut all ties with his friends when he met Kimiko, a pretty vivacious Japanese girl who must have been at least about thirty years younger than him. He was totally intoxicated with Kimiko and refused to listen to his friends who tried to tell him that he was making a fool of himself and that he would live to regret his decision to give up everything for her. They could all see that it was a relationship that was highly unlikely to have any future.

Sasha said that she did not know the whole story of what had happened after he left for Japan, it was snippets of information that she had gleaned from friends. She'd heard Gabriel resigned from his post at the university and travelled to Japan with Kimiko where they planned to marry. A few weeks before the ceremony was due to take place, Kimiko decided that the age difference was too great and broke off the engagement. It seems she had been having a relationship with a young architect that Gabriel had employed to design a house for them. Gabriel was devastated he had given up everything for this girl and he'd honestly believed that he would spend the rest of his life in Japan with her.

He returned to England and went straight from the airport to Akemi's flat in Ealing, where as far as Sasha knew he had stayed ever since. Sasha said that Gabriel had known Akemi for a very long time but she had only met her once or twice, she was rarely seen out socially with Gabriel and she had never thought of them as a couple.

Gabriel, she explained, had liaisons with many women, spending a few weeks with one and then a few weeks with another until he, or they, got bored or tired of the superficial relationship. Akemi was different, in spite of his indiscretions, of which she was fully aware, whenever Gabriel turned up at her flat, she would feed him, look after him and care for him until the next pretty face took his fancy. Gabriel was charming and great company and because of these likeable qualities it seemed he was able to use people and Akemi allowed herself to be used by him.

Sasha went on to explain that a few of their friends tried to contact him when they heard what had happened to him in Japan but that Akemi had told them that he was suffering from a nervous breakdown and didn't want to talk to any of them. Laughingly she said they referred to Akemi as the gatekeeper as she always made some excuse as to why they could not visit Gabriel or talk to him on the phone. After a while Sasha said they had all given up trying to contact Gabriel having decided that for whatever reason he didn't want to know them anymore. Some of them had speculated that he was embarrassed and didn't want to face his old friends who had clearly warned him about his inane decision to give up everything for a young girl less than half his years.

Malik listened with interest as Sasha talked openly and with affection about Gabriel. He'd known Gabriel for only a few days when he'd nursed him at the hospital but nevertheless recognised the colourful picture of him that she'd painted and realised that he too, like many others before him had been affected by the magnetism of Gabriel's personality.

He told Sasha how Gabriel had entertained him with tales of his travels during the long quiet nights at the hospital. How they had engaged in discussions about the reasons for the emergence of the Arab Spring and its consequences for the rest of the world. How he'd formed the impression that Gabriel was a well educated, perceptive and rational person but physically weak and fragile. He told Sasha about Gabriel's fears that there was a conspiracy against him, a conspiracy in which his carer was involved. Malik recounted how Gabriel had suddenly and unexpectedly been discharged and how Malik had managed to access his discharge notes and had read with disbelief the accompanying consultant psychiatrist's report. A report that said Gabriel had an incurable condition leading to a decline in his cognitive abilities and chronic psychotic symptoms which led him to mistrust his partner believing her to be abusing him. Malik confided to Sasha that the report he had read described the condition of someone who bore no resemblance to the patient he had come to know and that he'd become even more suspicious when he found out that the consultant psychiatrist who signed the report was not listed on the hospital register.

Malik told Sasha how he'd expressed his concerns to the ward manager but had been reprimanded for accessing and reading the report and was told the consultant that signed the report was a visiting consultant and not based at the hospital. He was warned firmly not to get involved any further in the case if he wanted to remain employed at the hospital. This was why, he explained, he'd tried to find some way of contacting the people on the list that Gabriel had entrusted to him. His intuition was telling him that something wasn't right and he was seriously worried about Gabriel's welfare and helpless to do anything about it. Moreover, Malik believed that Gabriel's fear of the woman who was caring for him was very real and that he'd been logically trying to work out a plan to escape from her, a plan he'd cryptically described as his itinerary.

Malik looked sadly at Sasha who seemed close to tears, they sat in silence together for a short while as if processing and digesting the information they'd shared with each other. When finally Sasha gave a deep sigh, Malik looked up from the empty coffee cup he'd been staring into and their eyes met, both instinctively knew they had complete trust in each other and were clearly united in their common concern for Gabriel's welfare.

He handed Gabriel's list to Sasha saying, "I know that this was important to Gabriel and I hope you and his friends can rally round and help him because I am sure that he for whatever reason has reached a point in his life when he needs friends." Sasha took the piece of paper folding it slowly and carefully placing it in her purse, then to Malik's surprise she put her arms around him and said simply, "Thank you."

15

Friends reunited

When Sasha returned home after her meeting with Malik she studied Gabriel's list, Albert, Max, Jake, Pete and Ollie, Alec and Yumiko, Simon and Maria, were all names she recognised as members of the old gang. An amicable group of professional people with whom she and Gabriel had shared so many carefree evenings in trendy London bars, but it was all a long time ago and she had had little contact with them for many years. She found their addresses and phone numbers in her address book but wondered if they were still relevant after all this time. She nevertheless set about trying to get back in touch with them all; her first call to Albert was greeted with a recorded message informing her that the number had not been recognised. Undeterred she dialled the number for Jake who to her surprise answered immediately. On hearing about Gabriel's situation he was equally as concerned as she was about him and assured her that he knew how to contact Alec as well as the other old friends whose names appeared on Gabriel's list. They chatted for a while catching up on the years gone by since they had last spoken. Jake came up with the idea of organising a reunion of the old gang and of course inviting Gabriel because as they both agreed it would not be the same without him.

As a consequence of Jake and Sasha's efforts over the next few weeks there was a steady stream of visitors calling at the flat. Akemi's gatekeeping tactics overcome by the insistence of the callers who proved determined to see Gabriel in spite of her excuses that he was not well enough to see anyone. Pete and his now long time partner Ollie were the first of Gabriel's old friends to call. They recognised Gabriel instantly in spite of the effects of his recent experiences which had taken a toll on the youthful appearance he had always managed to retain well into his mature years. They both embraced him fondly; Gabriel was taken aback and pulled away eying them with suspicion. The couple handled the situation sensitively by sitting close to Gabriel and showing him a photograph album they had brought with them. It contained photographs of the "gang" of which they had all been a part, photographs taken outside the bars where they had gathered on Monday evenings. Almost immediately Gabriel was engaged, looking intently at the scenes and to everyone's surprise excitedly announced that he knew the name of the pub where the crowd were sitting in a small garden. "This one's The Dog and Duck it's in Soho's Bateman Street," and then pointing to another of the snaps he announced, "and this one's The Cross Keys Covent Garden, I recognise the distinctive foliage around its façade." Gabriel slowly turned the pages of the album, pointing out and naming the various people in the snaps. Finally saying, "Yes, yes I remember it all as if it was yesterday," and with tears in his eyes he put his arms around the pair and said, "Thank you for coming here, thank you both so much."

They continued chatting about their mutually fond memories of those days until Akemi disappeared into the kitchen and Gabriel took the opportunity to try and explain his predicament and to ask for their help. She soon returned carrying a pot of tea, biscuits and tea cups. The conversation turned once again to their memories of the past and the many exploits they'd shared. When it was time for them to go, Gabriel once again embraced them both whispering as he did, "Please believe me, please, please believe me." Gabriel could not be sure but from the stern look on Akemi's face he suspected that she had overheard his plea.

Akemi left with them, she firmly closed the door to the flat and accompanied the pair down the flights of stairs leading to the main entrance to the apartment block. Gabriel could not hear what she was saying she began to explain to Pete and Ollie that although to them Gabriel might appear to be all right, she could assure them in no uncertain terms that he really wasn't. She told them he was severely depressed and had been clinically diagnosed with paranoia which is why he might have told them that he was being kept prisoner and that she was trying to murder him overdosing him with medication. As they said their goodbyes she implored them to believe her and not to take anything Gabriel might have told them seriously.

A few days later Gabriel's old friend Jake came knocking on the flat door. He was concerned following a long thoughtful telephone conversation with Pete and Ollie who had told him everything that had happened during their visit just a few days earlier. They had explained that Gabriel had aged considerably and was far from the exuberant fun loving personality that they had known but that he'd quickly remembered all the good times they had spent together and talked coherently and fondly about them. Gabriel, they had told him, appeared to be well cared for physically by Akemi but nevertheless there was clearly a tangible tension between them. They had voiced their very real concerns about the situation, Gabriel seemed genuinely afraid and they honestly didn't know whether to believe Gabriel's accusations or Akemi's explanations.

Jake's plan had been to take Gabriel out of the flat for a short walk to a local coffee shop where he'd hoped he would be able to talk freely with Gabriel and get to the truth of what was really happening to him. However this plan was instantly thwarted, when on his arrival Akemi explained that Gabriel was suffering from a slight cold and that she did not think it was a good idea for him to go out on such a cold day as it could lead to a chest infection to which she said he was prone. So Jake, just as Pete and Ollie had done, sat with Gabriel talking about the old days and the events that had taken place since they had last met. When Jake mentioned Kimiko, Gabriel became visibly upset telling Jake through his tears that she had died and he didn't want to talk about it. Worried at Gabriel's reaction to his mention of Kimiko, Jake glanced across at Akemi who was sat close by pretending to read a book, she shook her head and raised her finger to her lips which Jake took as a warning to drop the subject.

Jake thought this to be an opportune moment to suggest a get together of the "gang" and asked Gabriel if he'd like him to arrange a reunion in one of their old haunts. He went on to add that Gabriel would hardly recognise their old watering holes because they were no longer the friendly, cosy coal fired and smoke filled enclaves they had known. Many of them had been taken over by the large breweries and become eating houses with small bars and just a few bar stool seats which were more often than not occupied by local hardened drinkers. Jake asked Gabriel if he remembered the "The Nag's Head," Gabriel replied, "Course I do, it's down a little mews somewhere off Covent Garden."

"That's right," said Jake adding that it hadn't changed and that it was still a traditional old pub cluttered with portraits, bric-a-brac, pewter mugs, and curiosities with ale on tap and that best of all he'd heard that it was one of the few pubs in London that had dared to impose a mobile phone ban.

Gabriel was clearly delighted at Jake's suggestion of a reunion but Akemi did not seem too pleased about the idea. She told Jake that he didn't understand the nature of Gabriel's condition and that anyway Gabriel was far too frail to travel into central London on his own. Witnessing Gabriel's excited reaction to the idea of meeting up with his old friends, Jake was determined not to allow Akemi to jeopardise the plans and offered to personally collect him from the flat and accompany him in a taxi to the venue. Finally Akemi reluctantly agreed.

Jake rose to leave promising to be in touch soon with the details as to when he'd be coming to pick him up for the reunion evening. Gabriel embraced him warmly and just as he had done with Pete and Ollie attempted to secretly whisper a plea for help in his ear. Accompanying Jake down the stairs Akemi talked incessantly about Gabriel's terrible moods, his paranoia, his dementia, his violence towards her, his fear that there was a conspiracy against him. Jake was thankful when they reached the front door where he hurriedly said goodbye to her. Once out in the daylight his mind was in a whirl, the personality that Akemi had just so graphically described to him bore no resemblance to the person that he had known for so many years. He knew that Gabriel himself would freely admit to being narcissistic and self indulgent but he had never shown any signs of being of unkind. Jake was left with the same sense of confusion that Pete and Ollie had experienced after their visit. Jake was confused and really did not know what to think or who to believe.

* * *

As the days went by Gabriel grew anxious about meeting up with his old friends, worried about what they would think of the person he had become whilst at the same time desperately wanting to see them. At times he thought that perhaps Jake's promise to organise a reunion was just another one of his many drug induced dreams. He'd asked Akemi if it was true and she'd confirmed that yes, Jake had made all the arrangements for him to have an evening out with his old friends. The renewed excited anticipation he felt on hearing this was soon dampened when she quickly added, "But if you do not behave yourself, I will not let you go," Gabriel turned away from her, he resented the way she spoke to him as if he was a naughty child.

It was early on the morning of the day that the reunion was due to take place and Akemi had insisted that he wake up and get dressed because a taxi was booked. When Gabriel asked where they were going, she told him he had a pre-arranged hospital appointment and that if he didn't behave himself and get ready quickly she'd telephone Jake and say he was too ill to go out that evening.

Gabriel was frightened at the thought of going to the hospital and upset that Akemi was threatening to stop him going to the reunion. He started to feel anger rise within him and did something that he had never ever done before, he hit out at her and instantly regretted what he'd done. Akemi reeled back in shock; a bruise started to appear around her eye, she picked up a stick and pushed him towards the bedroom. Brandishing the stick she shrieked, "You get dressed now, now!" Her tone was menacing and Gabriel, too frightened and too frail to argue and with trembling hands managed to put on a pair of trousers and a jumper.

When he returned to the living room she was waiting at the door still holding the walking stick she held out his coat, picked up a small brown suitcase and said sternly, "We go now." He could not help but notice the swelling and bruising around her eye, knowing he was responsible for her injury, he really wanted to say he was sorry but felt it was unlikely that she'd accept his apology and it might even lead to another argument. He decided to simply comply and go along quietly with whatever it was she had planned for him that morning.

Sitting in the taxi he wondered why she had brought the suitcase with her and where they were going but knew better than to question her. It soon became clear that they were heading west across the city, passing well known landmarks. He recognised it to be the same route they'd taken in a taxi just a few weeks ago.

Leaving the North Circular onto the Marylebone Flyover, left over Gloucester Road Bridge towards the Octagon Building of University College London, Gabriel knew they were heading to the medical experimental centre. After meandering through the backstreets the taxi finally arrived at a large square and stopped outside a long low prefabricated building.

Once inside they were met by a young woman Gabriel recognised, the tag she wore identifying her as Eleanor Kozlowski, research assistant. Akemi handed her the small suitcase she was carrying, Eleanor, said "Thank you", as if she had been expecting it. Eleanor smiled at Gabriel and explained she was going to conduct some tests. "Why?" asked Gabriel. Trying to reassure him but in a manner Gabriel found disturbingly patronising, she replied, "There's nothing to worry about we just need to see the effects of the medication you are taking, please follow me."

Eleanor led him into a small room and presented him with a piece of paper on which was drawn a large empty circle. He was asked to write the numbers of a clock face in the correct sequence and draw in the hands to represent twenty five minutes to eight. "Well done," said Eleanor when he accurately completed the task. Another test where he was asked to recognise shapes drawn within shapes proved equally as simple to Gabriel and he completed it in seconds, this again evoking the obligatory positive reinforcement from Eleanor, "Well done Gabriel!"

Gabriel was led into another room, the same dark tiny room he remembered from his last visit. He was intrigued to see Akemi's brown suitcase had been opened revealing the distinctive old yellow Kodak boxes containing his photographic slides. A young man was in the process of transferring the images from the slides onto a computer. Gabriel was speechless unable to believe what he was seeing. The slides were precious to Gabriel; they provided a chronological record of his travels over his lifetime. Using an old fashioned projector they had been the visual illustrations that brilliantly complemented his university lectures. "Why do you have these?" he asked the young man at the computer who didn't reply instead looked up at Eleanor inviting her to respond to Gabriel's question.

In her usual condescending manner she answered, "There's nothing to worry about, we often ask our patients or their partners to bring some old photographs with them, and we use them to test one's long term memory." Akemi had told her that Gabriel didn't have any old photographs but that he had lots of old slides. Eleanor had explained they could easily transfer them onto a computer and use them for the test. Gabriel's reactions were mixed, for a long time he'd wanted to find a way of transferring his invaluable slides onto a computer. He could see this was an opportunity for his old slides to be reborn into the modern technological world and live on as an everlasting tribute to his life. But he was also angry with Akemi for not telling him about Eleanor's request and for even touching his precious slides without his permission.

Eleanor proceeded to connect the wires attached to a small helmet like contraption to a machine before placing the helmet on Gabriel's head telling him to relax whilst adjusting it around his ears. Then the light was switched off, the screen lit up and a slide show began. The first images to appear on the screen showed Gabriel with groups of young students in various locations throughout Europe. Scenes of Brussels, Gabriel and students having a meal at the Atomism restaurant, outside the United Nations Building, relaxing on a canal boat in Bruges. Scenes of Paris, typical Parisian cafes with Gabriel and students holding up empty wine bottles. Then a lively scene of street entertainers surrounding Gabriel in the Piazza Navona in Rome. The sequence of slides continued, vibrant colourful scenes taken in the cities of Europe, Gabriel correctly identifying each location as Eleanor had requested and in addition giving the names of the students in each of the scenes as a way of emphasising the accuracy of his memory. Admittedly, some he had forgotten but nevertheless instantly invented names rather than admit to any flaw in his memory recall. Surprisingly Gabriel had started to relax and to enjoy watching the colourful, vibrant reflections of his past life, when suddenly the screen went black and the words "End of slide show" appeared.

Almost immediately another show was being played out on the screen. These images showed Gabriel looking considerably younger than in the previous show. Standing with a rucksack draped across his shoulder outside a grand hotel the name clearly visible in the image as the Hotel Yugoslavia. Before she had time to ask the memory question Gabriel told Eleanor that the photo was taken in Yugoslavia in the mid '70s, and explained that he'd photographed the hotel because it was famous at the time for its modern architectural design and was the biggest hotel in the Socialist Federal Republic of Yugoslavia. Next, Gabriel sitting on the steps outside a very grand imposing building bearing the name Glavni Kolodvor. Gabriel was quick to point out that it was Zagreb train station and described it as a magnificent building a throwback to the days when it was on the route of the Orient Express. Many scenes of Gabriel in various cafes and bars that lined the hilly, narrow streets of Zagreb followed and in all of them he was accompanied by the same pretty young girl. Gabriel instantly recognised Jelena, the young idealistic student he'd met soon after arriving in Yugoslavia. Seeing her lovely smile on the large screen he distinctly recalled his attraction to her all those years ago.

Whilst continuing to correctly identify the various museums and tourist sites recorded on his visit to the old Yugoslavia Gabriel was relishing the intoxicating memories of his brief amorous relationship with Jelena. A slide appeared which quickly propelled him back into reality when he recognised the group of men outside a cafe in Zagreb. He and Jelena had been enjoying a drink in a cafe opposite and she'd pointed to the group identifying them as the Serbian State Security Service, SDB. She suspected that they were being watched by them, Gabriel decided to take photographs of them it would be an interesting story to tell when he returned home.

In the 1970s the SDB was focused on eliminating troublesome dissidents and Jelena because of her outspoken political beliefs and her participation in protests against the government was regarded as a dissident. Gabriel recognised the group of men because a few days later he had been interrogated by them because of his association with Jelena. Jelena was well known to the SDB as an active member of the movement known as "The Croatian Spring." A movement demanding more rights for Croatia and popular amongst students of those days who actively took part in the public protests and voiced their support for the cause. Jelena was aware of the danger of her involvement, many student activists had been detained and some even sentenced to years in prison.

Gabriel was questioned by the security forces over a few days, questions in which he was forced to disclose the names of Jelena's friends and contacts he'd met and to reveal any information he had about her future plans to travel abroad. Meanwhile his visa allowing him entry to the country expired, it was explained to him that this was a serious offence for which he could face a prison sentence. It took several phone calls to the British Embassy in Belgrade before he was allowed to leave the country.

The memories flooded back but it was a tale he was not ready to confess to Eleanor whom he suspected of being party to the conspiracy against him, so he simply denied all knowledge of anything to do with the ominous slide on the screen before him. More slides of the 1970s and 1980s continued to emerge on the screen. All showing people he recognised to be part of the secret services located in various Eastern bloc countries and Gabriel continued to deny knowing the identity of any of them.

Suddenly Eleanor disconnected Gabriel from the machine that he assumed was being used to measure his reactions to the pictures he'd been shown. She motioned to the young man operating the slide show to close it down saying, "That will be all for today Gabriel." Gabriel detected the frustration in her voice and suspected that he had not told her what she had wanted to hear. Gabriel moved across to the desk where the young man was sitting at the computer and spoke briefly to him asking if it was possible for him to have copies of the images he'd transferred. To Gabriel's surprise the young man didn't hesitate, he quickly copied the files and handed him a memory stick.

Gabriel joined Akemi in the reception area where she was talking to Eleanor, for a second she had her back him and he edged slowly towards the door, once there he took his chance and ran. He ran out into the car park, glancing at the waiting taxi, he saw the driver's head lowered as if asleep, he ran past him and out into the hustle of London, colliding with people as he ran momentarily interrupting their purposeful strides through the warren of streets.

Once away from the medical centre Gabriel felt it was safe to stop for a moment to catch his breath and to get his bearings. He knew the reunion in the Nag's Head was planned for that evening and he was determined to get there. He was familiar with this area of London and knew he was near Tavistock Square where he could rest a while before moving on to the tube station at Russell Square. Then it would be only a short ride on the Piccadilly Line to Covent Garden and then the Nags Head was just round the corner. It was a journey he'd made many times. It was late afternoon, he'd be early but it would be a pleasant surprise if he was there to greet his friends when they arrived.

He reached the gardens of Tavistock Square and rested for a while on a park bench close to the Gandhi statue. He'd walked this way so many times when he had been strong and healthy and was now finding it hard to accept that he had to sit down and rest because of his aching legs and overwhelming tiredness. He cursed the medication that Akemi forced him to take, convinced that this medication was experimental and unnecessary and was the sole reason for his debility. Nevertheless after a few moments' rest, resolute in his determination to see his old friends, he rose and made his way to the nearby tube station.

The station was crowded with people going about their daily lives, on reaching the turnstile Gabriel fumbled in his pockets searching for the wallet containing his Oyster card. The long line of people gathering behind him soon drew the attention of a station assistant. Gabriel close to tears explained that he'd mislaid his Oyster card. With the queue growing ever longer and seeing that Gabriel was frail and clearly upset the assistant made the decision to open the turnstile and let him through on to the platform.

The train screeched to a stop, the waiting crowd surged forward propelling Gabriel towards its open doors. He clambered aboard and reached for the leather strap suspended above him and hung on tight. The overwhelming sense of freedom he was experiencing was exhilarating and his heart was pounding as he travelled the short journey to Covent Garden. Once there he could feel the adrenalin running through his veins and made his way quickly up steep flights of stairs to reach the surface. He felt disorientated as he came out into the daylight and started running along the narrow street that led to the Nag's Head. He was finding it harder and harder to breathe but he knew that he was near his final destination and his determination to achieve his objective of meeting his old friends empowered him to carry on.

Turning a corner into James Street he could see the welcoming sign of the pub a slight breeze funnelling down the street causing it to sway gently. A clock chimed in the distance; Gabriel counted five chimes, it would be a while before his friends arrived. He stopped running, the sun was shining, it was a lovely day and he was free at last, he wanted to savour the luxury of that moment. Then it happened, a pain so sharp that it engulfed his shallow breath, his fragile frame slowly crumbling leaving him lying motionless on the pavement.

Although Gabriel had collapsed only a short distance from the busy Covent Garden tube station, the side street where he lay was unusually quiet and it was some time before a chance passer bye found him and called the emergency services. They responded quickly and realised that he was alive but was unable to see, hear or respond to what was going on around him. They wrapped him in a blanket, lifted him off the floor and carefully carried him to the ambulance. There was a long delay whilst the ambulance driver attempted to find the nearest hospital that was able to accommodate their patient. The combination of a multi vehicle pileup on the motorway and a norovirus infection in two of the city's hospitals had resulted in all new admissions being transported out of the city. Just as the ambulance crew were finally instructed to transport their charge to a hospital in Basildon, Gabriel's friends started arriving at the Nag's Head.

16

The Nag's Head reunion

Jake was looking forward to the reunion, having managed to locate and contact all of the old gang, he decided to hire a function room at the Nag's Head. Many of the old friends still lived in and around London and were delighted at the thought of seeing Gabriel after such a long time. It was going to be quite some party.

That morning Jake phoned Akemi's flat several times keen to tell Gabriel about the great response to that evening's planned reunion and arrange a time to collect him but each time he called he connected to an answering machine, the monosyllabic impersonal voice announcing, "Sorry, we are not at home at the moment, so please leave a message after the tone." Apprehensively Jake made the journey across London from his home in Bayswater to the flat in Ealing. There was no response to the buzzing of the intercom at the apartment block entrance. Jake reached in his pocket for his cigarettes, resigned to having to wait for the chance that a resident of the block might appear and allow him to gain entry into the flats.

Fortunately it wasn't too long before a lady pushing a young child in a pushchair arrived and opened the main door. Once inside Jake offered to help carry the pushchair up the flights of stairs, on reaching the top floor he realised that the lady with the pushchair occupied the flat next door to the one shared by Akemi and Gabriel. Jake knocked on their door but there was no answer. The neighbour told him that she didn't think that anyone was in there.

Jake explained that he was a long time friend of Gabriel and he'd recently got in touch with him again after not seeing or hearing from him for a few years. The lady told him that she had heard the couple arguing that morning, she hadn't thought anything of it because they often argued but unusually that morning when she'd looked out of the window she saw both of them get in a taxi. When Jake enquired if she knew what they had been arguing about, she introduced herself as Rosie, opened her flat door and invited him in. "I try not to get involved but these walls are thin and you cannot help but overhear and I do worry about the things that go on in there," she said, pointing next door. It seemed she wanted to talk to someone who was prepared to listen and Jake was more than ready to listen. The small child was fast asleep in her arms and she laid him gently down on a small settee carefully covering him with a blue baby blanket. She sat down beside the sleeping child and indicated to Jake to take the armchair. Speaking very softly so as not to disturb the sleeping child she told Jake that some of the arguments in the next door apartment were about money, it seemed that Gabriel was convinced that Akemi was stealing from him. Sometimes she was wakened in the early hours of the morning by raised voices coming from next door. These arguments were about medication, Gabriel was refusing to take his medication and Akemi was insisting quite aggressively that he must take it. A couple of times she had heard Gabriel shout out, "No, no, please don't hit me." Rosie told him that she thought she should report it to social services but her husband had emphatically forbidden her to get involved.

One day whilst taking the rubbish to the bins outside at the rear of the block, she had bumped into Akemi who had taken the opportunity to apologise for any disturbance that may have been caused to the family by noise from next door. She told her that she tried to keep the noise down but in her words, Gabriel was "a mad man", hastily adding, that it was not his fault, explaining that he was suffering from dementia. Not long after that conversation she'd happened to see Gabriel walking through the gardens that led to the flats, she'd said, "hello" to him and introduced herself as his neighbour. To her surprise he seemed perfectly normal and friendly, he'd told her he had just been to the barber's shop around the corner and commented on the fact that the gardens were not as well maintained as they used to be. He'd helped her to carry the pushchair up the stairs, "just as you did today," she told him. She laughed and said, "I had the strange bizarre impression that he was flirting with me." Jake grinned and replied, "You're probably right, that would be typical of Gabriel, he never could resist a pretty face." Their conversation was brought to a close by the wriggling of the small bundle that had been snugly sleeping, the movement soon followed by a loud ear splitting cry. "He's just letting me know it's feeding time," announced Mum, calmly picking the crying child up in her arms. Jake could see it was time to go and made his way to the door, thanking her for sharing her concerns with him and promising that he was going to do everything he could to help Gabriel.

Jake made his way to Ealing Broadway tube station just a short walk from Gabriel's flat. It was late afternoon and the station was crowded with commuters. Pushing his way through the throng and negotiating the network of underground subways he finally arrived at the platform and managed to squeeze through the doors of a crowded train heading towards central London. It was too late to cancel the planned reunion for that evening and he was making his way to the Nag's Head to meet the friends when they arrived and break the news that the VIP of the evening was not after all going to be there.

Jake held on tightly to the strap swaying above his head and with the train speeding through the darkness he reflected on his informative chat with Gabriel's neighbour. She had clearly wanted to unburden herself of her concerns about him; but passing these concerns on to Jake had served to further increase his unease about the situation. He looked forward to being with the old gang again and hearing their views on what they could do to help their old friend.

Leaving the train at the Piccadilly underground Jake made his way through the throng of tourists and turned into the narrow back streets, an ambulance sped by, sirens whirring and blue lights flashing forcing him onto the narrow pavement of the boutique lined Floral Street. Jake was blissfully unaware that his old friend Gabriel was laying unconscious inside,

The Nag's Head with its classic 'London pub' atmosphere was just as Jake remembered, explaining that he'd come for Gabriel Jones's reunion he was shown into a small, cosy and welcoming room with a roaring fireplace. To his surprise some friends were already there, Sasha who had arrived particularly early, Albert who'd travelled to London especially for the occasion and Simon and Maria who'd kindly agreed for him to stay overnight in their North London home. As the ambulance left James Street heading out to Essex, Albert, Sasha, Simon and Maria had been watching through the window of the Nag's Head. The publican had told them that an elderly man had collapsed in the street earlier that afternoon; one of the paramedics had come into the pub to ask if they knew the man. It seemed he had no identification on him but the publican had been unable to help them because he certainly wasn't one of his regulars and he couldn't recall ever having seen him before.

Jake was delighted to see them all again and greeted them warmly. As he was about to deliver the disappointing news that Gabriel would not be joining them, Pete and his partner Ollie came in followed almost immediately by Yumiko and Alec. With the exception of Gabriel and Max who'd sent his apologies from Australia all the members of the old gang were together once again. Jake quickly broke the news to them that he had been to Akemi's place intending to collect Gabriel but unfortunately he'd been informed that Gabriel left the flat in a taxi that morning with Akemi and had not returned and Jake had no idea where he had gone or why.

The jovial bubbly atmosphere was instantly subdued as Jake's announcement left them in a state of disbelief quickly followed by expressions of disappointment and ultimately concern about Gabriel. The barman came in with logs for the fire and took orders for drinks, soon returning with them on a tray. Slowly they began to take seats arranging them in a semi circle around the warmth of the roaring fire. Sasha told them about her meeting with Malik and the list Gabriel had entrusted to him, a list which included all their names. Pete and Ollie went on to describe what had happened when only a few weeks ago they'd visited Gabriel at the flat. Jake expressed his disquiet about the situation following his subsequent visit and particularly his increased concerns following his conversation with Gabriel's neighbour Rosie that very afternoon. Jake concluded by saying that he genuinely believed that Gabriel was asking for their help.

The group had sat quietly listening to the description of their old friend as frail, elderly and frightened a description that was hard for them to visualise because they could only remember him as he had been. Jake had told them that Gabriel believed there was a conspiracy against him and that Akemi had imprisoned him and was stealing his money. He also told them that Akemi had explained these fears as symptoms of Gabriel's paranoia.

Yumiko reacted defensively to Jake's suggestion that Akemi was in any way abusing Gabriel and refused to believe that Akemi could be party to any conspiracy. She had known Akemi for a long time; they had been close friends having arrived in London from Japan together. They had been together on the evening when they had met Gabriel and Alec. Yumiko and Alec's relationship flourished, Gabriel and Akemi went out together occasionally but Gabriel never hid the fact that there were other women in his life. Yumiko said she'd often warned Akemi that there was no future in the relationship but she chose not to listen to the advice and always welcomed him with typical Japanese hospitality whenever he chose to turn up at her place. "So if Gabriel is in trouble Akemi will be trying to take care of him, she loves him too much to cause him any harm," concluded Yumiko emphatically.

Maria had sat listening intently as Yumiko described Akemi's infatuation with Gabriel and her caring, unselfish nature. She agreed that Akemi obviously had strong feelings for Gabriel but she'd seen another side of her personality. She recalled a conversation when Akemi had actually threatened to kill Gabriel. She explained it was when Gabriel had met Kimiko and announced to Akemi in a cold matter of fact way that he intended to marry Kimiko and live with her in Japan. Maria said that at the time she was really quite worried about Akemi, she was so angry and felt her heart was broken and her world had come to an end and she wanted to kill Gabriel. Maria remembered at the time thinking that Akemi's anger and despair was so intense that maybe she was capable of murder. "Hell hath no fury like a woman scorned," cited Simon, putting his arm affectionately around his wife. Then Albert reminded the group that when Gabriel returned from Japan after the Kimiko episode, it was he who had met him at the airport and that Gabriel had specifically requested that he took him straight to Akemi's place. "Exactly," said Yumiko, "It's where he always went if he was in trouble."

However, Albert continued, saying that he had often had reason to think that Gabriel might have been involved in espionage activities back in the days of the Cold War. He'd accompanied Gabriel on many trips abroad and his suspicions had been triggered by the fact that Gabriel was always the one who was led away and interrogated at airports. Also when they'd travelled together he'd noticed that Gabriel was ever watchful and alert as to what was happening around him and always checked hotel rooms for listening devices. Albert paused as if debating whether or not to divulge an important piece of information that lent credence to his espionage theory. The group knew each other well and it was no surprise when Jake picked up on the momentary hesitation with the question, "Is there something else you need to tell us?" Albert went on to tell the story of the night of Max's leaving party before he left London to take up a prestigious neurosurgery post in a Melbourne hospital. The event had been held in the Jeremy Bentham pub in Bloomsbury, a well known haunt of Gabriel and the "old gang". At the end of the evening when most people had left Albert had wandered into the pub garden and found Max, both of them were rather the worse for drink and they sat together sharing a packet of cigarettes and drunkenly giggling about their shared escapades with their mutual and idiosyncratic mate Gabriel. Albert described how Max's mood suddenly changed when he recalled an evening sitting in this very same pub garden with Gabriel. It was an evening, he said, he would never forget because it was the evening that Gabriel revealed a very dark secret.

Albert paused, the others anticipating that he would enlighten them gasped with disappointment when Albert resumed saying that Max had refused to tell him the details of this dark secret. In spite of Max's inebriated state his loyalty to Gabriel and the trust he had placed in him remained strong. However, he had inferred that it was linked to Gabriel's youthful dalliance with the Communist party and his travels in Eastern Europe during the years of the Cold War. He'd told Max that he was haunted by the fear that one day he would pay dearly for the naivety of his youth.

The old friends sat quietly around the warm fire, digesting the information and each trying to imagine what Gabriel's dark secret might be. Soon the old group dynamics of the team came into play with Jake the organiser, summarising the situation as he saw it. "Well I'm sure he's in trouble now and I believe he has asked for our help." The group nodded in agreement and Jake went on to propose a plan of action.

He thought it would be a good idea if Sasha and Yumiko arranged to spend some time with Akemi and tried to find out what she had to say about what had been happening to Gabriel. Albert, he suggested contact Max in Australia explaining to him the seriousness of Gabriel's situation and inviting him to tell them any more about Gabriel's mysterious past that might be able to throw some light on the situation. Rather than all of them directly contacting and possibly overwhelming Gabriel in his seemingly vulnerable state he asked Pete and Ollie to call at the flat regularly and take note of what was going on there and what was being said by both Gabriel and Akemi. Simon was a solicitor and Jake suggested he look into the ways in which they could get legal help or protection for Gabriel if ultimately they found it was needed.

Naturally they all agreed to the assigned tasks, all clearly united in their desire to help Gabriel in whatever way they could. Jake rose and made his way to the bar to get another round of drinks. As the evening had progressed the bar had filled with a merry group of drinkers. The warm, relaxed and jovial ambience of the bar was in stark contrast to the despondent mood of the group of friends he'd left in the function room. He returned to the private room and suggested that they should joing the merry makers in the bar.

A table in the corner was occupied by some dapper-looking pensioners, one of them whipped out a pair of drumsticks from his jacket pockets and started drumming rock 'n' roll rhythms on the table. Before long the group joined in a sing-along of 'Rock around the Clock'. The atmosphere was light hearted, the glasses were full and once again life seemed good.

17

Gabriel's new identity

Akemi panicked when she realised Gabriel had disappeared from the reception area at the Medical Centre, she ran into the car park shouting to the cab driver, "Which way, he go?" The driver, who hadn't seen Gabriel run by, shook his head. Akemi raced out into the busy street pacing up and down erratically stopping pedestrians asking hysterically, "Have you see man in red coat?" People hurried by ignoring her question or simply shaking their heads. Catching a glimpse of a policeman in a fluorescent yellow jacket, she ran towards him, pushing people out of her way with no words of apology. She grabbed his arm shouting, "You must help me, you must help me find him, he ran away." The young policeman tried to calm her down, asking her to speak slowly and to explain her problem. "The man I look after, he ill, he need medication and he ran away from me, he wear red coat." The policeman at first was disinclined to get involved with the frenzied wild eyed woman who seemed unable to clearly explain her problem. She continued shouting in a loud, high pitched voice, "You must help me, you must help me," the noise attracting a small inquisitive crowd to gather around them.

The policeman attempting to take control of the situation took out his notebook and asked her the name and age of the missing person. Realising that he was at last going to do something she became a little calmer. She gave Gabriel's name and date of birth and paused struggling to remember the words a doctor had used to describe him, words she knew where significant. "He how you say, how you say? He vul… vul… he vulnerable adult," she stuttered. The policeman noted her name and address and mobile phone number and slowly explained that he would contact the local station who would radio all police cars in the area to look for an elderly sick man in a red coat and they would also contact all the local hospitals. He told her that the best thing she could do was go home because perhaps that was where Gabriel had gone. If he wasn't there then she should wait and the police would call her as soon as they had any news. He also gave her a card with a number for her to ring for any information.

Akemi was not happy with the response and continued pulling at his arm saying that he should go with her and search for Gabriel. Fortunately a passer-by who had joined the small crowd and was listening to the conversation interrupted and pointing to a coffee bar a little way down the street, said he'd seen a man with a red coat in there. Akemi immediately ran off down the street in the direction of the cafe with its distinctive red umbrellas overhanging the tables and chairs on the pavement. The passer-by winked meaningfully at the policeman who replied gratefully, "Nice one, mate," and walked off briskly in the opposite direction.

The cafe was crowded, Akemi brushed by the people seated at tables outside, she quickly looked round the inside room but there was no sign of Gabriel. She forced her way to the front of the people lining up to be served and shouted to the young girl who was busy pouring the drinks, "Man in red coat, he been in here, you tell me where he go?" The young girl taken aback by the rude interruption to her routine and the urgency in Akemi's voice shrugged her shoulders and turned away continuing to serve the coffees she'd prepared. Akemi threw her arms up in despair and ran out of the cafe. She continued to search all the shops and restaurants in the street until reluctantly as daylight started to fade she finally accepted that Gabriel had once again managed to escape from her.

Eventually she made her way back home, she knew that Gabriel would not be there but did not expect the overwhelming feeling of despair that the silence and emptiness of the flat created within her. Gabriel's daily medication was as she'd left it that morning neatly laid out on the kitchen table along with the dish of vegetables prepared ready for their lunch. Her eyes filled with tears and she lay on her bed and sobbed and sobbed until exhausted she fell asleep. If anyone could have witnessed her reaction to the events of that day they may have been forgiven for thinking that she really cared about him. Gabriel, however, would say to them that she was frightened and upset because she had failed in her duty of care.

On waking the next morning she found the card that the policeman had given her and called the number, she was informed that nobody fitting Gabriel's description had been admitted to any of the local hospitals and that there had been no reported sightings of him in the area but that they would continue to look for him. Then Jake rang and asked to speak to Gabriel, Akemi did not know how best to try and explain everything and so answered abruptly saying, "He not here, he gone missing," and hung up.

Naturally Jake was concerned; his immediate thought was to ring again and demand more information but on reflection thought it unlikely that she'd be any more forthcoming. So instead he emailed the group, repeating the terse conversation that he'd had with Akemi and sharing his concerns with them about the situation. The communication network between the gang flowed back and forth across the ether as the day progressed. Sasha contacted Malik asking if he could find out about local hospital admissions he replied later to say that all his enquires had proved negative. Yumiko had tried calling Akemi to see if she could glean any further information but there had been no answer. Pete and Ollie had called at the flat but got no reply. Jake had also visited the flat and when he received no answer at the door, crossed the corridor and knocked on Rosie's door. Rosie answered and confirmed that she had seen Akemi return alone and that she'd heard her sobbing in the night. Jake left his phone number and she agreed to call him if she had any news of Gabriel. Albert responded to say that he'd written to Max in Australia explaining as best he could the complexity of the situation and asking if he knew anything about Gabriel's past that might account for the problems he was facing.

As night fell Jake sent his final communication of the day in which he thanked them all for their efforts that day and expressing the hope that he knew they all shared that Gabriel was safe somewhere.

* * *

If only he had known Gabriel would have greatly appreciated the loyalty of the old gang but he lay semi-conscious on a hospital bed connected to machines controlling and monitoring his heart and a network of tubes radiating from his veins providing chemical infusions and the nutrients he needed to keep him alive.

Day after day passed, doctors and nurses came and went, consultants with students stood around the bed discussing the patient and all the time Gabriel was barely aware of anything happening around him. Until one afternoon when Gabriel felt someone gently stroking his body, it was a warm comforting sensation and he opened his eyes. He looked up to see a pretty young girl holding his arm and bathing him with a warm flannel. "Hello, you're lovely," were the words that instantly came into his head. The young nurse surprised at the apparent suddenness of his awakening smiled at him and asked if he was all right. Gabriel enchanted by her lovely smile which seemed to light up her face, thought for a second before answering, "Yes, I think I'm OK." His eyes followed her as she gently patted his limbs dry with a fluffy warm, white towel and indulging in the pleasurable sensation of the moment he thought, yes I really am OK and I'm alive.

A doctor passing by stopped and stared at Gabriel for a second with a mixed expression of surprise and relief. Moving closer he said, "Welcome back, you've had us worried." He instructed the nurse to carefully disconnect the electric wires and remove the intravenous tubes. Then he sat on the edge of Gabriel's bed and told him that he had been found alone and unconscious in a street. He was admitted to the hospital where there was concern because his heart rate was dangerously slow. Tests had revealed that there were toxins in his blood that had caused his heart to fail. It was very unusual he said, but so far they had been unable to identify the toxins, samples had been sent to a specialist laboratory for further investigation and they were awaiting the results.

He looked kindly at him saying, "You must rest now." As he rose to leave he remembered that his patient as yet had no name. "By the way what's your name?" Gabriel didn't reply immediately and the doctor took the opportunity to explain that he was alone when he was found and was carrying no means of identification. Gabriel was quick to realise that a lack of identity might be to his advantage and closed his eyes pretending to be sleepy, the doctor checked his pulse and finding it to be normal left him to rest.

Later the pretty young nurse came by; she smiled and asked if he was OK to answer some questions. Gabriel instantly replied flirtatiously, "I'll answer anything for you, my lovely," patting his bed inviting her to sit down close to him. The young nurse seemed quite at ease with her patient, having tenderly cared for him over the past weeks when he had lain unconscious and seeing him now awake and cheekily responsive was most pleasing to her. She said she needed to update a form with his personal details and started by asking for his full name. "I'll tell you mine if you tell me yours," he replied jokingly. "My name is Marianne," she smiled. Gabriel had anticipated that this question of identity would arise and had time to think how he would reply, "Wilfred Owen Jones, date of birth, 27th of December 1952, he said, the nurse looked up in surprise, "I know I look young for my age," responded Gabriel, she smiled and shook her head in disbelief. Gabriel in his deception had deliberately deducted many years from his actual age. When asked for the name of his next of kin, he thought of Lucas but quickly replied saying that there was no next of kin. His place of birth he truthfully answered was Swansea and his current address he gave as 23 Wind Street, Swansea which is where he'd lived as a child. As regards the name of his GP he simply explained he didn't have one because he had never needed to see one. The remainder of the questions about his health he answered truthfully or so he thought, saying no to all questions relating to any serious illness or disability.

When she'd finished the nurse said cheerfully, "All done Wilfred, I'll see you later." Gabriel lay back relishing in his new found identity which he believed would be his passport to a new life. Watching the young nurse going about her duties on the ward he secretly wondered if it might be possible that he could persuade her to play a part in this new life.

* * *

Every morning Akemi presented herself at the local police station to ask if there was any information about Gabriel and every morning came the same response that their efforts to find him had proved negative. The police had been obliged to take this particular missing person case seriously because of Akemi's insistence that Gabriel's life could be in danger if he did not take his prescribed medication. A photograph of Gabriel, with the headline MISSING PERSON and a contact number below was displayed prominently on public notice boards in Ealing.

When Akemi left the police station she was reluctant to return to the loneliness of the flat that she had shared with Gabriel for the past few years. She spent her days searching for any clue as to his whereabouts wandering through the streets of Ealing, calling in the cafes and bars; the banks and the barber's shop all the places that she knew Gabriel had frequented in the past. Eventually she would return disheartened to the flat, where she would play the numerous telephone messages that were left on the answering machine every day. The only message she wanted to hear was one that said Gabriel had been found and that he was safe. She didn't want to listen to the messages from Jake or Sasha or Yumiko or anyone else and simply deleted them.

Yumiko who had once been a close friend of Akemi had repeatedly left messages asking Akemi to call her with no success. The pair had a lot in common, they had met many years ago when they were both recent arrivals in London at a college where they were attending evening classes to learn English, and Akemi was from Kobe and Yumiko from the nearby city of Osaka. They happily shared a flat in Holland Park for a short while until one summer evening they happened to meet Gabriel and Alec in a London bar. Soon after this first meeting Yumiko moved in with Alec and couldn't understand the subsequent animosity Akemi displayed towards her. It was Alec who'd explained that Akemi was jealous of their commitment to each other. Alec and Gabriel had been friends for many years and Gabriel had boasted that Akemi was totally infatuated with him. Of course Alec explained, Gabriel being Gabriel toyed with her feelings being too independent and too promiscuous to commit to any long term relationships.

The friendship between Yumiko and Akemi had briefly rekindled when Gabriel left London to live in Japan with Kimiko. It was Akemi who'd made the first approach, calling Yumiko to say that she was desperately unhappy and needed to talk. Yumiko was naturally concerned about her old friend and immediately agreed to drive over to see her that evening. Remembering the cosy evenings when they had shared their dreams for the future over a few glasses of wine, she pulled into a store on the way to buy some bottles and a large bunch of flowers.

That evening for the first time since Yumiko's marriage to Alec, Akemi openly confided in her. She told her that many years ago on the evening after Yumiko and Alec's wedding Gabriel had unexpectedly proposed to her and she of course had instantly accepted. She'd never been so happy, but a few days later he said he'd been drunk at the time and didn't really mean it. She was heartbroken and turned for advice to a local fortune teller who had helped her with kind words and spiritual healing when her father had died a few years earlier. She had told her that she and Gabriel were meant to be together because she had been chosen to care for him. She could foresee that the road ahead would be difficult for both of them but they would always be together. With tears welling up in her eyes she went on to tell Yumiko how over the many years that she had been with Gabriel he had lied to her and cheated on her. She had always known when he was lying. There were often weeks when she never saw him or heard from him, and then he'd turn up and say he'd been away at a conference or staying with Albert in Oxford because he was busy with work. After these absences he'd be quiet and withdrawn and Akemi knew instinctively he'd been with another woman. She'd come to accept these liaisons because she knew he'd come back when the novelty and infatuation wore off and he always did.

When he'd told her that he had met an amazing woman who was unlike anyone he'd ever known and he really believed he'd found his true love, this time she had known it was different and one day she'd followed him wanting to see for herself this perfect woman. She followed him to the tube station in Ealing where he took the District Line to Acton Town. Akemi described how she was worried that he would notice her when he disembarked because the station was small and above ground but he immediately boarded a waiting train on the Piccadilly Line and Akemi selected a seat at the end of an adjacent carriage from which she could keep him in her sight. When he got out at Leicester Square and ran up the escalator leading to the streets above Akemi knew where he was heading, The Photographers' Gallery in Great Newport Street. Gabriel had a passion for photography and the gallery was well known for displaying informed, imaginative, thought provoking, presentations from visionary photographers. Gabriel always dreamt that one day some of his vast collection of photos might find a place within the gallery.

Akemi described what happened next, Kimiko was waiting for him and he ran towards her with his arms open and she welcomed him allowing his arms to fold around her. She was so young and so pretty and so full of life and youth and it was as if some of that youthful vitality had somehow been transmitted to Gabriel who appeared spritely and far younger than he really was. He couldn't take his eyes off her and she was giggling flirtatiously as they went arm and arm into the gallery. This was the last time she saw Gabriel before he left London to start his new life with Kimiko in Japan. She was left with the image of them so happy together and when he didn't even bother to call her to say goodbye she felt bitter and betrayed.

Yumiko had listened patiently, as Akemi tearfully revealed the feelings that she'd kept hidden for so long. Yumiko put her arm around her attempting to console her but this act of kindness resulted in Akemi's pent up emotions erupting into a flood of incontrollable tears. Yumiko knowing that little she could say would make any difference went into the kitchen, she remembered the wine she'd brought with her and filled two large glasses.

18

Gabriel embraces his new life

Gabriel was busy creating his new identity and was completely unaware of the efforts being made by the police and his friends to find him. He'd decided that he wanted to be known as "Wilf," the name Wilfred sounded rather outdated and didn't fit the image he wished to portray.

He unexpectedly had found himself starting to enjoy life once again; he flirted jokingly with all the nurses and was totally captivated by the lovely Marianne. Secretly he suspected that the attraction was mutual because she paid more attention to him than she did to the other patients on the ward. It was Marianne who had brought in a small radio so that he could listen to the current debate on the EU referendum. It was Marianne who gently brushed his hair and trimmed his beard when he returned to the ward after a shower each day. He looked forward to his intellectual conversations with the doctors when they made their daily rounds. In his eagerness to demonstrate to them that his educational standing was on a par with theirs he'd admitted to part of his real identity, informing them that he also had letters after his name and was a retired Oxford University lecturer.

When the results of the toxins investigation arrived they revealed high levels of a drug in Gabriel's blood. Unusually the doctor did not immediately recognise the name of the drug but after some research discovered that it was an experimental drug being used to treat a variety of neurological disorders. The doctor unsuccessfully scanned the national database which listed patients registered for clinical trials with such drugs but found no trace of Wilfred Jones. The doctor liked the man he knew as Wilf, he'd spent time debating with him the issues around the UK membership of the EU. Perceiving him to be an intelligent person he decided to show him the results of his blood test hoping that he might be able to offer an explanation. The doctor explained that the markers on the printout showed a high concentration of a drug that was not on regular prescription in the UK. This confirmed what Gabriel had always suspected, that he was part of some experiment. He wanted to tell the young doctor the truth about the nightmare scenario he had become involved in, about his conspiracy theories but knew if he did he would have to tell him everything and in so doing reveal his true identity. He remembered that this was what had happened before when he was in hospital and they simply contacted Akemi and he was back in the nightmare once again.

Desperate to hold on to the freedom that he felt his new identity had given him, he quickly called on his overactive imagination to offer the doctor an explanation for the toxins found in his blood. It must have been a couple of years ago, he told him, he was on holiday with some mates in Vietnam and he met a beautiful young girl, her name was Mai. Gabriel explained that he really liked this girl and of course he wanted to have a relationship with her but he knew he was getting older and for the first time in his life he'd become worried about his virility. He'd shared his concerns with one of his mates who told him that he'd experienced the same problem and recommended a traditional Vietnamese doctor in Hanoi. Gabriel was dubious at first, but his mate who had once lived in Hanoi explained that both Vietnamese traditional medicine and oriental medicine formed an integral part of the national health care system in Vietnam and were frequently used in hospitals. Gabriel, seeing that the young doctor was intrigued by his story decided to elaborate on the detail to add authenticity to his tale. He told him that his mate had taken him to the old quarter of Hanoi to Lan Ong Street named after a famous old Vietnamese physician where numerous stalls and shops sold herbal potions proven to cure all ills. From there he took him to meet the physician he'd recommended who was based in a modern clinic on the outskirts of Hanoi. After a short consultation, he was handed a prescription for some tablets with an assurance that they were guaranteed to produce the desired effect. When Gabriel announced with a glint in his eye, "and yes they did work," the young doctor shook his head in disbelief and couldn't help but smile.

The doctor knew very little about traditional Chinese medicine but thought it highly unlikely that any herbal preparation prescribed for the condition Gabriel had described could have produced the effects of the experimental drug he had discovered in Gabriel's blood. When he expressed his doubts, Gabriel quickly recalled that when he was in Vietnam he'd also been given many other prescriptions for headaches and for all his allergies. The doctor scratched his head and finally in the absence of any other information made a written note of Gabriel's explanation, following it with a series of exclamation marks.

The hospital had been unable to locate the medical records for anyone with the name Wilfred Jones and date of birth as given to them by Gabriel. The address in Swansea he'd offered as his last place of residence was checked and was found to be the location of a lively nightclub. With no next of kin and no one named as a person to contact in case of emergency Gabriel thus fell into the category of a vulnerable and frail elderly adult and his case was referred to the hospital social work team. He was visited in turn by the team manager, a senior practitioner, a social worker and various therapists all attempting to complete assessments of his physical and mental capacities and issues regarding his future welfare. Gabriel, intent on preserving the freedom given by his new identity, used his well rehearsed skills of diversion, distraction and deceit to successfully confuse them all. He told them that he prided himself on being a free spirit who loved to travel. He deliberately interrupted their probing questions with elaborate tales of his travels to distant places and his opinions on current affairs. His love of travel was the reason he had not settled anywhere and not laid down any roots. He had many friends spread around the world but nobody in London who he could ask to be responsible for him or guarantee his well-being if he was discharged from the hospital

At a hospital assessment team meeting the complexity of Gabriel's case raised many concerns. A medical report showed that he met the clinical criteria for discharge. A mental capacity assessment described an intelligent individual with good memory recall. The problems highlighted were those of safeguarding and the inability of the assessment team to formulate a discharge plan for this patient. The team were expected in the case of someone as frail as Gabriel to undertake forward planning by sharing his expected date of discharge and information on the complexity of his case with community services and relatives. As the team manager explained Gabriel had no address to which he could be discharged and no relatives that they could contact. A decision was made to discharge Gabriel to a local community hospital in Essex.

Gabriel was sad when he learnt that he was being transferred to another hospital, he had become accustomed to the daily routine and to the people caring for him. He had come to regard them as his friends, he trusted them and he felt safe here with them. This was the place where "Wilf" had been born and where all the nightmares of his recent past had been buried. He was frightened and felt his pulse quicken and his hands start to tremble, his plan to establish a new identity had worked but now he needed to move on to the next phase of his new life as Wilf. If he could get to a bank and draw enough money to buy a plane ticket then he could disappear, as the nomadic Wilf he would be able to go anywhere and live anywhere. The weeks of bed rest had weakened his muscles and although he'd been religiously following the exercises that the physiotherapist had suggested he could still not walk very far unaided. He knew that he would need help for this next stage of his plan.

When Marianne reported for duty that day she noticed that Gabriel did not greet her with his usual flirtatious grin but looked rather downcast. "Wilf, what's the matter?" she asked kindly. No way was she expecting to hear what he was about to say. He told her that it had been decided to move him to another hospital; he looked imploringly at her and told her that he was so very fond of her and he couldn't bear to ever leave her and that he had a plan for them to be together. "You're a nurse you can look after me until I am strong again and then I promise that I will look after you forever. I have money we can buy tickets and go anywhere in the world. We can go anywhere, I'll let you choose." Marianne could scarcely believe what she heard, she didn't wish to upset Gabriel by telling him that he was a likeable old man but that she did not wish to go anywhere with him. Instead she humoured him, explaining that she was flattered by his comments and sorry that she could not accept his offer because she loved her job at the hospital and she could never move away from her family in London. At that moment the doctors came on the ward to start their daily rounds and Marianne was thankful for the opportunity to move away from Gabriel.

A consultant and his entourage of young trainee doctors were gathering around Gabriel's bed but for once he wasn't interested in trying to impress them with his extensive knowledge of world affairs or listening to whatever they had to say about his medical condition. He was still coming to terms with the fact that Marianne had rejected his proposition. He had made her such an attractive offer and all he'd asked was that she nurse him back to health in return for which he'd promised her financial security and the chance to travel anywhere in the world with him. It was incomprehensible to him that she would choose to stay in London with her family and continue to work as a lowly paid nurse.

"Are you all right Wilf?" asked the consultant having noticed that his patient was unusually silent. The question brought Gabriel sharply back to the reality of the moment and he became aware of the presence of the consultant and the faces of the young trainees staring at him. The consultant was describing the unusual features of Gabriel's case. He'd turned to his trainees with a smile and explained that the patient was admitted with heart failure caused by an overdose of a drug taken to improve sexual performance. A drug that the patient said he'd obtained during his travels to Vietnam. The trainees were trying to resist laughing and Gabriel noticed that one of them raised his hand slightly and seemed to wave briefly as if giving a subtle gesture of recognition. As the group moved on to the next patient Gabriel realised there was something familiar about the young man.

This was a teaching hospital and as was customary when the ward round was completed the trainees gathered round the consultant who fired questions at them testing their understanding of the medical conditions and treatments of the patients they had observed. Gabriel was still trying to remember where he had seen the young man before and it was during this question and answer session that he heard the distinctive heavily accented voice of the young man and immediately he knew it was Malik.

* * *

Malik had recently been assigned to the Essex hospital to complete his foundation training. A routine part of that training was to accompany the consultants on their ward rounds. Today was the first time he had been to the James Mackenzie ward where Gabriel was being treated. He recognised him instantly and wanted to tell him how good it felt to see him there alive and looking well and how concerned everyone had been about him but protocol demanded that he stay silent and listen to the wisdom of the revered consultant. He was surprised when the consultant, when delivering a spiel about the patient's diagnosis and treatment, referred to him as Wilf. Then looking at the whiteboard above the bed he saw the name Wilfred Jones written clearly with a red marker pen. Malik tried to give Gabriel a signal that he recognised him by raising his hand slightly and gently waving at him but Gabriel seemed unresponsive to the motion.

As he and the other juniors accompanied their master on his rounds, Malik pondered on how best to deal with the situation. Malik had often wondered over the past few months how and why he had come to form such a close bond with this vulnerable elderly man. Ever since Gabriel's disappearance Malik had been in regular contact with Sasha asking for any news of Gabriel's whereabouts. Malik was aware that he had a responsibility to inform the hospital authorities that the man calling himself Wilfred Jones was really Gabriel Jones and that he had been reported missing weeks ago. Then he remembered the many conversations that he'd had with Gabriel in which he'd expressed genuine fears about his personal safety and his mistrust of the woman who was supposed to be caring for him. He also recalled the suspicious circumstances surrounding his previous discharge from the central London hospital where he had first met Gabriel. His instinct now was to protect Gabriel and he decided to wait before reporting Gabriel's real identity to the hospital authorities. He decided that he would come back later and talk to Gabriel when he was alone, he would explain that he was in contact with Sasha and she and all his other friends were really concerned about him. He would tell him that there were posters with a picture of him headed "MISSING PERSON," displayed around Ealing and near the Nag's Head pub where he had collapsed. He would ask him why he was pretending to be someone called Wilfred Jones.

Later that day, Malik, as he had planned, made his way back to the James Mackenzie ward hoping to be able to talk to Gabriel in private. As he entered the ward he was overcome with a sense of "déjà vu", the bed Gabriel had occupied that morning lay empty. Pristine white sheets lay folded upon it and the white board above the bed that had borne the name Wilfred Jones had been wiped clean. As he stood looking in despair at the empty bed a young nurse came by, it was Marianne. "Can I help you?" she asked.

Malik replied, "I was looking for Gabriel."

"Who?" asked Marianne.

Malik quickly rectified his mistake, "Sorry, I mean Wilf."

Marianne told him that Wilf had been discharged that afternoon and enquired whether he was a relative. Malik shook his head struggling as to how he'd explain the complicated relationship he had with the man she knew as Wilf. "I met him when I was working in a London hospital and found him to be quite a character." Marianne nodded in agreement, saying, "I know exactly what you mean, Wilf's a real charmer, can you believe that this morning he proposed to me?" Malik grinned asking if she knew where he'd gone. He followed her to the work station where she checked Wilf's discharge notes and gave him the contact details of the community hospital in Grays.

"So nobody came to take him home," remarked Malik. "I don't think he has a home in London and he said there was nobody we could contact; no next of kin or friends," Marianne explained. As she was speaking an elderly man was being lifted off a hospital trolley and laid onto the bed where Gabriel had lain just a few hours before. "You can see we are under pressure to discharge patients," continued Marianne. She admitted to Malik that she had become a little fond of Gabriel and was sad to see him go but the doctors had agreed that he was medically fit for discharge although still too frail to care for himself and it had been decided that the best place for him under the circumstances was the local community hospital.

Malik thanked her and left, he was beginning to understand why Gabriel had chosen to give a false name and deny having anyone who would be able to care for him. It was part of his master plan to escape from Akemi. Malik could not foresee how Gabriel could make such a plan work in the long run. He was still reluctant to let the hospital authorities know the truth about the situation but the responsibility of what he knew was beginning to weigh heavily upon him and he decided to call Sasha and see if she had any ideas as to how they could best help Gabriel.

19

A memory stick goes missing

Gabriel was confused, it had happened so quickly, a porter arrived with a wheelchair and a nurse hastily packed his few belongings into a large white carrier bag emboldened with a green cross. Gabriel's eyes became fixated on the green cross; the symbol was familiar to him from his international travels. His anxiety levels heightened his mind went into overdrive and for a brief second he thought that he was abroad and asked the porter, "What country am I in?" The porter laughed and replied, "You in London, England."

Gabriel detected an East European accent and said, "But you are not a Londoner?"

"No, I from Estonia," replied the porter, wheeling him out of the ward and along a corridor to the lift.

Gabriel had a fear of lifts, always opting to run up and down flights of stairs rather than use them. When the lift door opened and he looked into the void before him, his heart was pounding, he tried to speak but couldn't, his hands were trembling and the palms were wet with sweat. It was not only his phobia of travelling in a lift that was causing the panic attack. The nationality of the man taking him into the lift triggered the paranoia that lurked deep within the dark corners of his mind. Gabriel had visited Estonia at a time when it was a part of the old USSR. His mind had instantly slipped back into the dark depths of fear leading him to suspect this man might not be a porter but an employee of the Russian Security Services. He was aware of their undercover surveillance methods, placing operatives in inconspicuous and mundane positions – roles such as cleaners, waitresses and hospital porters allowing them close contact with the person under surveillance without arousing suspicion.

His heightened awareness of such tactics had led him to be ever vigilant, never leaving anything incriminating in a hotel room and always on guard whenever he sensed that a waiter or waitress was hovering at his table. Perhaps this was the moment that finally they had caught up with him, a moment they had cleverly used to their advantage, he was immobile and panic stricken and confined to a wheelchair being transported by a porter who had complete control and could take him anywhere and do whatever he liked with him.

Although physically shaking and frightened Gabriel knew that he had to draw on every ounce of mental strength if he was to survive any interrogation by the Russian Security Services. His mind leapt into overdrive and old questions that over the years he'd struggled to find answers to were at the forefront once again. "Why after all these years are they still interested in me?"

"What is it they want? What is it that I know that is so important to them? Do I have something they want?"

Suddenly Gabriel remembered the small memory stick onto which the technician at the institute had electronically transferred the images from his slides. Nervously he fumbled in his coat pockets but to no avail, the pockets were empty. Gabriel's thoughts were racing, "Where is it? Who has it? If someone has accessed the data will they realise its significance? Can the contents of the memory stick have revealed my real identity and my secrets?"

It was such a long time ago during the years of the Cold

War when he'd worked as a translator at the Russian embassy and travelled to Leningrad with classified files unaware at the time of their importance having been more concerned with accurately translating them than delving into the details of the information they contained. There was the map of the secret cities he'd inadvertently seen on a wall of a room in the fortified government building in Leningrad. There were also the hundreds of photographic slides, some with pictures of government officials of the old USSR and some of officials of the old Yugoslavia.

Recently, Gabriel had seen the TV coverage of the mass exodus of refugees crossing the Mediterranean and travelling through Greece, Albania and Serbia heading for Western Europe. These images had profoundly affected him evoking memories of his travels in Eastern Europe at a time when countries one by one had dramatically severed their umbilical cord with the USSR.

Gabriel had been inspired by Mikhail Gorbachev's policies of glasnost and perestroika and the revolutionary fervour taking place in the Eastern Bloc. It was 1989/1990 and Gabriel had successfully applied for a sabbatical year. It was a time when obtaining travel visas to the Eastern Bloc was notoriously difficult. However, to the amazement of his friends and colleagues Gabriel's visa applications were speedily and unquestioningly granted, enabling him to travel freely behind the Iron Curtain. With a sleeping bag in a rucksack and his camera he'd set off alone for Eastern Europe. He saw this as a momentous opportunity to witness and record the events as they happened.

In June 1989 he was in Poland when Solidarity won an overwhelming victory in a partially free election in Poland, leading to the peaceful fall of Communism in that country. In October he was in Hungary when a section of the physical Iron Curtain was dismantled and he'd witnessed the mass exodus of East Germans through Hungary. That same month he was caught up in the mass demonstration in Leipzig and had joined the crowd walking around Leipzig's ring road, past the Stasi headquarters and towards the train station carrying nothing but candles and banners reading "We are the people." Fellow marchers had told him that the Stasi had planted plainclothes officers in the crowd to cause trouble, but they were quickly surrounded by the protesters chanting "no violence." All of these famously historical moments Gabriel had systematically recorded both in his diaries and on camera.

His camera had also recorded the fall of the Berlin Wall in November 1989, the crowds cheering as bulldozers tore down the Wall and the emotions on the faces of East Germans as they ran into the freedom of the West. In December 1989 he was in Bucharest when the military sided with protesters and turned on Communist ruler Ceausescu who was later executed after a brief trial that lasted only three days. He recorded the events in Tirana in July 1990 when hundreds of Albanian citizens gathered around foreign embassies to seek political asylum and flee the country. What amongst his memories of these historic events or amongst his photographic images of them could be so important to them all these years after the end of the Cold War?

Suddenly his mind which had been busily occupied reliving these memorable events was propelled back into the moment. He was outside the building now, it was late afternoon and the sky was heavily laden with dark ominous clouds. The chair was bouncing across rough ground and his small frame was rolling precariously from one side to the other. They seemed to be heading towards a small outbuilding which to Gabriel looked no bigger than a garden shed. On reaching the building Gabriel realised it was a small three sided shelter. The porter pushed the chair into the shelter, turning it so that Gabriel faced the outside. Immediately they were joined by another man also wearing a porter's uniform. The pair spoke briefly in a language Gabriel could not understand. They stood close to his wheelchair, one either side of him as if on guard. They lit cigarettes and Gabriel sensed that they too were apprehensive; it felt as if they were waiting for instructions and were unsure of what might happen next. Gabriel was becoming more and more afraid with every minute that passed. The pair had stopped talking and the silence was broken only by the striking of matches and the whisper of smoke curling lazily into the air. Eventually a car could be heard approaching and a black Mercedes with darkened windows appeared. The "guards" greeted the driver conversing in a common language and offering him a cigarette. They appeared to be in no hurry to take Gabriel anywhere and were still waiting for something. After a while, the driver's mobile phone rang, he spoke briefly and then shouted instructions to the others.

Simultaneously, both men stubbed out their cigarettes and Gabriel felt himself being lifted from his chair and transferred to the back seat of the car, the porter who had claimed to be from Estonia sat next to him and the driver took off at speed. Gabriel tried peering through the darkened windows hoping to recognise anything that might give some indication of where he was or where they were likely to be heading. The daylight had faded and Gabriel could tell only that they were racing along a dual carriageway his line of vision sucked involuntarily into the river of light coming from the never ending stream of traffic flowing in the opposite direction. His jangled nerves had left him exhausted and he closed his eyes hoping to close down the confused messages flooding into his mind. He held his trembling hands over his eyes attempting to control the fluttering of his eyelids.

He felt the car slowing down and uncovered his eyes to see that they had moved off the motorway and were now driving along an unlit single track. With the numerous twists and turns in the road he thought they must have travelled away from the city and out into the countryside. A light beckoned in the distance and as they drove nearer Gabriel could make out a large country house set in its own grounds. They stopped at a tall wrought iron gate, the Estonian man alighted spoke into an intercom and the gate slowly opened. They proceeded along the tree lined drive arriving at what Gabriel perceived to be an architecturally very old and very impressive country house. The wheelchair was retrieved from the large car boot. Gabriel's legs were weak and gave way under him as he struggled to manoeuvre himself out of the car. Seemingly unconcerned the porters lifted him off the ground and carried him in the chair up the stone steps and through the huge wooden door. He was wheeled along a corridor, lined on either side with numbered doors. When they reached room number 5, they pushed the door and switched on a dim light bulb hanging from the high ceiling. To Gabriel it looked like a cheap hotel room housing only a single bed and a small wardrobe with an old fashioned washbasin in one corner. Once again sign language, this time a firm tapping of the bed inviting Gabriel to move onto it. Gabriel followed the hand signals and tentatively managed to hoist himself up onto the bed where he sat trembling, the porter made a brief phone call and moments later an elderly lady dressed in an old fashioned nurse's uniform came. She simply nodded at the porters as if to accept their delivery and they folded up the chair and left.

The elderly lady took his trembling hands and held them tightly in hers. "I don't know where I am," Gabriel whispered. She looked directly into his wide eyes that were full of dread and said in a kind, reassuring voice, "Don't worry Wilf, you'll be safe here, you are in a convalescent home in Grays." Gabriel consumed by fear was not expecting anyone to demonstrate any compassion towards him. Slowly she lifted his legs up resting them on the bed and gently moved his shaking body into a comfortable position resting him against two large pillows. She smiled and said "I'll be back in a minute," and left the room. Gabriel lay back on the soft pillows. The old lady soon returned carrying a tray with a large glass of what looked to Gabriel like hot milk and two digestive biscuits, She held the glass to his lips and said, "Drink this, it will help you sleep." Gabriel immediately knew that something had been added to the milk but drawn in by the kind expression of the lady holding the glass to his lips and too exhausted to speak he swallowed the liquid. Seconds later he was asleep; the nurse lowered the glass, lay his head down on the pillows and left the room locking the door behind her.

* * *

As soon as he arrived home that evening, Malik sat at his computer and sent a message to Sasha.

"Hi Sasha,

At last some good news, I have been based at an Essex hospital for the past two weeks and today completely by chance I was selected to accompany a neurological consultant on his weekly ward rounds. I could hardly believe it, but on one of the wards I saw Gabriel. He was sitting up in bed, he's gained a little weight and looks well. He seems to have assumed a new identity calling himself Wilfred Jones, which explains why we were unable to trace him in the lists of hospital admissions. I went back to find him on the ward when my shift was over and was told he's been discharged to a community hospital in Grays. I believe it's a place that provides for people who require rehabilitation following illness and have no one who can care for them in the community. I've enclosed the address and phone number of the Grays hospital.

I know Gabriel's life is complicated and I didn't want to betray the trust he placed in me by telling anyone at the hospital that I know who he really is. But also I do not want to put my job in jeopardy by not revealing what I know about a patient.

So Sasha, I feel it is best if I leave the matter in your hands. I know how worried you and everyone else have been

187

about Gabriel, so please let them all know that he's leading a
double life but thankfully is still alive.

Kind regards
Malik.

On receiving Malik's message, knowing that Gabriel was alive, Sasha felt an overwhelming sense of relief. Immediately she forwarded the good news to the recently reunited circle of friends. As she clicked "send"she felt grateful that the friends were all out there and that between them they'd be able to work out what to do next. She had complete trust in all of them and was thankful she was not facing this difficult situation alone.

She opened a bottle of wine, raised a glass in a silent toast to Gabriel and reflected on the resilience of the close friendships made so long ago. Years had passed since they were a band of merry, hedonistic drinkers frequenting the bars and pubs of the city. It was Gabriel who had been instrumental in bringing them together then, captivating them with his infectious energy and joie de vivre. They were all older and wiser now, most of them settled with families and all progressing in their professional careers. It was indeed remarkable that after all this time they had come together again now, united once again by memories of those carefree evenings and the camaraderie they'd shared and in their concern for the old friend who'd introduced them to each other all those years ago.

When Alec and Yumiko received Sasha's message, Yumiko immediately picked up her phone to tell Akemi the news that Gabriel had been found but was quickly deterred from making the call by Alec who after numerous conversations with Jake since Gabriel's disappearance had grown increasingly suspicious of Akemi's motives. Pete and Ollie holidaying in Majorca received the message and answered simply, "*Sorry we're not there to celebrate with you all but great news that he's OK.*" Jake on receiving the message had long telephone conversations with Alec and Simon and Marie before finally calling Albert. Jake was surprised when Albert revealed that he'd arranged a meeting with Max who was visiting family in the UK. They had all unanimously agreed that someone needed to pay a visit to the community hospital in Grays as soon as possible and try to find out what exactly had happened to Gabriel and offer to give him any help and support he needed. They all were now aware that the situation was a delicate one and needed careful handling. So it was decided that Jake should go alone and he agreed to contact the hospital and make the necessary arrangements to visit Gabriel the following evening.

20

Albert and Max share their thoughts

Following their reunion at the Nag's Head the gang were committed to helping to sort out the confusion surrounding the affairs of their old friend Gabriel. Albert had contacted Max in Australia, attempting to explain the seriousness of Gabriel's situation. He reminded Max of a conversation they'd had years ago in the garden of the Jeremy Bentham pub when Max had hinted that Gabriel was burdened with a dark secret. Albert asked Max to reveal anything about Gabriel's mystery past that might be able to throw some light on what was happening to Gabriel now. Albert was delighted to receive a reply from Max saying that he was returning to the UK for a short holiday and was keen to meet up with him.

They agreed to meet in one of their old haunts, The Dog and Duck in Soho's Bateman Street. Max arrived first and on entering the pub was struck by the familiarity of his surroundings; it was as if he had walked back into the past. He was staring at the plaque displayed on the wall which laid claim to the fact that the pub had once been once frequented by John Constable and George Orwell when Albert tapped him on the shoulder. Almost twenty years had passed since Max and Albert had last met; both displayed the inevitable signs of aging but nevertheless recognised each other instantly. They greeted each other warmly and were soon sitting comfortably chatting together, pints in hand, happy and relaxed as they had always been in each other's company. Naturally their initial conversation focussed on their own lives and the key events that had taken place since they had last met. Max was keen to show Albert the many photographs he'd brought along, photos of his Australian born wife and his two children and of the hospital where he currently worked as an eminent neurosurgeon. Albert, older than Max and recently retired, proudly showed him the photo of his two young grandchildren that he carried in his wallet, saying how lucky he was now to have the time to spend with them.

The conversation paused and both knew the time had come to address the ultimate reason for their meeting, their old friend Gabriel whose idiosyncratic life was now in sharp contrast to the stability and conventionality of their own. Max was under the impression that Gabriel had married a Japanese girl; Gabriel had sent a postcard from Japan telling him of the intended marriage and their plans for a honeymoon in Australia. Max had replied inviting them to spend time with him and his family in Sydney but was surprised when Gabriel did not respond. In fact that was the last time he had heard anything until Albert had written telling him that Gabriel was back in London and that he was in trouble.

Albert explained that he actually knew very little about what had actually happened in Japan except that the marriage never took place. Albert thought Gabriel had suffered a nervous breakdown as a result but couldn't be sure about that. Albert told Max how he had met him at Heathrow when he had returned from Japan and he was unusually quiet and subdued on the journey back to central London where Albert left him at Akemi's flat. After that, Albert continued, nobody heard anything from him, "Some of us rang

Akemi's flat but were told that he didn't want to talk, inevitably over time we gave up trying to contact with him."

Albert went on to tell Max that he'd visited Gabriel a few months ago when he'd been in London. He'd rung and Akemi had answered, she was at first evasive but eventually had agreed to him calling in to see Gabriel. Albert recalled the meeting, Gabriel was thinner and looked much older and had stared at him with blank wild eyes as if he wasn't sure who he was. He went on to tell Max how Gabriel had persistently interrogated him about Max, desperately wanting to know if he had heard from him. Aware of Gabriel's fragile state he'd been reluctant that afternoon to enter into a conversation with him about Max and resurrect old wounds by revealing that they had kept in touch with each other and were still close friends. Albert confessed that he'd diverted the conversation away from Max, saying he'd lost touch with him because of his vivid recollection of Gabriel's disapproval of their close friendship. Max nodded, confirming that he too remembered Gabriel's angry reaction to their practical jokes and his obvious resentment of the close bond they shared. Albert concluded, "I don't think he has ever forgiven us, he never did have a sense of humour and things were never the same between us after he realised we'd been taking the p... To us it was a bit of harmless fun but he got really angry with me, accusing me of disloyalty but I always suspected that he was jealous of our relationship, it was as if he thought of it as a betrayal of him."

Albert went on to describe that on the afternoon of his visit, Gabriel seemed anxious and was constantly watching Akemi, appearing to be frightened of her. When she left them alone for a moment he'd whispered that she was keeping him a prisoner and being paid to monitor him because he was part of an experimental drug testing programme. Albert explained how sad he had felt to see Gabriel in that state but didn't want to get involved. Gabriel had changed from the fun loving crazy guy they had once known.

It was obvious that he wasn't well and that there was a tangible tension between him and Akemi who appeared to him at the time to be doing her best to look after Gabriel.

It was a long time after that visit when Sasha had contacted him and the others telling of her meeting with the young Egyptian junior doctor who was seriously concerned about Gabriel's welfare and had a list of all their names he'd given to him. Albert explained that they had collectively decided that it was Gabriel's way of asking for their help, Jake had organised a reunion at the Nag's Head, it was a great evening with the old crowd but Gabriel didn't show and later they found out that he had inexplicably disappeared.

Max had listened intently as Albert tried to explain what he knew of the facts relating to Gabriel's situation. Then decided that in spite of his promise made to Gabriel all those years ago it was time that he revealed what he knew and recounted the conversation that he'd had with Gabriel in a pub garden so long ago. A conversation in which Gabriel had told him that he'd worked as a translator at the Russian embassy and accepted an opportunity to travel to Leningrad to personally deliver the translated documents. While he was there he'd seen certain things that he could never admit to having seen and overheard conversations that he should never have been a party to. He also had a liaison with a Russian girl with whom he'd naively confided his concerns about the things he'd heard and seen, later when he saw her talking to one of the officials he'd spoken about he suspected she was part of a "honey trap".

When he returned to England he was approached by another lecturer from the university assuring him that when he graduated he would be offered a post in the London British Civil Service. Following his graduation, he was immediately offered the post but asked if he could defer his acceptance of this post because of a planned trip to Afghanistan. Gabriel was surprised when the Ministry agreed to his request. Their agreement to comply with his request, however, came with a condition that he would provide a series of first hand reports specifically on Soviet Union involvement in the construction of transport infrastructure assets and general observations of Soviet influence on the People's Democratic Party of Afghanistan which had come to power in 1973.

Gabriel believed that his irresistible yearning for adventure and his naivety had led him to inadvertently become involved in espionage, the Russians had used him and the British had used him, the result of his involvement with both sides meant that neither trusted him and he genuinely believed he had become identified as a double agent. He was convinced that his frequent sojourns into foreign countries had lent credibility to these suspicions. "These are the things that Gabriel revealed to me that night and until now I have never spoken of them with anyone," concluded Max.

They sat in silence, the minutes ticking away, Albert struggling to digest the mind boggling information that Max had just shared with him whilst Max was feeling a sense of relief, having unburdened himself of a long kept secret. Albert was the first to break the silence, picking up the two empty lager glasses from the table, saying, "I find it incredible."

"Yes," replied Max, "It sounds unbelievable, I know some parts of Gabriel's story are undeniably true but I suspect that other parts are pure fantasy. I have no doubt that Gabriel sees truth as a highly elastic concept."

Max thought for a moment before continuing, debating whether or not to share his personal opinions and professional diagnosis of their long time mutual acquaintance Gabriel. When Max had first met Gabriel he had been impressed by his congeniality and surprised at how easily he'd been drawn into Gabriel's close circle of friends. As time passed Max, a trained psychiatrist, recognised in Gabriel many of the traits characteristic of a narcissistic personality and had asked Gabriel to participate in a research project aiming to understand the neurological basis of

194

personality. Gabriel had readily agreed to take part in the research which Max assumed had continued after he'd left the institute and moved to Australia. Max was now an eminent neuroscientist who had devoted years attempting to understand the complexities and mysterious workings of the human mind.

Max hesitated for a moment debating whether he should divulge his objective psychoanalysis of their mutual friend's personality. Finally he decided that in the light of recent events it was appropriate and relevant to share such observations. He explained that he did not want to appear to be disloyal to Gabriel but felt it important that Albert was aware of his thoughts and the possible impact of his observations on Gabriel's present state of mind. Max explained people like Gabriel surround themselves with people who are attracted to them by their magnetism, charm, energy, joie de vivre. Like Gabriel, they often fail to form stable close interpersonal relationships because they have an unhealthy belief that anything less than perfect is unacceptable.

Albert nodded, expressing agreement and reflecting his understanding that Max was accurately describing their friend which encouraged Max to expound on his theory. Max continued, describing Gabriel's personality type as having an excessive need for admiration and affirmation and a tendency to cultivate a self image in which they always had to appear to be special, successful and important. Such people, he said, may find it virtually impossible to accept any imperfections in their life and that perhaps it is precisely now when Gabriel has aged and seems to have become excessively concerned about his own health and welfare that his reaction is to blame others for his situation. If this is the case it can develop into paranoia and Gabriel could be using the persecutory beliefs and conspiracy theories to explain what is happening to him. Max concluded, "Please understand that this is a hypothetical scenario based on my own professional opinions but nevertheless it is one that we do have to consider."

Although Albert respected Max's professional expertise

and recognised the accurate portrayal of many of Gabriel's characteristics, he was reluctant to accept that Gabriel could be suffering from a paranoid type illness. Albert was now of an age when he frequently reflected on the past. When he looked back to the days when he and Gabriel had been young, carefree travelling companions he felt lucky to have met someone with Gabriel's adventurous spirit at a time in his life when he was young and free. He was thankful that he had taken advantage of the opportunities and knew that he would be forever grateful to Gabriel for the memorable experiences they had shared. He could clearly remember the rush of adrenalin he always experienced when Gabriel presented the intricate itineraries he'd prepared for their journeys. He remembered the excitement of spontaneously disregarding the itineraries and boarding local buses or trains just to see where they might take them. He remembered with merriment how they enjoyed the attentions of many attractive women they met on their travels. Wherever they were Gabriel's charm never failed to attract the young ladies.

Albert was not surprised to learn that Gabriel was perhaps a secret agent. It was something that he'd suspected many times when they'd travelled together. Gabriel was frequently apprehended by men in dark suits and interrogated at custom points. He'd watched incredulously as Gabriel meticulously checked their hotel rooms for listening devices. Yes, he had been aware that while traveling Gabriel was always on his guard but Albert had never asked any questions, simply accepting that whatever was going on, it was Gabriel's business.

The pair had been sitting quietly next to each other each preoccupied with their individual personal memories of Gabriel when their thoughts were abruptly interrupted by a young couple dressed in red sweaters and red jogging bottoms, noisily jangling charity tins. As Max and Albert reached into their pockets for loose change they were drawn back into the moment and the communal ambience of the Dog and Duck, the melodic refrains of a street musician busking just outside the pub window and the laughter of children in a nearby playground all offering a welcoming reassurance of the ongoing normality of everyday existence.

Max and Albert left the pub and walked the short distance along Bateman Street and into the busy thoroughfare of Oxford Street heading for Tottenham Court Road tube station. Arriving at the station, reluctantly they said their goodbyes; both knew it was unlikely that they would ever see each other again. Max was due to fly back to Australia within the next few days and they agreed to keep in touch. Albert thanked Max for revealing the details of the private conversation that he'd had with Max all those years ago and said that he would pass on the information to the rest of the gang. Albert grinned, saying they would be intrigued to learn of Gabriel's dubious connections to the secret services of both the UK and Russia. He also assured Max that he'd inform them of his professionally based speculations about Gabriel's condition and would ask the friends to face up to the possibility that Gabriel's mind may have become disturbed and unbalanced.

21

Jake's eventful encounter with Gabriel

Gabriel had been classified as a "bed blocker," an elderly patient who had been deemed medically fit for discharge but continued to occupy a bed. Hospital managers were under pressure to release beds and the decision to transfer Gabriel to a rehabilitation unit in Grays once made was enacted suddenly and chaotically. The fast moving sequence of events around Gabriel's relocation to the community hospital triggered his deep rooted fears and anxiety. There had been no explanation of where he was going and he knew nothing about the people who were transporting him. Once again his life was out of his control, he was afraid that in spite of his ingenious success in creating a new identity the dark forces that haunted him had returned. It was late evening when he'd arrived at his destination he was trembling, confused and frightened. He'd been grateful for the glass of milk laced with sedatives given to him by the old lady.

The following morning awakening from a long drug-induced sleep the room, that had previously been so bare and uninviting had undergone a transformation. The curtains had been opened to reveal a glass door opening out onto an ornate, well cared for garden. The scent of freshly cut grass filled the air, an easy chair with soft comfortable brightly coloured cushions had appeared and there was even a small TV on a table in the corner. Fluffy white towels had been neatly layered along a rail and a row of colourful toiletries were lined up on a shelf above the washbasin.

As Gabriel slowly began to take stock of his new environment a young doctor appeared. With a broad boyish smile he said, "Hi Wilf, welcome to the rehabilitation unit," and politely enquired how he was feeling after a night's sleep. Gabriel on hearing the doctor refer to him as Wilf, was reassured that his real identity was still unknown. After the terror that had engulfed him the previous evening, Gabriel was surprised that he did not perceive this young man to be in any way threatening; on the contrary he seemed friendly and genuinely concerned about his welfare. Gabriel found the young doctor's manner completely disarming as he chatted about football and shared his thoughts on reasons why England's team had been knocked out of the World Cup. Gabriel felt quite relaxed as the young man proceeded to give him a routine overall examination. Gabriel asked the doctor which university he'd attended thereby leading the conversation on to the subject of academic qualifications and taking the opportunity to list the letters he could claim to cite after his name. The young doctor smiled and said, "Wow that's impressive, I'll have to give you your full title and call you the Professor from now on." When his brief examination was complete he went on to tell Gabriel that he was doing remarkably well considering his age and after everything he had been through, adding that he certainly didn't look anywhere near his chronological age. Gabriel smiled and thanked the young doctor who was accustomed to dealing with people of Gabriel's age and knew that he'd managed successfully to stroke Gabriel's ego.

There were two female nurses regularly caring for him, the lady who had attempted to settle him in when he'd arrived and one just a little younger. They were both very attentive and content to help him with his personal grooming and provide him with whatever he fancied to eat or drink. However, Gabriel had always been somewhat of a voyeur and observing them closely had decided that one showed premature signs of ageing and the younger one was far too plump and matronly for his liking. He was disappointed that they were so unattractive; he'd have liked the chance to indulge in a harmless flirtation.

Gabriel was feeling stronger and becoming more confident as every day passed and had even dared to think about plans for his future. The younger of the two nurses had kindly provided him with a writing pad and a biro and he was busy compiling a complicated escape plan in a diagrammatic form. The kind nurse had told him that he was in a hospital in Grays, Essex. This, his current location he represented with a circle at the centre of the page. A series of arrows radiating out were his optional escape routes, a variety of mathematical symbols denoting the likely probability of the success of each option. Gabriel engrossed in the task didn't hear Jake tap lightly on the door and didn't look up when he tapped him on the shoulder saying, "Hello Gabriel old boy, great to see you, we've all been so worried about you." Gabriel didn't recognise the voice and was alarmed at hearing the name Gabriel. Without raising his head he replied, "You've got the wrong person, mate, my name's Wilf," waving the back of his hand dismissively towards Jake clearly indicating that he wished to be left alone.

Gabriel's hands started to tremble, the pen he had been holding dropped to the floor, his heart was racing, he tried to speak but his breathing had become laboured. Jake witnessing the sudden dramatic change, immediately summoned a nurse. "What's the matter Wilf?" she asked, taking him by the hand and turning to Jake saying accusingly, "What have you said that's caused him to be so upset?" Jake shook his head in disbelief at the suggestion that he may have caused the reaction and replied curtly, "I only said hello."

Gabriel's frail body was now quivering, as if he was freezing cold and the nurse wrapped a blanket around his shoulders. He looked up and with wide eyes stared directly at Jake and Jake knew instantly that Gabriel recognised him. Gabriel looked away and although struggling to catch his breath, he managed to utter, "Go, go, go away."

Jake was upset to see Gabriel in such a frail and vulnerable state and not wishing to cause him any further distress decided that it was better that he leave the room and leave Gabriel in the hands of the capable young nurse who seemed to have developed a close rapport with him. As he made his way along the long corridor Jake felt helpless, he wanted to help Gabriel but if Gabriel was denying that he even knew him then how could he be of any help. He emerged from the long corridor out into a sunny summer evening, the hospital was set in large grounds; this must have once been an old stately home he thought. He sat down near a small fountain, the sound of the water gently cascading down was surprisingly soothing and Jake began to relax and to think more clearly about the situation. He reached in his jeans pocket for his mobile phone; there were a series of text messages from the "gang". His heart lifted as he read them, all the messages were sharing his concerns and asking for the latest news about Gabriel. It was good to know he was not alone in trying to find answers to help solve the crazy complex situation in which Gabriel had somehow become embroiled. The last message he had received was from Albert who had written,

"How is Gabriel? I met up with Max a few days ago; he was over here for a few weeks. He had some very interesting information about Gabriel. A lot of what he told me could be relevant to his current situation. Will explain when I see you. We need to meet up soon." Albert.

Jake was about to call Albert and arrange a meeting when he was distracted by a piercingly loud repetitive sound emanating from the hospital building. Minutes later he watched as people in orderly groups emerged from the main door, some identifiable as in-patients by their night wear attire and accompanied by porters, nurses and doctors. It was clear to Jake that an evacuation procedure was being implemented. He made his way towards the crowd that was assembling on a courtyard some distance away from the main building and mingled amongst them hoping to find Gabriel but there was no sign of him. He stopped and looked back towards the main building where patients in wheelchairs were being brought out. It was then that he saw Gabriel, a blanket still wrapped around his shoulders and being wheeled along a pathway towards the courtyard by the young nurse who had asked Jake to leave. He watched as they came nearer to him and deliberately moved to the back of the crowd fearful that the nurse would once again insist that he left the premises. "Is this a routine fire drill ?" Jake asked a young man standing next to him. "Don't think so mate," replied the man, pointing to the east side of the building where plumes of smoke were appearing out of an open window, adding, "Some old geezer's probably lit up a fag and fallen asleep."

Jake looked towards the near edge of the large crowd where Gabriel had been parked alongside other wheelchair patients, he was relieved to see that the young nurse had left him there with the others and was chatting with a group of nurses assembled in a corner of the yard. Jake knew this could be his chance to try and talk to Gabriel on his own and he slowly made his way over to him. Jake was surprised to see that Gabriel appeared to be quite relaxed, observing with interest everything that was going on around him. Jake fearful of Gabriel's reaction at seeing him again approached tentatively but as he got closer to him, Gabriel waved and began to lever himself out of the wheelchair with his arms. Once standing he beckoned to Jake to follow him and began walking with short shuffling steps but moving remarkably quickly across the grass towards a large tree. Jake soon caught up with him and gently took Gabriel's arm as a gesture of support. "Over there," ordered Gabriel pointing to an impressive weeping willow tree. Together they made their way to the back of the tree where Gabriel parted the leafy low overhanging branches of the tree to reveal a secluded space where they stood hidden from view protected by a curtain formed by the cascading leafy branches. "In here, where no one can see or hear us," said Gabriel. Gabriel stared at Jake intently for a while before saying, "I need your help but I'm not certain that I can trust you?"

"Of course you can trust me Gabriel and I'll do whatever I can to help you," replied Jake.

In spite of the sincerity of Jake's reply, Gabriel looked angry and shouted, "Don't call me Gabriel my name is Wilf, you must promise never to call me Gabriel or to tell anyone that my name was ever Gabriel. I've worked hard to create a new identity and I want a new life, it's a crucial part of my plan to escape from the people who are searching for me and from Akemi who is trying to kill me." Jake's instinctive reaction was to laugh but instantly refrained from doing so when Gabriel, his voice shaking in trepidation pleaded, "Jake, I want to trust you and I desperately need you to help me."

Gabriel's persona changed; no longer did he appear the frail, confused character that Jake found when he first arrived at the hospital. Now he was standing erect assuming the well practised air of a confident distinguished university lecturer as he proceeded to dictate a list of tasks that he needed Jake to undertake for him. Jake listened in disbelief as one by one Gabriel reeled off his incredible demands. He was being asked to find a way to get into Akemi's flat when she was not there. Once inside he was to search for Gabriel's passport and his bank cards which Gabriel said Akemi had hidden somewhere in the flat. Then he needed him to draw money from a cash point using his bank card and bring the cash and the passport to the hospital. He must also collect boxes of Kodak slides which were in a cupboard in Akemi's bedroom, take them away from the flat and find a safety deposit box in London where they could be stored.

Jake hoping that he had found an obvious reason why it would be impossible for him to carry out Gabriel's demands said simply, "I won't be able to get into the flat, I don't have a key." But Gabriel had an answer, reminding Jake that Akemi had kept him a prisoner in that flat and that she was in the habit of locking the door behind her whenever she went out and leaving the key under a plant pot in the hallway where the neighbours knew where to find it in the case of an emergency. "She's a robotic creature," Gabriel explained disdainfully, "She'll never deviate from her routine, and you'll find the key there."

Remembering a recent conversation he'd had with Akemi's neighbour Rosie, Jake knew that Akemi and Gabriel's relationship was not a happy one, but why would she hide his passport and bank cards, a question he put to Gabriel. Gabriel's response only served to add to the intrigue. "She's being paid by the people who are trying to kill me; she is getting cash for keeping me a prisoner in the flat and forcing me to take medication that will ultimately destroy my brain cells. Jake you must believe me, do these things I've asked of you and tell no one and I mean no one."

Jake was well aware of the problems he needed to overcome in order to do what Gabriel was asking of him and hoped that he could persuade Gabriel to allow him to get help from their mutual friends. "But what about the others in the old gang, they are all concerned about you and I'm sure they would want to help." Gabriel reacted angrily to the suggestion, "No, no, you must not say anything about this to any of them I don't know who I can trust anymore. The people who are looking for me are clever and ruthless; they will have been monitoring all my friends and will not hesitate to use them to get to me. They've done it before, they knew Max was my friend so they funded his research project and persuaded him to use me as a participant in a clinical trial. One of their agents pretending to be Albert visited me in Akemi's but I knew immediately that he wasn't Albert. You must be very careful because they will be watching you and they will try to get you on their side by telling you that I am crazy and imagining all these things."

Jake was becoming increasingly uncomfortable, sensing that he was inadvertently being drawn into a dark world of conspiracy and deceit and it was a world that he wanted no part in. It was with welcome relief that he heard the reprimanding voice of the nurse charged with Gabriel's care demanding to know what was going as she brushed apart the low lying tree branches with Gabriel's empty wheelchair. Jake stared in amazement at what happened next, the articulate and confident Gabriel completely transformed right before his eyes. Lowering his head, hunching his shoulders and stumbling into the chair, he feigned breathlessness and his hands were shaking, once again slipping effortlessly into the role of a vulnerable helpless old man. The nurse tucked a blanket over Gabriel's lap and legs, saying, "Everything is OK Wilf, we've been told it's safe to go back inside now." She glared at Jake saying, "I don't know what has been going on but I think you should leave now."

Gabriel was staring at the grass and refusing to make eye contact or give any sign that he knew Jake. Jake quickly made his way to the car park wanting desperately to get away from the place and regretting that he'd been the one who'd volunteered to visit Gabriel. As he left the car park and turned on to the main highway, his mind was in overdrive frantically trying to make sense of Gabriel's astonishing accusations and the enormity of what Gabriel had asked of him. Jake was naturally a cautious driver but that day his attention was not focussed on the road ahead; he was unaware that he had driven through a red traffic light when an unmarked police car overtook him; an arm through the open window placed a blue flashing siren on the car roof and indicated to Jake to pull into a nearside lay-by. Two plain clothed policemen approached Jake's car opened his door asking him to step out. Jake remembering Gabriel's warning that he would be watched was immediately fearful and mistrustful. He was informed that he had gone through a red light at speed and was asked for his documents which fortunately he was able to produce. It was a brief encounter; he was given a warning and informed that he would acquire points on his licence. The officers drove off and Jake shaken by the episode sat in the lay-by watching the cars speeding past, his mind replaying over and over again Gabriel's incredible revelations about the complicated network of conspiracy surrounding his life. Inadvertently his decision to visit Gabriel that day had thrown his simple orderly life into confusion. He reached for his phone desperately needing to talk to someone. He sat for a long time grasping his phone tightly in the palm of his hand, torn between his loyalty to Gabriel and a desperate need to share the burden of what he knew with someone. Something that Gabriel had expressly made him promise not to do. It was a well timed call from Sasha that helped with this dilemma, the welcome sound of a familiar voice, "Hi, Jake I've been waiting to hear from you, how was Gabriel?" Jake hesitated unsure of what he was going to say, Sasha picked up immediately on the hesitation and asked, "Jake are you OK, is something wrong?"

In spite of Gabriel's warnings Jake wanted to tell Sasha everything, he believed without any doubt that he could trust her; they had been close friends and confidantes for years. But he didn't know where to start it was far too complicated to explain in a phone call and the seeds of mistrust and conspiracy that Gabriel had planted led to the thought that his phone might be tapped. Jake simply said, "Sasha, it's so good to hear your voice, I'm on my way back to London and I'd appreciate it if I could call in for a chat and a coffee."

"Of course, I've nothing planned for this evening, it'll be good to see you Jake," replied Sasha.

22

Gabriel's plan

Gabriel's nurse concerned that night was falling and sensing a chill in the air wrapped a blanket around Gabriel and wheeled him back to the hospital. Gabriel sat with his head lowered and his shoulders hunched giving the appearance of a lost soul locked in his own little world. But in reality he was taking the opportunity to assess the layout of the hospital. Out of the corner of his eye he could see the car park and the direction that the cars were taking as they left, deducing this must be the direction needed to reach the long driveway and the impressive gate that he remembered from the night that he'd arrived. Approaching the main doorway leading into the hospital he could see there were CCTV cameras strategically focussed on the car park. Once inside he made a mental note of a telephone number for a taxi clearly displayed on the side window of the reception desk. Seeing that the desk was unmanned he noted the time on the large round wall clock above the desk which read 7.30pm.

It was the first time since he'd arrived at the hospital that he'd been outside of his room and now knowing that he was returning, he focussed on mentally mapping the maze of corridors. First left, second right, first left past a nurse's station and through a long ward until they reached Room 5, one of the few private rooms and the one which he had been allocated. Once inside the room he deliberately refused to speak to the nurse whilst she helped him out of the chair and onto the bed. There were so many facts in his head and he didn't want any distractions that might erase them. He wanted her to leave him alone so that he could retrieve his notebook from under the mattress where he had hidden it and accurately record the observations that he had so carefully made. He had always prided himself on having a photographic memory but was aware this precious asset had been adversely affected by the medication that Akemi had forced upon him. He could remember past events in great detail but had realised with alarm that sometimes he could not remember if he had eaten breakfast that day.

His nurse seemed disinclined to leave, busying herself by pouring a fresh jug of water for him and insisting on taking his temperature saying she was worried that he might have caught a chill. Gabriel was growing more and more frustrated with her procrastinations and had difficulty in controlling his strong impulse to tell her to "– – – - off." Instead he laid his head back on the pillow and closed his eyes hoping that if she thought he was asleep she'd leave. He felt her gentle hand on his brow as she brushed his hair away from his forehead. It was a tender touch evoking memories of his many flirtatious liaisons; he opened his eyes and closed them again quickly. She was moving towards the door before closing it quietly behind her. It was a shame, he thought, that this nurse was not younger and more attractive because she did seem to be very kind and attentive to him. He smiled to himself believing that he could still woo any woman of any age He reached for his precious notebook containing his secret escape plan. He began filling in details on a map tracing from memory the twists and turns of the corridors that would lead him to the reception desk and the main entrance/exit. A rectangle marked the reception desk and inside the number that he might need to call for a taxi and a note of the time when it might be unmanned; in Gabriel's inimitable way substituting the numbers he'd remembered with letters corresponding to their numerical location in the alphabet. The map continued to represent the area of the car park, the location of the CCTV cameras and the direction he'd concluded that he would need to follow to reach the main gate.

If only he could get to the main gate then the next part of his escape plan would be easy. His starting point of Grays in Essex was fortuitous he thought, it wasn't too far from London, it must be straightforward to get from here to Tower Hill underground in East London and from there the Circle Line would take him directly to St. Pancras and the Eurostar. The final leg of his journey would take him through the Eurotunnel to Paris. He'd then simply jump in a taxi to one of his favourite hotels; the Hotel Cluny in the Latin Quarter. He'd discovered the place when he was presenting a paper on European Rail Networks at the Sorbonne which was just across the road from this small hotel. Perhaps the lovely Nicole might still be working there, the lovely Nicole who delivered coffee and croissants to his room every morning although room service was definitely not one of the facilities provided in the small establishment.

Gabriel preoccupied with the details of his plan and his dreams for his future suddenly awakened to the reality that it all depended on Jake whom he was relying upon to provide him with the cash he needed and his passport. If Jake did not do as he'd asked then all his plans would be to no avail. On reflection Gabriel began to question the wisdom of his decision that day to confide in Jake. It had been an impetuous decision taken at an opportune moment. These days Gabriel trusted no one so why in that moment did he think that he could trust Jake? Jake was a steady sort of guy, an accountant who true to form would organise information in a simple linear fashion and insist on getting things right. Gabriel had often stayed at Jake's Bayswater flat after a night out in that part of London. Jake had purchased the flat in the late 1970s when property prices in London were within the reach of an aspiring accountant. Gabriel had advised him against the decision, telling him that he would lose his freedom if he shackled himself with a mortgage. Now Gabriel envied Jake's fashionable London property, although he disapproved of Jake's taste in furniture and general decor. He disliked the orderliness of the flat, the towels lined up neatly and the meticulously tidy cupboards where nothing was ever out of place. Gabriel took pleasure in teasing Jake about his fastidious traits and his unadventurous lifestyle. If he was being honest with himself he would have to admit that he thought of Jake as a rather boring character but of all the people that he knew he was probably the most reliable.

* * *

Meanwhile Jake had made his way back to London. After his brief telephone conversation with Sasha he'd regained his composure and had made his way safely back to his Bayswater home. Sasha's small flat that she rented above a cafe on the Portobello Road was just a mile away and as Jake walked along the busy London streets he wondered how Sasha would react to what he was about to tell her. Instinctively he knew his decision to confide in Sasha and tell her everything that had happened during his strange meeting with Gabriel that afternoon had been the right one.

He mounted the fire escape steps that led to the front door of the flat and knocked on the door expecting Sasha to open the door with her usual welcoming manner and was taken aback when it was not Sasha but Alec who greeted him warmly, "Hi Jake, Sasha rang me to say you were calling in, it's good to see you mate." Jake had never been more pleased to see anyone, he and Alec were good friends and since Gabriel's disappearance they had spent time together discussing and sharing their concerns for their old friend. Neither Jake nor Alec trusted Akemi and both were suspicious about her motives. Jake knew that he had to relieve himself of the burden Gabriel had laid on his shoulder and having already made the decision to confide in Sasha in spite of Gabriel's warnings not to trust anyone, he knew it would be safe to go one step further and include Alec in the revelations They moved through the small hallway into Sasha's small cosy living room where Sasha embraced him with an affectionate hug and Alec held up a bottle of Shiraz asking Jake's approval of his choice before he uncorked it. Jake sank into a comfy arm chair with a large glass of red wine in his hand feeling safe at last.

When Sasha said, "Go on tell us everything Jake, how was Gabriel? Why did he disappear?" Jake needed little encouragement to talk, the words pouring out as he recounted everything as it had happened. He told how at first Gabriel had pretended that he did not know him and his insistence that his name was Wilf. Then the strange sequence of events that followed when the fire alarm had sounded and the hospital was evacuated. The conspiracy theories revealed under cover of the willow tree where Gabriel had appeared to be frightened but rational and very much in control. The list of demands Gabriel had made of him, demands that Jake felt placed unrealistic expectations on him, demands that he was not sure he could or should undertake Finally Jake described how he had witnessed Gabriel's incredible ability to physically transform himself into a vacant frail old man when his nurse had appeared. Jake spoke quickly the words pouring out like a gushing stream allowing Sasha and Alec no opportunity to interrupt the fast flowing verbal torrent.

Finally Jake picked up his glass of wine and gasped with relief before drinking, the tension within him had slowly unwound as his story had unfolded. Sasha and Alec who had silently listened in wide eyed amazement and disbelief were speechless. Alec was the first to speak, "Bloody hell, Jake, what a mess." Sasha was more sceptical saying, "But how do we know if any of it is true, he could just be making it all up in order to get attention, we all know what he's like?" Jake so relieved at having recounted the day's events at last felt he could relax. He slowly sipped his red wine content to sit back and listen to the pair as they voiced their thoughts on what he had told them.

Alec went on to say that he also had some information that he needed to share with them. He'd recently been in touch with Albert who said Max had been over from Australia and that he'd met up with him in the Dog and Duck. It was about the time Gabriel went missing so naturally they had a conversation about their mutual old friend. Apparently many years ago Gabriel had confided in Max about his dubious connections to the secret services of both the UK and Russia. When Albert had explained the problems Gabriel was experiencing with Akemi and his very real fears that she was poisoning him with unnecessary medication, Max had laughed. Max explained that as a neurologist he found Gabriel to be a very interesting character, describing him as having a tendency to cultivate a self image in which he always had to appear special, successful and important. Now Gabriel had aged he could not accept the consequent imperfection in his life and had to find someone or something to blame.

"It's a possibility that Gabriel could be using persecutory beliefs and conspiracy theories to explain what is happening to him," commented Sasha.

"I know it sounds a likely possibility given Gabriel's psychological profile," replied Alec, he'd thought a lot about Max's professional opinion as recounted to him by Albert but there were many things that didn't add up. Firstly, Max had admitted to Albert that Gabriel had agreed to take part in a neurological research project many years ago but denied that he had any involvement in the research after he left London and as far as he knew the funding for the project ended years ago. But Gabriel genuinely believed that he was part of a drug trial and that the medication that was being forcibly inflicted upon him by Akemi was poisoning him.

Secondly, Alec wanted to emphasise that Gabriel, before taking up the lecturing post at Oxford, had been employed by the British Government that he'd studied Russian and these were the days of the Cold War when young graduates with the right profile were targeted by the international spy network. Albert had told Alec that he had often had reason to seriously think that Gabriel might be a spy and had recalled the strange things he'd experienced when travelling with Gabriel. He'd described how many times Gabriel had been singled out at an airport for questioning. The way Gabriel inspected his hotel rooms as if looking for listening devices and his vigilance when out and about, constantly looking over his shoulder. His insistence on never taking the first taxi that offered a fare but waiting for a second and sometimes a third to pull up.

Finally, Alec raised the question of Gabriel's relationship with Akemi. He and Jake had already had a number of discussions about this and had agreed that although Akemi was keen to demonstrate to any visitor that she was caring for Gabriel and had his best interests at heart neither of them were convinced of her sincerity. Alec had for a long time had suspicions about Akemi's motives in spite of his wife Yumiko's insistence that Akemi cared deeply for Gabriel and that it was Gabriel who had always used Akemi. They had all assumed that he had finally decided to settle down with Akemi after whatever had happened with that other woman in Japan but perhaps things were not what they appeared to be. Jake's suspicions had been heightened after his conversation with Akemi's neighbour Rosie on the day Gabriel had disappeared. He recounted how Rosie had told him about hearing raised voices from next door with Akemi shouting aggressively that Gabriel must take his medication and how a couple of times she'd heard Gabriel shout out, "No, no, please don't hit me." Akemi had tried to explain these things by saying to her that Gabriel was "a mad man". But Rosie had spoken to Gabriel one day as he was returning from the barber's and to her surprise he'd seemed perfectly normal and friendly, he'd just been to the barber's shop around the corner and helped her to carry the pushchair up the stairs. She'd laughed, saying she'd had the strange feeling that he was trying to flirt with her. Sasha grinned and said, "She was probably right."

Suddenly, there was a heavy silence; it was as if all three of them were struggling individually to process the seriousness and complexities of the situation. Sasha went into the kitchen, returning with another bottle of wine and proceeded to fill the empty glasses on the coffee table. Alec unsure of Sasha and Jake's reaction to the thoughts he'd expressed was the first to break the silence, announcing, "I'm simply trying to be objective about the situation."

Alec sipped his wine before revealing the conclusion that he had personally reached, "It seems to me that we have a choice, we can simply accept Max's hypothetical assessment and diagnosis of Gabriel's condition, in which case we simply have to sit back and watch as he deteriorates. The alternative is that we take Gabriel's fears seriously and we try and do as he asks. I am very fond of Gabriel as I know you both are and I want to help him and I have a strong inclination to try and find out the truth." Alec hesitated briefly before stating firmly, "I will carry out the instructions that he gave you Jake, I will go into the flat and try to find the things he needs, and I know that I have to do it for Gabriel's sake and for my own peace of mind."

Sasha and Jake had sat quietly and patiently listening to Alec and he felt very uneasy, unsure of what their reaction might be to the decision he'd just made. Sasha sensing Alec's unease reached across and laid her hand on his, "You're right Alec, we have a choice and I don't want my choice to be that I do nothing and I'll help in any way I can." Jake, a cautious individual by nature had nevertheless also been persuaded by Alec's arguments and he too wholeheartedly gave his approval for taking any actions necessary to find out the reality of what might be happening to their friend.

A muffled sound of a phone ringing distracted from the intensity of the moment. Alec delved into his coat pocket to retrieve the phone to see that it was Yumiko. On answering he was greeted with Yumiko's reprimanding tone, "Are you still at Sasha's because it's getting late?"

"Yes, I'm still here," replied Alec, adding, "I'll be home soon and by the way, have you spoken to Akemi lately?"

"Yes," she replied, "I called her, she's really at her wit's end with worry about Gabriel, I tried to comfort her and wished that I could give her the news that he's been found."

"Please tell me that you did not tell her?" said Alec.

"No, I didn't because you were so insistent that I shouldn't, but I am worried about her and I don't understand why we can't tell her." Alec quickly saw an opportunity to take advantage of his wife's friendship with Akemi and suggested that she invite Akemi over to dinner one evening soon. Yumiko was quick to agree to the suggestion saying that she would ring Akemi in the morning.

It was already late in the evening but the friends seemed unaware of the time as they held up their refilled glasses, offered a toast to Gabriel and swore their commitment to him and to each other. Enthusiastically they set about devising a strategy to accomplish their intended mission. They agreed that for the time being they would not reveal anything about their plan to anyone and that they would go together to Akemi's flat and search for the items Gabriel had requested. Alec outlined his plan to ensure Akemi would be out of the flat, a plan which he'd hurriedly formulated during the short conversation with his wife. "Yumiko will invite her to our place for an evening meal and when she arrives, I'll make some excuse to leave them alone, they'll be free to talk incessantly in Japanese and I'm sure they won't mind if I pop out for a while and join you two on our mission."

The friends relieved at the consensus of their response to Jake's bizarre encounter with Gabriel at the hospital that day refilled their glasses and made another toast, this time, "to a successful mission". As they reflected with a sense of almost disbelief on the absurd reality of the decision they had just made, Sasha burst out in laughter immediately followed by giggles from Jake and Alec. Sasha, normally a very reserved person, seemed to lose her inhibitions when fuelled with red wine and suggested they should go in disguise in case anyone recognised them. She disappeared for a moment into the bedroom returning with a pair of tights and proceeded to pull them over her face. Jake amidst his hiccups brought on by laughing, added to the hilarity by pointing out that these days gangsters always wear plain, dark tracksuits with the jacket hoods pulled over their heads and with October Halloween celebrations already in full swing they could easily hide their faces with masks. Sasha trying to appear straight faced and serious announced, "I have something that might be very useful," she left the room returning with something covered in a tea towel. Alec and Jake's infectious giggling stopped suddenly, when Sasha removed the tea towel to reveal a small, black pistol. "Bloody hell, Sash where did you get that?" demanded Alec.

"I thought it might come in handy if we get followed by any secret agents," she replied nonchalantly. Seeing the alarm on their faces, Sasha once again burst into uncontrollable laughter, finally managing to gain her composure to explain that it was only a toy gun, nonetheless a very realistic looking one and that it belonged to Alfie, her five year old nephew.

When Alec and Jake bid Sasha good night and went their separate ways, they knew they would remember that night when together they shared their concerns for their mutual friend. Little did they know, however, that as future events unfolded, they would relive those moments time and time again and come to question the rationality of the decisions they had made that night.

23

The complicity of friends

The next morning Sasha woke with a heavy head and a vague nagging recollection of the previous evening, she pulled the quilt over her head momentarily blanking out the world. Eventually she arose and headed for the kitchen where the neat line of empty red wine bottles lined up on the kitchen table had the sobering effect of bringing her memories of the past evening sharply into focus. "Oh my God," she said out loud, as she robotically went through the motions of making a cup of tea.

Grateful that it was a Sunday and that she hadn't made any plans for the day Sasha was about to curl up in the comfort of her armchair, hands cupped around her mug of tea, when she noticed a new message flashing on her answer machine. It was Alec, Sasha listened to the message and hearing Alec speaking slowly with a slightly slurring voice, she could tell that he too was suffering the effects of the previous evening's over-indulgence on red wine.

"Hi, Sasha, don't expect you're up and about yet. What a night! Anyway Yumiko is going to invite Akemi to come over for dinner on Friday evening. Have spoken already to Jake

*and he's got nothing on that night. Hope you're free on Friday;
it's our chance to get on with the plan. Are you still up for it?
Call me when you get this message."*

Sasha felt her heart racing and couldn't be sure whether it was
excitement or fear, everything was happening so quickly and she
had never done anything so daring before. She decided to call Alec
straight away to confirm that she was free. She knew that if she
stopped to contemplate her decision to go along with their plan
she was likely to get cold feet and change her mind. They arranged
to meet in the coffee bar on Ealing Broadway at 7pm on Friday
evening from where it was only a five minute walk to Akemi's flat.

At regular intervals throughout the day Yumiko called Akemi's
number to be greeted only by an answering machine and the
monotone of an impersonal pre-recorded message. Yumiko was
reluctant to offer her invitation to dinner with a few words left on
a machine and decided to keep trying. When late in the afternoon
Akemi eventually answered her call, Yumiko could not hide her
frustration, "Where have you been? I've been trying all day to call
you."

Akemi's voice was shaky and faltering as she explained that
she'd spent the day walking around the streets of Ealing calling
in the local cafes and bars Gabriel frequented and asking if
anyone had seen him. She added that it was what she did every
day. Yumiko did not know how to reply to this, she desperately
wanted to tell her that Gabriel was safe in a rehabilitation hospital
but she had made a promise to Alec that she would not tell her
until he said that she could. She was torn by her divided loyalties
but decided to keep her promise to her husband and say nothing
about the matter. Instead she offered the invitation to dinner,
"Alec and I haven't seen you for a while and we thought it would
be nice if you'd have dinner with us on Friday evening." Akemi
was a little hesitant at first saying that she was afraid that she
wouldn't be very good company but Yumiko was persuasively

insistent and in the end Akemi very kindly agreed to accept the invitation.

Akemi considered it very bad manners to be late for any social gathering and she would always arrive five minutes early. On Friday evening, Akemi rang the doorbell at exactly five minutes to six, six o'clock being the agreed arrival time. She brought with her a large bouquet of flowers, a box of chocolates and a bottle of red wine. Yumiko greeted her with a hug and Alec kissed her gently on both cheeks. Alec, well schooled in Japanese etiquette knew exactly what time she would arrive and had arranged for Jake to call. On cue Alec's mobile rang, it was Jake pretending to be a work colleague and reminding him of an important staff meeting taking place that evening. Yumiko pleaded, "Alec don't go, tell him we are entertaining a guest, I've spent all afternoon preparing the dinner for us." But to no avail, Alec made his apologies to Akemi, pecked Yumiko on the cheek, saying "It's important, I must go, I promise I won't be long," and he quickly disappeared out of the door. With Akemi safely out of the way, he was on his way to meet Sasha and Jake and put the final stage of their daring plan into action.

Sasha was surprised at how excited she felt as she made her way to Notting Hill Gate and negotiated the labyrinth of underground passages to board a Central Line train to Ealing Broadway. Sasha's sense of anticipation and the feeling that she was embarking on an important mission grew as the train hurtled its way through the blackness. The train was busy, passengers rushing on and off as it abruptly came to a stop at the stations en route, Holland Park, Shepherds Bush, and White City. Since that eventful evening and the revelations about Gabriel's life, Sasha seemed to have developed a heightened sense of awareness of what was going on around her. She discreetly scrutinised the other commuters, all clearly intent on avoiding any communication with anyone else. Some boarded the train and immediately closed their eyes, the clearly observable earphones an indication that they were pre-occupied. Others had eyes firmly rooted on an open book but never turning a page. Sasha sensed the underlying tension that to these city dwellers had become the norm.

Sasha was the last passenger to leave the carriage when it terminated at Ealing Broadway and as she made her way along the platform she reflected on the experience of her short journey. It had revealed to her a depressing picture of the futility and alienation of everyday life in a city as crowded as London. It was at that moment that she knew for certain that her decision to cooperate in a plan with Alec and Jake to help their old friend Gabriel was the right and the humane thing to do.

The agreed rendez-vous was just across the road from the tube station; Alec had driven across London and parked up in the road outside Akemi's flat just a short walk away from the cafe where Jake had been waiting for him. They rose to greet Sasha taking it in turns to give her a warm hug and a peck on her cheek.

"Afraid we don't have time for a coffee, Sash. We need to get over to the flat. Akemi's happily tucking into Yumiko's cooking, right now, I've made an excuse to pop out for a couple of hours but I suspect Yumiko will be ringing soon to see when I intend to return."

It was only a short distance to the block of flats, the first challenge was to gain entry through the main door into the block, and access could only be gained via an intercom. Jake had an answer, he pressed number 22 and when a female voice answered, he said, "Hello Rosie, this is Jake, do you remember me I'm a friend of Gabriel."

"Yes, hello I do remember you," came the reply. "Can you let me in?" A buzzer sounded and the door swung open. They quickly climbed the flights of stairs and found Rosie waiting for them at the door of her flat. Jake took control of the situation introducing Alec and Sasha as close friends of Gabriel and explaining to Rosie that Gabriel had been found and was safe and well in hospital and he'd asked them to get some things from the flat. Jake knowing that Rosie shared their concerns about Gabriel's relationship with Akemi asked her to trust them and not tell Akemi that they had been to the flat or that Gabriel had been found. Rosie said that she understood and quickly agreed to do as they asked.

Jake retrieved the key from the plant pot and the three of them entered the flat, they moved quickly through the small hallway, cluttered with carrier bags, walking sticks and umbrellas and into the lounge which in comparison was tidy, video cassettes lined up neatly and alphabetically next to the TV and books tidily displayed on a tall narrow bookcase. Cautiously they peered into the two sparsely furnished small bedrooms. Each of the rooms had a single mattress on the floor covered with dark blue quilts and an opaque sliding door with a little round handle opening to reveal a big wall closet built into the wall. Alec, who frequently accompanied Yumiko when visiting her family in Japan, commented that the rooms were typical of Japanese bedrooms.

Jake opened the closet, inside, Gabriel's clothing hung neatly along a rail, parting the clothes he could see that the closet went from the floor to the ceiling and was cut deep into the wall, lining the wall at the far back of the closet were yellow Kodak boxes stacked neatly one on top of the other. "I've found the slides he wants," he announced excitedly. Sasha peering into the deep closet said jokingly, "Is this the entrance to Narnia?" She opened the drawers of a small chest that stood inside the closet, there were jumbled mounds of socks, underpants, handkerchiefs and scarves. Sasha guiltily ferreted through the piles, these were Gabriel's personal things and she could not help but feel uncomfortable with the thought that she was intruding into his personal space. Her hands rested on a rolled up pair of socks that felt unusually bulky. When she uncoupled the pair a bundle of rolled up £20 notes tumbled out. "Look, there's a stash of money hidden in these socks." Alec unfurled the roll and counted twenty notes, announcing to the others, "There's £400 here." Sasha discovered five more bundles rolled up in the socks. Simply comparing the size of the rolls they estimated that in total there was at least £2000. "Any sign of his credit cards or his passport?" Sasha systematically searched all the drawers and replied, "No luck."

Alec had moved into the other bedroom and was searching the wall closet containing Akemi's clothes, shoes, handbags and suitcases. Alec searched through the suitcases finding only clothes neatly packed into them. The handbags were mostly empty save for some loose change and some odd make-up items. He was about to give up on the search when he noticed what appeared to be a book amongst the shoes that lined the floor of the closet. He picked it up and realised that it was actually a small box designed to look like a book. Tentatively he opened it and eureka, the box contained passports all of them belonging to Gabriel. There were old blue British ones that had long expired and a few of the less impressive small red European ones which also had the corners of the cover trimmed showing they were no longer valid.

"Jake, Alec, come see this there's a virtual pharmacy in here it's incredible," shouted Sasha from the small kitchen. She was standing in front of an open cupboard where every shelf was filled with hundreds of different coloured boxes of tablets, sterile packets of syringes and plastic yellow boxes for the disposal of needles. "God, that's an amazing amount of medication, either Gabriel is seriously and I mean seriously ill or perhaps what he's told me is true and he really is an unwilling participant in a drug trial," said Jake. Shaking his head as if not wanting to believe what he was seeing, Jake quickly shut the cupboard door urging Sasha and Alec to hurry. He showed them the many missed calls from Yumiko on his phone and a text message enquiring where he was and when he'd be home. "But we haven't found any of his credit cards," pointed out Sasha.

They were interrupted by the piercing wail of police car sirens, the pitch and intensity increasing as they came nearer, Alec peering through the blind on the kitchen window into the street below could see blue flashing lights coming down the hill heading directly towards the flats. The cars skidded, tyres squealing on the tarmac, eventually coming to a stop and effectively blocking the exit from the flat car park.

Jake, Sasha and Alec stood transfixed in the hallway of Akemi's top floor flat as the police officers approached the main entrance to the block. Alec moved quickly to retrieve the yellow Kodak boxes which had been stacked outside the door of the flat, placing them inside the door, and then he locked the door from the inside and turned off the lights. "I'm scared," whispered Sasha, Jake put his arm round her hoping to reassure but knew it was in vain when he felt her trembling beneath his touch. Alec put his finger to his lips gesturing to them both to stay quiet.

There was a lot of noise coming from downstairs, people were shouting angrily, there was the sound of glass breaking and repeated loud thumps as if a door was being battered or kicked down. Alec gently lifted the letter box flap and peered through the slit getting a brief snapshot of the events taking place on the ground floor, a young woman wearing a head scarf and head lowered was seated on the first step holding a small child wrapped in a blanket. Two men dressed in Arabic style clothing were struggling unsuccessfully to resist being handcuffed by the police. Jake watched as they were forced to lie face down on the floor and their hands bound with the cuffs behind their backs before being led out to the police cars. The remaining officers went into the flat beckoning to the young women with the baby to follow them.

Jake whispered what he'd seen to Sasha and Jake. "Let's get out of here," cried Sasha. Alec looking out of the kitchen window could see that the three police cars were still there blocking the exit. Alec sighed and said, "We have to wait, just sit it out until they leave."

"I really thought that it might be something to do with all this Gabriel business and they had come to get us." said Sasha, her voice trembling. "To be honest, so did I," agreed Jake, reminding them that Gabriel had warned him that there were people out there who would try and harm anyone who tried to help him. Alec knew that he needed to disperse their fears if they were to continue in their plan to help Gabriel and pointed out that what they had just experienced was unfortunately part of everyday London life. "Those men sitting in the police cars out there may be illegal immigrants, potential terrorists, human traffickers, who knows? It's just an unfortunate coincidence and has nothing whatsoever to do with Gabriel," argued Alec. He hoped this pragmatic explanation would allay their fears but seeing the worried expressions on both faces he couldn't be sure.

It wasn't long before once again the night sky was lit up by the rhythmic rotation of blue light followed by the wailing of sirens signaling the departure of the police cars. The three had anxiously awaited that moment, "Let's go," said Jake. They cautiously dismounted the stairs, Jake and Alec with their arms encasing yellow Kodak boxes held securely by their chins rested on top of each pile. Sasha gripped an inconspicuous plastic carrier bag containing Gabriel's out of date passports and his "money socks". On reaching the ground floor they could see a flat door had been broken down and the opening bore the blue and white plastic tape indicating a police scene and forbidding unauthorised entry.

Once outside, they lost no time in loading the boxes into the car and driving away, Jake having to remind Alec of the 30 mile zone limit as he raced through Acton and Shepherd's Bush towards central London. Alec was heading for a self storage unit near Paddington Station where they'd already planned to deposit the boxes of photographic slides. Once the boxes were safely locked away the friends relaxed, Sasha suggested that they stop for a drink in the Victoria pub which was close by, an old haunt of theirs back in their carefree days. Their mood instantly uplifted when they entered the warm welcoming atmosphere of the Victoria in Strathearn Place. It was the last day of October, and Halloween night and the pub was full of party goers dressed in macabre style costumes, The merriment was infectious, the trio raised their glasses in a toast to Gabriel, followed by another to congratulate themselves on having achieved their objective and done what he'd asked in spite of the dramatic events of the evening.

24

Akemi reveals the cross she bears

Fireworks cascaded across the London skyline and the streets thronged with Halloween party revellers, red devils their arms linked with zombies danced on the pavements. As Alec and his fellow passengers tried to negotiate their way through the narrow old streets, faces hidden behind spooky, scary masks pressed against the car windows. The London Ghost Bus Company offering a sightseeing tour in an elegantly refurbished vintage double-decker drew up beside them at a traffic light. The loud recording playing inside the bus was clearly audible to them and told of London's murky past as a city of execution, murder and haunting. The festivities they had inadvertently become caught up in left the trio feeling pleasantly light hearted after the earlier drama laden events of the evening. Continuing to navigate his route through the revelling crowds filling the London streets Alec drove to Sasha's Portobello Road flat, Jake was happy to walk the short distance from there to his home in Bayswater. Alec thanking them both for their cooperation that evening bade them both good night.

When Alec finally arrived home he was surprised to find the

house in darkness. He peeped through the lounge door to find Akemi, covered with a duvet and fast asleep on a settee. He glanced at the clock in the hall and was shocked to see that it was 2am. Perhaps because the city streets were so busy and vibrant it had genuinely seemed much earlier. He crept quietly up the stairs and carefully climbed into bed next to Yumiko and was relieved to see that she was in a deep sleep.

* * *

Alec knew that his wife had not been happy when he had made his excuse and left the planned dinner party that evening but he had his own plans for the evening and gave little thought to the fact that Yumiko was upset. Over the years he'd grown accustomed and come to expect her servile almost deferential manner towards him, accepting and welcoming her deference as a reflection of their cultural differences.

Yumiko's cultural inclination towards and demonstration of subservience, however, masked a growing discontentment with her life. She could not help but compare her marriage to those of her female work colleagues whose husbands seemed to pander to their every whim. Increasingly of late she had begun to feel that Alec took all that she did for him for granted and had little consideration for her needs. Every evening she cooked a nutritious meal for them both and decorated the table with flowers and candles but often she ate alone, Alec eventually arriving home with the excuse that he'd been in a meeting that went on late into the evening. Yumiko could tell that he'd been drinking and assumed his meetings took place in a pub but she always welcomed him home politely, reluctant to give voice to her frustrations. But when Alec left for one of these meetings on the particular evening that he'd suggested they entertain Akemi, she felt she had been embarrassed in front of her friend and she was very angry.

As soon as Alec left she went into the kitchen and stood staring at the platters of food that she'd so lovingly prepared. Akemi, who understood the embarrassment that Yumiko was feeling, followed her into the kitchen, asking simply, "You OK?" Yumiko burst into tears, the anger and the resentment that she secretly harboured flooding to the surface. Akemi instinctively put her arms around her in an attempt to comfort her.

Yumiko quickly regained her composure, conforming to her ingrained cultural norm which emphasised the separation of one's private emotions and one's public expression of them. She apologised to Akemi for Alec's rudeness and for her own silly tearful over reaction. Together they carried the platters of traditional Japanese food, steamed fish, rice and pickled vegetables, placing them on the beautifully laid up table in the dining room.

They sat down together at the table, comfortable enough in each other's company to eat in silence whilst processing their personal thoughts. Yumiko was first to break the silence, the pair had once been close friends; they'd arrived together in a strange country and adapted to an unfamiliar culture together. That evening Yumiko tried to draw Akemi back to the memories of those days. She started by asking, "Akemi, do you remember the romanticised vision of London we'd shared before we left Japan and how different everything was when we got here?" Akemi responded that she remembered it well, particularly how unpredictable they'd found life in London to be. How the public transport was often delayed or cancelled without notice and how delivery services said they'd come on a certain date and didn't. Yumiko recalled, "I remember how isolated we felt because we didn't speak or understand the language very well," and mentioned the time they'd seen students queuing in a fish and chip shop and decided to buy some. Akemi remembered that time, "Yes, they were wrapped in newspapers and they tasted so horrible." The pair laughed at the memory, reliving these moments had left the girls feeling a little more relaxed and very grateful for each other's company on that evening.

Yumiko could not help but notice that Akemi had aged, she looked pale, tired and very thin. Yumiko was far too polite to comment on this change in her friend's appearance but nevertheless felt that she should ask if she was OK and how she was coping with the trauma caused by Gabriel's disappearance. Akemi replied instantly; it was as if she had been waiting for Yumiko to voice these very questions. "I tired, I so tired, I look for him every day, he all I think about," she replied tearfully. Yumiko put her arms around her knowing that it was now her turn to offer comfort. Akemi's tears began to flow and Yumiko gently took hold of both her hands. "I have to talk, I have to tell, I cannot keep the secret, I cannot keep it in me any more," spluttered Akemi between wiping her tearful eyes. She hesitated before continuing, "I know he would be so angry with me, he's forced me to keep so many of his secrets, but I cannot carry them inside me any longer.

"You and Alec and Jake and all his friends think you know Gabriel, but you do not know him," the tears had gone now replaced by anger and frustration that was clearly evident in her voice. "Did any of you know he has a son?" She asked, staring directly into Yumiko's eyes. "No," exclaimed Yumiko, shocked by the disclosure.

Having turned the key and opened the box of secrets that she'd kept locked away for so long Akemi just kept on talking. She told Yumiko that she knew Gabriel told his friends that she treated him cruelly and that he'd accused her of stealing his money but that it was all lies and she would never hurt him in any way. On the contrary it was he who was abusive towards her and although she was embarrassed to admit this, he had at times physically assaulted her. She paused; Yumiko was appalled at what she was hearing, it was very apparent from Akemi's distress that she was telling the truth. Once again she put her arm around her friend, this time as a gesture of support, a way of saying it was OK and that she believed her. "Why, haven't you told anyone? Why have you stayed with him? "she asked

Akemi remained silent for a long while before saying that in spite of everything that had happened between them, she still cared deeply for Gabriel, adding that when he was not angry he could be charming and affectionate towards her. "That's the familiar pattern of a woman who's being abused, it's the way they exert control over you," observed Yumiko wisely. Akemi responded that she was well aware of this but there was something else that was more important to her. Akemi had lost both her parents when she was very young and this had had a profound effect upon her. She had always felt her parents' presence in her life and truly believed they guided her. She attended spiritualist meetings and more than once had been told that her parents believed that the gods had chosen Gabriel for her to love and it was her duty to care for him. She genuinely believed that she and Gabriel were destined to be together and the inevitable troubles she would experience in the relationship were part of the cross that was her destiny to bear.

Akemi held her head despairingly in her hands and fell silent. Yumiko was lost as to what to say and believing that Akemi had unburdened herself of the "secrets" decided a cup of tea might be the answer to lifting their mood but as she rose to go into the kitchen Akemi cried out, "I haven't told you everything, there's more and this is something that Gabriel never wanted his friends to know," she hesitated for a second and Yumiko could see genuine fear in her eyes before she announced, "Gabriel would kill me if he knew that I was even contemplating telling you what I am about to tell you." Akemi lowered her voice almost to a whisper and glanced around the room as if afraid that someone else would overhear the secret that she was about to divulge.

Akemi still whispering reminded Yumiko of the disastrous relationship that Gabriel had entered into with "that woman". Yumiko nodded, knowing that she was referring to Kimiko, the young Japanese student who he had planned to marry. "But that was years ago," interrupted Yumiko. Akemi agreed, "Yes it was a long time ago," and continued, explaining that when the relationship ended, as his friends had predicted it would, Gabriel had a complete nervous breakdown. "As you know, he moved into my place when he returned to London and I nursed him but it took a long while for him to recover and now I don't think he ever did recover."

Akemi went on to describe how a year or so after his return from Japan, his doctor who had been treating him with anti depressants referred him to a consultant. After many tests it was confirmed that he was suffering from Parkinson's, a degenerative disease. From the start Gabriel had refused to believe it, dismissing the diagnosis as part of a conspiracy, he was still in complete denial. She told Yumiko that he'd invented all sorts of stories that he used to explain what had happened and what was continuing to happen to him. Tearfully she told of how he accused her of poisoning him because she administered the prescribed medication that was essential to keep his illness under control. Akemi went on to describe how he'd become totally paranoid, not trusting anyone, believing the flat was bugged and how he had told her that special agents were out to get him. When she'd asked him why they were after him he'd told her that it was because he'd acted as a double agent for the Russians and the British back in the 60s and 70s.

"Oh, Akemi, how have you lived like this without telling anyone?"

"How could I tell anyone? Gabriel threatened to kill me if I breathed a word of it to his friends and anyway who would believe me, Gabriel is so convincing and somehow always manages to charm everyone into doing what he asks and accepting what he tells them." Her reply resonated with Yumiko; it was consistent with and typical of Alec's relationship with Gabriel who always appeared to do what Gabriel asked of him and accepted at face value everything he told him. Yumiko glancing at the clock on the mantelpiece realised she had been so intent on listening to Akemi's tragic story that she'd lost track of time and was astonished to see that it was already midnight. Whilst Akemi was opening her heart to her, Yumiko had been struggling with the fact that she knew where Gabriel was and it was only her promise to Alec that was preventing her from telling Akemi. When she realised how late it was her anger towards Alec returned, he'd not even rung to explain where he was and why he was not yet home. His inconsideration towards her was unforgivable and she made a decision; he was undeserving of her loyalty but her friend who for so long had coped so unselfishly and alone with such a complex and demanding situation was deserving of her loyalty. Ever since the breakdown of his relationship with Kimiko, Akemi had in effect become Gabriel's carer, a role that she had so unselfishly accepted although unrecognised and unsupported

"I have something to tell you and please don't be angry with me Akemi," said Yumiko, "Gabriel is safe, he's in a rehab unit somewhere near Grays." Yumiko expected a tirade of questions, "How do you know? How long have you known? Why hadn't anyone told her?" But the questions never came instead Akemi fell onto her knees and with hands placed together as if in prayer, murmured "Thank you, oh thank you, Lord."

Then she was up on her feet, collecting her shoes and coat from the hallway and heading for the front door. "Wait, wait," cried Yumiko, "Where are you going?"

"I have to go to him, I must go to him now," answered Akemi excitedly. Yumiko had not anticipated this sudden and dramatic reaction to the news she'd given her, "Akemi, it's far too late to go tonight, please come back and sit down." Gently but firmly Yumiko led Akemi who was still holding her shoes, back into the sitting room. Yumiko explained that Alec had made her promise not to tell of Gabriel's whereabouts. He was likely to walk through the door any minute now and he'd be really angry if he was to find out that she had broken her promise to him. Akemi nodded, "I understand and I don't want to get you into any trouble."

Yumiko knew that evening Akemi had been close to breaking

point and this was why she had revealed to her the appalling situation that she had endured silently and without complaining for years. Now that Yumiko knew the facts that she genuinely had no reason to doubt she was determined to help her and if this resulted in conflict with Alec, then so be it. Yumiko's inner strength was growing as a result of her defiance and she found herself in the unfamiliar role of taking control of a situation.

Akemi was sitting quietly staring into space with vacant eyes; it was as if the shock of knowing that Gabriel was alive and safe had completely mesmerised her. Yumiko quickly ran upstairs, collected spare bedding from the cupboard and returned to the sitting room to prepare a bed on the settee for her friend. When she'd finished she knelt before Akemi and took her hand successfully awakening her from her trance-like state. She then proceeded to tell Akemi what she thought they should do. Akemi should stay the night and in the morning after Alec had left for work they would go together to see Gabriel. Akemi nodded, she looked relieved and happy to accept Yumiko's suggestions.

25

Akemi's brief respite

The next morning, after a restless night Alec headed for the kitchen, drawn by the welcoming aromas of coffee and warm toast. He greeted Yumiko and Akemi, "Morning," as he joined them for breakfast. His greeting was not reciprocated; Yumiko poured a cup of coffee and handed it to him, then to his astonishment, casually began conversing with Akemi in their native Japanese. Such behaviour was a marked deviation from her traditional Japanese culture with its extreme emphasis on politeness and was a deliberate indication of her anger towards him.

Absenting himself from a pre-arranged evening meal to which a guest had been invited would be seen as disrespectful to Yumiko and an affront to their guest. Moreover, he'd promised to return soon and had not even called to explain why he was late; this would further be seen as yet another example of bad manners. Alec realised that he had transgressed social norms that were important to Yumiko but was nevertheless shocked by her reaction. In all the years that he had known Yumiko she had never behaved in this way.

Alec felt unusually uncomfortable in his own home but

soon realised that Yumiko's hostility towards him offered him an opportunity. It was Saturday and she had provided him with the excuse he needed to disappear for the rest of the day. Collecting his jacket and car keys from the hallway he left without a word, deliberately slamming the door behind him.

Ironically, Alec's reaction was exactly what Yumiko had anticipated and also gave her the opportunity to get on with the plans she and Akemi had already made for the day. Akemi was anxious to return to her Ealing flat to collect clean clothes and toiletries for Gabriel and Yumiko feeling very protective of Akemi after hearing her account of the facts and the true nature of her relationship with Gabriel was insistent on accompanying her.

As they made the journey across London by bus, Akemi was in good spirits, talking excitedly about how happy she felt knowing that Gabriel was alive and how she was so looking forward to seeing him. When they arrived at the flat, Yumiko watched as Akemi busily began collecting the items that she thought Gabriel would need, placing them all neatly into a rucksack, completely unaware of the previous evening's uninvited intrusion into her home. They were about to leave when Akemi remembered that there was something else that she needed to take to the hospital with her. "What are you doing?" asked Yumiko in amazement as she saw Akemi emptying the contents of the fridge onto the kitchen table and then struggling to manoeuvre it away from the wall. Akemi still struggling to move the appliance failed to answer. Yumiko watched as Akemi finally squeezed into the gap she'd created, emerged with a file, brushed the dust off the file and explained, "These are some of Gabriel's medical records, they're the only ones I've managed to keep because whenever he finds them he destroys them."

They left the apartment block and walked the short distance to the Ealing Broadway tube station calling in at a supermarket where Akemi bought grapes, apple juice and chocolate digestive biscuits, informing Yumiko they were Gabriel's favourites. Akemi was accustomed to the London transport network and knew that the District Line from Ealing would take them directly to Tower Hill from where it was only a short walk to the main line station of Fenchurch Street from where they could get a train that would take them east into Essex.

They boarded the train, found seats next to each other and settled down comfortably, it was mid morning and the congestion of the rush hour had passed. They sat quietly together at first as the train rattled between the stations, Acton Town, Chiswick Park, Turnham Green, Stamford Brook and Ravenscourt Park. Yumiko reflecting on their conversation of the previous evening and a question she wanted to ask. She glanced at Akemi who appeared relaxed as she stared out of the window and thought perhaps this might be the right time to ask the question. "Akemi, do you remember that last night you told me Gabriel has a son?"

"Yes, of course I remember," she replied. "Who's the mother?" asked Yumiko.

"I don't know her, but I can tell you what Gabriel told me," she answered, stressing that Gabriel was always inclined to interpret events in the way he wanted them to appear to be rather than perhaps how they actually were. What he had told her was that a long time ago he had been "going out" with a young art student and she had become pregnant, her family insisted that he do the "right thing"and so he married her. After the birth of the child, he'd told Akemi that his wife started behaving strangely and so he left her and the child. He'd insisted that, "he'd done the right thing" and paid for the maintenance of his child until his ex wife remarried and her husband legally adopted him. It was his son Lucas who'd traced his biological father. Akemi's tone took on a serious note when she added, "Lucas knows nothing about his father's illness, and Gabriel says he must never know."

The train screeched to a halt, Akemi looked out of the window and cried, "We're here, it's Tower Hill, we have to get off," engrossed in conversation the pair hadn't realised the time passing. They disembarked and jostling through the crowds of sightseers around the Tower of London made their way along the narrow back streets to Fenchurch Street. "Train for Southend via Chafford Hundred and Grays leaving platform 2 in five minutes," the ticket office clerk announced. They ran towards the platform managing to jump aboard before the guard slammed the doors, he waved his flag and the train started moving. Swaying from side to side negotiating the aisle of the train as it pulled out of the station, the pair managed to find two adjacent empty seats. This was a short half hour journey and as it neared its end Yumiko noticed that Akemi who had been quite relaxed until then seemed to become agitated, at first opening and closing the zipper on the rucksack, then checking the contents of the supermarket carrier bag, intently inspecting the fruit and the biscuits she'd purchased for Gabriel. "Are you feeling nervous?" Yumiko enquired, adding reassuringly, "it's only natural, given everything you've been through."

"I'm worried that he'll say bad things about me, that is what he always does in front of nurses and doctors and he can be so convincing that they believe him, it's happened before," said Akemi tearfully.

Yumiko was grateful to find a cheerful, chatty taxi driver who assured them that he knew exactly where the rehab unit was and he'd get them there in ten minutes, traffic permitting. "It seems like a nice place Akemi," commented Yumiko as they drove up the long tree lined drive. Once inside the building, they headed for the reception desk where Yumiko supportively holding Amekl's hand, enquired politely where they could find a patient called Mr. Gabriel Jones. The receptionist spent a few minutes, scrolling through lists of the hospital wards, and patients' names on her computer. Eventually, shaking her head, she said apologetically, "Sorry but I can't find any record of a patient with that name, are you sure you have the right hospital?"

"Yes, we were definitely told that he was here," replied Yumiko.

The receptionist once again navigated her computer, searching through the records of discharged patients. "No, no," she repeated, "I cannot find any record of him ever having been here."

Akemi, sensing that the brief exhilarating respite from the profound despair she'd endured since Gabriel's disappearance was over, turned abruptly and walked away from the desk. Yumiko politely thanked the receptionist for her help and hurried after her. Akemi, desperately trying to hold back her tears of frustration, was heading away from the hospital, the rucksack loaded on her back bobbing rhythmically from side to side as she limped along the driveway leading to the gate. Yumiko caught up with her, catching her by the arm, Akemi turned to her, "You lie to me, Gabriel not here, he never here, why you lie to me?" she shouted angrily. Not waiting for an answer she pulled herself away from Yumiko's grasp continuing to hurry towards the main gate. An approaching black car slowed down as it turned into the driveway, as it drew near to Yumiko and Akemi it gained speed quickly accelerating away from them spinning into the hospital car park and stopping suddenly with a screech of brakes. "Bloody idiot," shouted a fellow pedestrian. Yumiko turned to look back towards the car park and was surprised to see Jake getting out of the black car. "Akemi stop," she shouted to her friend but to no avail as Akemi stubbornly kept striding away. She ran, caught up with her, saying "I've just seen one of Gabriel's friends go into the hospital. Perhaps Gabriel is in there, why else would Jake be here?"

"I'll run and catch up with him, follow me." Akemi receptive to any glimmer of hope turned round and limped after Yumiko as she ran back to the hospital.

Jake was standing in the reception area, the first in a queue of visitors, he collected a visitor's badge then Yumiko watched as he turned down a corridor to the left, clearly he knew where he was going. She looked out of the window to see Akemi had reached the main door, Yumiko met her at the door telling her to, "Wait here," pointing to the long corridor and adding, "I need to follow

238

him and he's walking fast, I'll come straight back to you." She hurried after Jake who she could see turning right at the end of the corridor, she followed at a discreet distance as he passed a busy nurses' station and walked through a long ward until he reached Gabriel's private room.

When Yumiko reached the room, she stood next to the open door listening. She heard Jake's voice, "Hello Wilf," enquiring, "How are you feeling today mate?" Immediately Yumiko assumed she'd jumped to the wrong conclusion, Jake was not after all here to visit Gabriel but was visiting another person called Wilf. She moved aside to allow a porter pushing a patient in a wheelchair to pass and in that moment managed to steal a glimpse into the room and saw Gabriel sitting in a chair, looking older than she remembered him but there was no mistaking that it was Gabriel.

She lost no time in making her way back to Akemi waiting anxiously for her in reception, unable to hide her excitement Yumiko cried, "He is here, I've seen him, come I take you." Akemi was physically and mentally exhausted, in less than twenty four hours she had been transported from the height of elation to be plunged once again into the depth of despair. Her reluctance to believe Yumiko was not surprising, "No, no, you lie again," she was shouting and the receptionist at the nearby desk thought it necessary to enquire if everything was OK. Yumiko explained to her that although they had asked about Gabriel Jones she now believed the patient they had come to visit was known to them as Wilf Jones. The receptionist once again scrolled through her computer and smiled as she looked up at them to say, "Yes, we do have a Wilf Jones here, he's in Room 5, Darwin Ward, he's been here for a few weeks," then handed over two visitor's badges to Yumiko. "You see it's true, come," insisted Yumiko offering Akemi her hand which she accepted wearily allowing Yumiko to lead her to Darwin Ward.

Jake as promised had delivered the money and out of date passports retrieved from the raid on Akemi's flat. Gabriel had already hidden the socks full of £20 notes under his pillow and was intently scrutinising his old passports when the two friends appeared at the door. "How you get them," shrieked Akemi pointing to the passports, Gabriel dropped the pile on the floor and screamed, "Murderess, murderess, go away." Jake jumped up from the bed where he had been sitting and moved towards the women and attempted to usher them out of the room. Gabriel, still shouting abuse at Akemi had his finger pressed firmly on the alarm button next to the bed and the ear piercing noise resounded in the room.

Gabriel's assigned nurse was the first on the scene, she knew her priority was her duty of care to her patient and seeing that he was upset and distraught she had no choice but to ask the three of them to leave immediately. A security officer was called to escort them away, Akemi burst into tears, "I knew this would happen, it's what always happens and everyone believes him," she cried. She turned to the man leading them away pleading, "I'm his carer, I look after him and he went missing, now I found him and you won't let me stay with him." The security officer replied that unfortunately he had often witnessed these situations; he told Akemi sympathetically that there were a lot of elderly people with dementia here and for whatever reason it was not unusual for them to be accusative of their carer. Having escorted them safely away from the ward and stripped them of their visitor's badges as were his instructions, he pointed them in the direction of the hospital cafe where he suggested they could wait and see if the patient calmed down.

Akemi still verging on hysteria sat at a table with her head in her hands crying, Yumiko gently put her arms around her, asking if she'd like a cup of tea, Akemi nodded. Jake was feeling distinctly uncomfortable and was struggling to understand this latest twist in the already bizarre scenario. He was beginning to question why he had ever allowed himself to get involved. Taking the opportunity to move away from the tearful Akemi he followed

Yumiko to the serving counter only to be accosted by a jolly yellow teddy bear jangling a bucket of coins. Jake's everyday world was familiar, predictable and organised and he began to seriously think that today he'd slipped into a disorienting alternate reality. Yumiko gently reminded him that it was Comic Relief day.

Although he already knew the answers, he felt he needed to ask the questions, "Why is she here and how did she know where to find him?" Clearly referring to Akemi in what Yumiko considered to be a derogatory manner she quickly jumped to the defence of her friend. "She's here because she has a right to be here, Gabriel has problems, and Akemi has been caring for him and has spent every day searching for him since he went missing." Reluctant to accept her response to his questions, Jake said curtly, "She's part of the problem." He could sense the frustration in her voice when she retorted, "No, no, there is a lot that you don't know, come and let her tell you what has really been going on."

With Yumiko carrying the tray of beverages they returned to the table where Akemi now seemed a little more composed. "Akemi, please, please tell Jake everything that you needed to confide in me last night." Akemi reached for her rucksack and drew out the file that Yumiko had watched her retrieve from its hiding place behind the fridge, the file she'd said contained some of Gabriel's medical records. "Here, I show you," she replied, opening the file and handing it to Jake. Whilst Yumiko began pouring the tea into the cups, Jake opened the file.

There were a number of letters from a neurology department of a London hospital. The letters had been neatly compiled in chronological order. There was a lot of medical terminology that he did not understand but the concluding sentence of the first letter dated March 2005 was clear and left him in no doubt that Gabriel had been diagnosed with Parkinson's disease. This was followed by numerous letters sent over the years which recorded details of Gabriel's regular attendance at the institute and listed the medications prescribed as part of the treatment plan for the disease. He flicked past the pages until he came to what seemed to be the most recent communication from the institute, it was dated July 2013, alarmingly he read, Gabriel's mental condition had deteriorated markedly and he was demonstrating signs of paranoia and the latest diagnosis was advanced dementia. Immediately Jake recalled Alec's account of a meeting between Albert and Max when Max had offered his professional assessment of the link between dementia and Gabriel's egotistical personality which could explain the persecutory beliefs and conspiracy theories. They had all been quick to dismiss Max's observations as a hypothetical scenario which they were reluctant to accept.

Jake looked up at Akemi and Yumiko who had sat silently watching the expression on Jake's face change from one of total disbelief into one of sad acceptance, "Akemi, I'm so sorry, if only we'd known," he gasped, remembering how he, Alec and Sasha had all been complicit in hiding Gabriel's whereabouts from her. Unaware of Jake's misgivings, Akemi went on to explain that she'd been unable to tell any of his friends because Gabriel was in denial about his illness and refused to accept the diagnosis, he'd threatened to kill her if ever she spoke of it to anyone.

Ever since his strange encounter with Gabriel in the hospital garden just a few days before Jake had been struggling to try and find rational explanations for the things Gabriel had confided in him. Now, Jake although having a deep sympathy for his friend was nevertheless relieved that at last everything was beginning to fall into place and his own life could resume in the organised, predictable way to which he was accustomed.

Pragmatically Jake quickly took control explaining to Akemi that when Gabriel was admitted into hospital he had no means of identification with him and had given his name as Wilf Jones and his address somewhere in Wales. "What?" Akemi cried out in shock. Jake dismissed her questioning, "Please listen, and we must act quickly." He continued to explain that the hospital unaware of Gabriel's true identity had not been able to access his complicated medical history. "We need to find someone in authority here and give them this information," he said pointing to the file Akemi was once again clutching.

Akemi nodded her agreement, willingly handing over the file. Jake had the feeling that she was discharging herself of the burden and gratefully passing the responsibility on to him. It was a responsibility he was more than willing to accept, Gabriel had been a good friend to him, and now, knowing the truth, he would continue do everything he could to help both him and Akemi. Seeing Akemi distressed and tearful and fearful she might behave irrationally, he suggested she stay in the cafe with Yumiko while he endeavoured to pass on the crucial information about Gabriel that she had entrusted to him.

On reaching the cafe door, Jake was apprehended by the security man who had accompanied them to the cafe. "Excuse me sir, but I have been instructed to ensure that lady over there does not return to Darwin Ward because of the distress she caused to one of our patients. I have to follow orders and escort the lady off the premises."

"Please," begged Jake, "it's urgent that I deliver the patient's medical records, this file contains details of a serious diagnosed condition that nobody here is aware of."

The man, tall and stockily built towered over Jake but in spite of his stereotypical appearance he had a sensitive nature. He'd been observing the trio talking whilst they were sat in the cafe; he'd seen the anguish in Akemi's eyes and the genuine concern shown towards her by Yumiko and Jake. He reached for his walkie-talkie, and spoke to reception. "I have a gentleman here with me who says he has some important information about one of our patients; can I send him over to you?" Turning to Jake, he asked, "What's your name Sir?" Jake gave his name adding that the patient was the man known to them as Wilf Jones. Relaying the information, the guard motioned to Jake that it was OK for him to take the file to reception. Once there Jake tried to explain but the receptionist having waited for him was now anxious to simply take the file off him, close up the desk for the day and leave. Fortunately a doctor passing by and hearing the name Wilf stopped, he told Jake that he had been treating Wilf and enquired, "What's the problem."

Jake handed him the file calmly informing him that it contained details of the medical history of the man known to them as Wilf, that his real name was Gabriel and that weeks ago he had been reported to the police as a missing person. The doctor at first seemed just to give the notes a cursory glance but then Jake sensed his interest was aroused when he asked if he'd accompany him to a tiny room that led off the reception area. There he invited Jake to have a seat whilst he turned to the computer, the file was open on the desk and Jake watched him input Gabriel's NHS number which was emboldened at the top of the letters.

A few minutes later, he stood up and moved towards the door clearly indicating their meeting was over, he thanked Jake for the information but said it was a complicated case which he was unable to discuss any further with him because of patient confidentiality. He did, however, let it be known that they would contact the police to check their missing person's records and that already their procedures were in place to investigate the serious accusations made by Wilf following a visit from an Asiatic lady he'd named as Akemi Hakashami.

26

Gabriel's journey continues

The hospital authorities liaised with the Eastwood police station where Gabriel had first been reported missing. The details they had recorded at the time and the date corresponded with his admittance to the hospital in Basildon. The numerous blood tests Gabriel had undertaken at the neurological institute meant that Gabriel's DNA had been recorded on the national database and matched a sample that had been taken recently at the rehab unit. Gabriel's true identity was proved conclusively.

Nevertheless, Gabriel remained in the rehabilitation unit, the complexity of his situation a constant source of frustration to the hospital manager. It was winter, a time of the year when there was always increased pressure to release beds for urgent admissions. Numerous meetings were held where Gabriel's case was discussed but Gabriel's unusual circumstances and the overall complexity of the case refused to fit neatly into the boxes that required a tick. The series of ticks that would demonstrate that the criteria necessary to discharge him back into the community had not been met.

A steady stream of practitioners including psychiatrists, hospital almoners and social workers, dieticians and physiotherapists were regular visitors at his bedside. Gabriel welcomed their company believing the attention he was receiving to be a sign of his importance. He had always enjoyed the opportunity to talk to anyone who was prepared to listen to him and succeeded in perpetuating the confusion surrounding him by telling tales of his world travels and adventures, deliberately diverting their attentions away from the questions they needed him to answer.

He had not given up on his plans to escape and saw an opportunity late one evening at a time when he knew the nurses were changing shifts. Over the past few weeks he'd carefully observed them during this process and saw that in their preoccupation with the changeover routine they paid little attention to their patients. He had planned this earlier in the day and had already filled a pillowcase with his day clothes, a toothbrush and a clean handkerchief. He simply walked out of the room, along the corridor and past the reception area which he remembered was unmanned at this time. Then he was out in the grounds of the building and heading for the gate that led on to the main road where he could hitch a lift back to London.

The nurse's changeover completed, the night nurses started their rounds and soon discovered that Gabriel was missing. The procedures for dealing with an absconded patient were set in motion. Security were notified and ordered to search the wards and the grounds, matron contacted the local police and Gabriel's designated night nurse searched his file for his next of kin or name of person or persons to contact. The only name listed as a telephone contact for Gabriel was Jake Newcombe. The nurse rang and left a message for Jake to contact her as soon as possible.

Security personnel were combing the grounds equipped with search lights and fortunately it wasn't long before one of them noticed a slight figure bare footed and dressed only in pyjamas crouching behind a waste disposal bin. As the guard approached him Gabriel became extremely agitated at realising that his escape had been thwarted, he tried unsuccessfully to lash out at the guard before running off in the direction of the main road. The guard soon caught up with him, Gabriel, was in tears and shivering with cold, he pleaded with the guard to let him go. The guard kindly took off his own warm jacket and placed it round Gabriel's shoulders and did his best to try and calm him down whilst firmly escorting him back to the main building.

Following his attempted escape Gabriel was reclassified as a patient with high risk and moved into a room close to the nurses' station where he could be monitored closely. At the meetings that followed the incident, the hospital authorities argued that they were responsible for the safety of their patient and they could no longer guarantee his safety by providing the 24 hour care Gabriel needed. It was now of even greater urgency that an alternative place be found for Gabriel. The psychiatrist agreed to finalise his report following his observations of Gabriel and the hospital almoner updated them with the news that she had contacted Eastwood Social Services who were in the process of investigating the allegations made by Gabriel against Akemi who according to Gabriel's close friends had unselfishly cared for him for a number of years.

The process was hurried through because of the urgency of the situation. The psychiatrist's report confirmed that Gabriel had been diagnosed with Parkinson's disease some years ago and since then his mental condition had deteriorated and that he was now suffering from dementia and exhibiting signs of paranoia.

Eastwood Social Services visited Akemi in her flat where they endeavoured to establish the exact nature of her relationship with Gabriel. When they raised questions about the financial arrangements between her and Gabriel, Akemi quickly produced files of bank statements clearly showing Gabriel's substantial monthly income and his minimum expenditure. She also produced records of her personal transactions; it was clear that Akemi was paying for and providing everything for Gabriel. The social worker inspected the flat, it was clean, tidy and well organised, she noted that Akemi looked tired and from her experience of working with such cases she could see that Akemi needed help. When she suggested this, Akemi burst into tears telling her that Gabriel refused to pay for any extra help, he had a friend called Alicia who occasionally helped and that was the only time she ever had any time away from him. Having completed her assessment the social worker left, informing Akemi that she would compile a report for the meeting of the safeguarding team.

A week later a meeting of the Eastwood safeguarding team was held where the psychiatrist's report and the social worker's reports were presented. Whilst visiting Gabriel, Jake had been informed that the meeting was to take place and that the next of kin or near relative usually attended such meetings in order to represent the interests of the patient. Knowing Gabriel had no next of kin Jake had contacted the social services team and it had been agreed that he and two other close friends of Gabriel could be there to represent his interests. Sasha, Alec and Jake attended the meeting where the decision was made to discharge Gabriel into the care of Akemi with the recommendation that Jake as his named contact and in the absence of a next of kin apply for a Court of Protection Order.

When he returned home that evening Jake sent this electronic message to all of Gabriel's old friends asking for their support in the decisions that had been made.

Dear all,

Just to let you all know a meeting was held about Gabriel on Thursday April 14th at Eastwood Council. The meeting was organised by the social services safeguarding of adults team following Gabriel's complaint (whilst in hospital) of violence and theft against Akemi. The meeting was attended by two social workers, a representative from the memory clinic and also the lady from the dementia clinic along with Sasha, Jake and I.

The meeting was useful if only in that the ladies from the dementia and memory clinics gave the social workers a better understanding of the nature of Gabriel's condition and resulting behaviour. The general agreement was that Akemi needs support. They recognised that the situation of Akemi looking after Gabriel virtually 24/7 was because Gabriel had refused to pay for help and rejected the council social services approaches.

I have been advised to apply for a Court of Protection Order to get control of Gabriel's finances which will enable Akemi to get the support necessary to maintain Gabriel in his own home and provide a level of 24/7 care that gives him the best quality of life.

I would also add that Gabriel has deteriorated mentally in the last six months and I think it would be very sensible for me and Akemi to be appointed Deputies by the Court of Protection for Gabriel's "Health & Welfare." Gabriel is requiring medical intervention more often and there needs to be somebody to speak on his behalf.

With the approval of you all I will draw up the application form to send to the Court and will send it to you for your signatures. I will list myself as a Deputy also so that I can handle the administrative/paperwork.

Let me know if you support this approach.

Best regards
Jake

* * *

Jake, with the help of Simon, the solicitor amongst the group of friends, systematically undertook the process of applying for the

Court of Protection Order and when it was granted completed the bureaucracy with the banks to get access to funds to pay for care. He organised a meeting with the Swallow Care Agency and arranged for a carer to attend once a week.

Akemi was grateful for the help but continued to shoulder the brunt of the relentless burden of caring for Gabriel alleviated only by the one day support of a private nurse and Alicia who helped out whenever she could. Simon and Maria and Alec and Yumiko visited often as did Albert, Pete and Ollie, whilst Jake and Sasha kept a careful eye on Gabriel's finances and his general welfare. Lucas who was now aware of the reality of his biological father's condition also visited whenever he was in London.

* * *

Gabriel was now 84 years old and living on the edge of reality, the year was 2016, and he'd finally stopped fighting the inevitable deterioration and fragility of both body and mind. Forced to accept that his freedom loving adventuresome lifestyle was over he'd sunk into a depression so profound it was indistinguishable from perfect bliss. With the veil between past and present ever thinner Gabriel spent his days staring at the television compulsively digesting the news headlines and commentaries. Living within the world's changing events as they unfolded daily on the screen absorbed his mind, distracting from the reality of his personal mental anguish and dispelling the negativity of his depression. Slowly and briefly he unlocked his innate creativity of thinking and began to analyse the world situation albeit in his own unique blinkered manner.

Gabriel's inability to untangle subjective schemas from objective reality led him to believe that only he could see through the dark mist of a fractured and fragmented geo-political landscape. Such ego-stroking thoughts stimulated Gabriel's intellectual agility to stubbornly seep through the cracks in his rusting neurological gateways. He grew more and more agitated believing that it was imperative that he find a way to give voice to his thoughts in order to save the world from the inevitability of the apocalyptic scenarios he could foresee. As ever he formulated a plan, he would deliver his thoughts in a lecture to a selected intellectual audience at his old college in Oxford. He would ask his old friend Albert to make all the necessary arrangements for the event.

Gabriel unbeknown to his friends was learning to manage his condition. He understood that there was a glitch in the matrix, some neurological gateways had closed down and he needed to re-create the neurological pathways by updating his model of mind control. At first he'd practised on the physical control of his body by concentrating intently on where to place each foot whilst negotiating a path and deleting all other thoughts from his mind. It was a technique that would prove invaluable in enabling him to now focus his mind.

Akemi was surprised when Gabriel asked for a pen and a writing pad. His eyesight was failing and he struggled to hold a pen because of his shaking hand. Once Gabriel committed himself to a course of action he was still as he had always been unswerving in his determination to complete what he had set out to achieve. This characteristic had survived the onset of old age and mental deterioration. Now, sitting staring through the window of the flat he focussed on processing the thoughts that he intended to deliver to an audience. He closed his eyes, visualising the scene, he could see himself standing upright and confident before the lectern in the huge tiered lecture theatre. The theatre was full of academics all renowned in their field and waiting expectantly for him to deliver his spiel. Such ego-stroking thoughts had the effect of stimulating his innate intellectual agility. An intellectual agility, well exercised over a lifetime was still there and was now stubbornly seeping through the cracks in his rusting neurological gateways.

His thoughts came quickly in rapid succession far quicker than his shaking hand could commit them to paper. His frustration with his condition never far from the surface, he threw the note pad and biro pen across the room aiming them deliberately at Akemi. She responded calmly being accustomed to such unprovoked outbursts, hoping that this time she could appease him by letting him know that Lucas was in London and would be calling in to see him today. Gabriel was quick to jump upon the opportunity his son's visit offered. He would dictate his thoughts to Lucas, Lucas could type them onto his laptop, Lucas could print the document and hey presto his lecture would be prepared.

Lucas hadn't been looking forward to this visit, the last time he visited his father he'd found him staring vacantly into space and mumbling incoherently in response to any attempt Lucas made to communicate with him. But today was different, his father seemed genuinely pleased to see him and spoke clearly when he asked for Lucas's help in writing an important lecture. Lucas astonished and happy to see this remarkable change in his father readily agreed. As Gabriel poured out his thoughts Lucas did his best to accurately make notes on his laptop which he carried everywhere with him. Then Lucas dutifully spent time unravelling these hastily jotted notes to compile as accurate a record as he could of the profound thoughts that Gabriel believed he could deliver as a lecture. Lucas knew that Gabriel could never deliver his lecture but felt it important to record his father's observations on the modern world which he had so clearly expressed in this rare moment of lucidity.

Gabriel's Lecture
Reflections on the post millennium world

The images of refugees from Africa and the Middle East have had a profound effect on me. I believe that Britain throughout the years has arbitrarily drawn lines in the sand creating artificial boundaries dividing tribes that had once interacted seamlessly. I've travelled widely in the Middle East having taught students from

Egypt, Iraq, Libya and Syria and accepted their invitations to travel to their countries and stay with them and their families. I remember the kind hospitality of ordinary people with a reasonable standard of living, content with their lot and with no real desire to see their regimes replaced with secular democracies. Now before my eyes these ordinary people of the deposed regimes in Libya, Egypt and Iraq and Syria are fleeing their countries beset by tragedy.

I believe that the Arab spring demands for freedom and democracy are not the result of the invasion of Iraq but are fuelled by the invasion of satellite TV, mobile phones and the internet after 2000. I believe that the explosion of these influences has had a profound effect on the young people of these nations who previously had been safely insulated from the outside world. Now any attempts by governments to control these influences are doomed to failure.

I understand the term "Post truth" to mean that there are no longer any objective facts from which we can scientifically deduce the validity of a course of action. Now, everything can be seen as subjective, irrespective of conventional wisdom, reason, or morality. I believe that it is such a distortion of facts and a campaign of misinformation that has resulted in Britain breaking away from Europe. It's a decision that saddens me, having lived through the creation of the European Union and taken full advantage of the opportunities it has offered me.

I have always believed myself to be a free thinking liberal, I travelled widely in Eastern Europe before the fall of the iron curtain and I witnessed first-hand the impact of the loss of individual freedom resulting from totalitarian states. Now I am disturbed to see the western world swing so suddenly to the election of right wing authoritarian figures. I await with trepidation the results of forthcoming elections in France and Germany.

I see a world where subjective opinions are expounded, are nurtured and fed upon by like minded people in social media bubbles and ultimately they are deemed to be facts. I believe this distortion of reality and the truth devalues democratic principles,

I believe it to be the reason why we see a TV celebrity become leader of the free world. I foresee that the election of right wing megalomaniacs inevitably will lead to the loss of individual freedoms and potentially to the underlying tribal world tensions between east and west re-emerging with potential catastrophic consequences.

Gabriel sighed and sat back with his eyes closed; indicating to his son that he'd finished his oratory. He was unable to sustain the intense mental control required for this episode of rational, lucid analytical thinking and his neurological pathways were once again encountering roadblocks.

But the furrows in his brow and the intense look of concentration on his face suggested that he was still deep in thought. Gabriel's head was filled with a murky sea of disconnected thoughts, memories of times past ebbing and flowing amidst his prophetic visions of a future world. He held his head in his hands and started to rock backwards and forewords in his chair. Lucas, seeing that his father was clearly in distress, gently took hold of his hand. Gabriel stared at him with an all too familiar blank expression and asked, "Who are you? Where am I?" They sat together in silence until Gabriel once again closed his eyes and lay back in his chair. Lucas carefully let go of his father's hand as Gabriel appeared once again to be resting peacefully.

When he'd briefly opened his eyes Gabriel's confusion had forced him to face the ruthless reality of his everyday life, an unfortunate situation which he still believed was linked to his past. Now his eyes were closed again but Gabriel was not asleep; he was struggling mentally to piece together the floating individual pieces of a jigsaw. Slowly he began slotting some pieces neatly together but still he needed to find the final fragments which, once in place, would unite the jumbled pathways of his mind and solve the puzzle. As the last piece fell into place the muddy pathways of Gabriel's troubled mind finally connected to reveal a clear mental image of a long and winding road, the arrows on the road indicating the direction to follow. He mentally superimposed a picture of himself onto the scene which was now firmly imprinted on the forefront of his mind. Following the direction of the arrows he travelled from the past through the present and continued striding purposefully along the road heading for the future new world of "post truth". Gabriel had found the solution to the puzzle he had struggled so desperately to find. He had found his road to freedom.

He opened his heavy lidded eyes, peered over his gold rimmed spectacles delicately balanced on the end of his nose and announced to his son with a wry smile, "Everything's going to be OK, I have a plan."

Lucas and Akemi watched in amazement as Gabriel stood up tall and erect and walked with renewed confidence across the room. Leaning out of the open window, he shouted out to the world below:

> *"If I believe something to be true then it is true, I will create my own reality, I will have the freedom to do whatever I want and to be whoever I want to be."*

Gabriel had announced to the world his determination to continue his extraordinary journey in his own inimitable way.